You Only Get Letters from Jail chronicles the lives of young men trapped in the liminal space between adolescence and adulthood. From picking up women at a bar hours after mom's overdose to coveting a drowned girl to catching rattlesnakes with gasoline, Jodi Angel's characters are motivated by muscle cars, manipulative women, and the hope of escape from circumstances that force them either to grow up or give up. Haunted by unfulfilled dreams and disappointments, and often acting out of mixed intentions and questionable motives, these boys turned young men are nevertheless portrayed with depth, tenderness, and humanity. Angel's gritty and heartbreaking prose leaves readers empathizing with people they wouldn't ordinarily trust or believe in.

YOU
ONLY GET
LETTERS
FROM JAIL

YOU ONLY GET LETTERS FROM JAIL

STORIES by
JODI ANGEL

 TIN HOUSE BOOKS / Portland, Oregon & New York, New York

Published by Tin House Books, Portland, Oregon, and New York, New York

Distributed to the trade by Publishers Group West, 1700 Fourth St., Berkeley, CA 94710, www.pgw.com

Library of Congress Cataloging-in-Publication Data

Angel, Jodi.
You only get letters from jail : stories / by Jodi Angel.— First U.S. edition.
    pages cm
ISBN 978-1-935639-57-2 (paperback)
1. Men—Fiction. 2. Masculinity—Fiction. I. Title.
PS3601.N553Y68 2013
813'.6—dc23

                                        2012045369

These stories appeared, sometimes in slightly different form, in the following publications: "A Good Deuce" and "Firm and Good" in *Tin House*; "Snuff" in *One Story*; and "You Only Get Letters from Jail" in *Esquire/Byliner*.

First U.S. edition 2013
Interior design by Jakob Vala
www.tinhouse.com
Printed in the USA

To Laura

CONTENTS

A GOOD DEUCE

I was on my second bag of Doritos and my lips were stained emergency orange when my best friend, Phillip, said he knew a bar in Hallelujah Junction that didn't card and maybe we should go there. We had been sitting in my living room for eighteen or nineteen hours watching Robert Redford movies, where Redford had gone from square-jawed, muscled, and rugged to looking like a blanched piece of beef jerky, and we had watched it go from dark to light to dark again through the break in the curtains. The coroner had wheeled my mother out all those hours ago and my Grandma Hannah had stalked down the sidewalk with her fists closed and locked at her sides, insisting that a dead body had every right to stay in the house for as long as the family wanted it there. My mother was no longer my mother; she had become Anna Schroeder, the deceased, and my Grandma Hannah had been on the phone, trying to track my father down. The best we had was a number for the pay phone at the Deville Motel, and only one of two things happened when you dialed that number—it either rang and rang into lonely nothing or someone answered and asked if this was Joey and hung up when the answer was no. My grandma called the number twenty-two times and the only thing that changed was the quality of the light, and my mother went out, and Phillip came in, and my sister, Christy, packed her things so she could go, and I did not.

I understood why my grandma didn't want to take me. There had been that time when I was eleven and smart-mouthed and full of angry talk and I had made her cry. I still thought of that sometimes, what it looked like to see her in her bedroom, staring out the window in the half darkness, and how I walked up beside her and said her name and then realized that she was crying. I can still smell the room she was standing in, talcum powder, stale lace, but I try very hard to forget what I said, though it hangs in my mind like the dust caught in the weak shafts of sun. It did something to my heart to see her like that, something that I can't explain, and it did something to hers, too, I guess, because after that she never looked at me directly with both of her eyes. And now Christy was hand-ed a suitcase and I was handed a brochure for the army recruiter office in the strip mall by Kmart and told I could take my mother's car over as long as I gave it back when my bus left. Christy was thirteen, and I was seventeen, and what she had was no choice, and what few choices I had were being made for me.

"It doesn't smell," Phillip said. He was standing in front of my mother's room, both of his arms braced in the doorway so that he could lean his body in without moving his feet. From over his shoulder I could see the bed against the wall, and the flowered mattress stripped and the blankets on the floor. The bed stood empty and accusatory, waiting to be made.

It was Christy who found her, and I wished it had been me—not because I wanted to spare Christy the sight of what she'd seen, but because for the rest of Christy's life she could fuck up or give up or not show up, and nobody would hold it against her because, Jesus Christ, you know her mother died, and she was the one who found the body. Christy had a free ticket to minimum. I came in when Christy had called for me, but when your mother dies, there is no prize for coming in second. No one was ever going to keep some slack in my rope. The one who comes in second is the one who is supposed to spend the rest of his life cleaning up the mess.

"I keep feeling like I'm waiting for something and it isn't coming," Phillip said.

"I wanna go out," I said. My fingers were stained yellow like weak nicotine or old iodine, and I thought about all the ways that iodine can cover and stain—clothes and fingertips, forearms that have gone through bedroom windows, scraped knuckles from walls. My Grandma Hannah kept a jug of it under her bathroom sink, called it something in German that I could not understand.

Outside, a dog started howling, and I listened to its voice rise and fall, over and over again, and then I remembered that Oscar had been chained to the back fence since the paramedics came, and he had cried like that at the sound of the sirens, even though they were all for show and not for need, because my mother's lips had been blue and there hadn't been breath between them for a while. I went out back and saw that his water bowl was tipped and his chain was wrapped around the post, and when he saw me he started straining at the clasp and coughing out barks, because his throat had gone hoarse from the spilled bowl or the tight chain or a combination of both.

My mom's car was cold inside and smelled like tired cigarettes. Phillip wanted to drive, and I didn't care enough to fight about it, so we put Oscar in the backseat and I leaned against the headrest and closed my eyes. It was the first time I had done that in more than half a day and I realized my pupils felt grit-rubbed and sore. Phillip cranked the engine over a few times, pumped the gas pedal, and the car started and he gunned it once, and then twice, so that I could smell smoke from the tailpipe coming through my window. There were lights on in houses and my watch said six and there was a second when I couldn't decide if it was a.m. or p.m., and I thought maybe I could just make myself faint if I thought hard enough about it. It was a tempting thought, but Phillip couldn't handle surprises well, and I knew that if I fainted and let the whole damn mess go, when I woke up I would still be in my mom's car, breathing in the smoke stain that she had exhaled, and we would still be in front of the house, and it would still be this day, and nothing about anything would be changed.

"Let's roll," Phillip said, and he dropped the stick on the tree to drive, and when we pulled away from the curb, the wheels caught the wet leaves in the gutter and we spun in place for a minute, the back end trying to fishtail, and then the tires gripped the street and we put the neighborhood behind us, and in twenty minutes we put the town behind us, and if Phillip kept the car pointed east, we could put the state behind us, too, but east kept bending north, and then we finally turned west and the thought of escaping faded from a spark to an ash.

There had been rain and the road was hard obsidian that threw back the reflection of taillights every time Phillip came up on a car. Hallelujah Junction was ninety minutes out of town and nothing but a general store full of hunting and fishing supplies and a roadside bar and a place for people to stop on their way to Bear Lake for ice or more beer.

Oscar ate dog chow from his bowl on the floorboard in back and every now and then the radio picked up intermittent stations that came in when we broke through the pine trees for a minute or two, and then turned to static as the signals blurred. The tape deck was broken, just like the heater, and the window crank in back and the speedometer, but Phillip was able to wedge a Van Halen tape in place with a crumpled Viceroy pack and we listened to side one over and over again as the road hairpinned and climbed until the asphalt thinned out and there was a gap in the trees and the sudden neon promise of cold beer. Phillip did not talk to me and I was grateful for that.

The parking lot was thick with lifted trucks and muddy tires, and we found a place to wedge the Chevy between a couple of Fords. We got out of the car and stretched and kicked at the gravel for a minute. Neither of us wanted to be the first one through the door, and even though Phillip had been positive that we could drink here without a hassle, I could tell that he wasn't so sure now, and maybe he wished he hadn't opened his mouth back at the house and we were still watching movies in the dark and debating over whether to order a pizza, because when push meets shove, it's a lot of responsibility to have an idea.

"Let's give it a try," I said. The air was crisp and it snapped at my clothes in long sighs. We had showered before we left the house, and now we were both clean and new, and I had the bottle in the front pocket of my jeans, an amber cylinder with a name on it that was not my mother's shoved deep in the cotton that my shirt hem covered, half full of blue ovals the innocent size of Tic Tacs. When me and Christy had rolled my mom over, not for the first time, she still had the bottle in her hand, and I had to pry it loose because I didn't want her to be seen like that. People are quick to judge because sometimes it is easier to not understand.

We walked across the short parking lot and up to the building, and there was the steady increase in volume of steel guitar and snare drum, and when we pushed the door open there was a moment of huddle and wait that we had to fight before we stepped in far enough to let the door close behind us, and both of us stood there, blinking into the darkness, as if we had come in late to a movie and we were standing in the back, waiting until our eyes adjusted before one of us finally took the lead and made the brave walk in the dark to find a seat. The place was small and full, maybe fifteen people along the bar to the left and knots of men around the pool table at the back of the room. There was a handful of tables against the wall opposite the bar, and the center of the floor was clear and big enough to dance on if maybe the night was right.

I was immediately disappointed.

I had wanted the stuff of movies and TV, the mountain bar, the big men with shaggy beards and leather vests and a band playing loose and loud and a barefoot lead singer and a sea of hats bobbing in time to the kick. I wanted a fight in progress, breaking glass, splintered pool cues, and a lot of ducking punches.

But there was no band, and the men at the bar were old and thick and slow, and what few women I saw didn't look as if they were in much need of having their honor defended. Phillip seemed as disappointed as I was, but he got over it faster and went up to a break in the barstools and leaned in far enough to get the bartender's attention. Phillip was six months older, four inches taller, and thirty pounds heavier, with shoulders built for the football he thought he might someday play. I watched his mouth move with no sound, and the bartender adjusted his greasy baseball hat and Phillip pulled money from his pocket, and two bottles of Budweiser were uncapped and set down in front of him and that was that. No emergency, no joke, no *get the fuck out of here*, no bouncer gripping our collars and

tossing us to the gravel outside. Phillip brought me a bottle, and I swallowed as much as my mouth could hold, and
it was over. I had my first drink in a bar.

We found a table in the corner near the jukebox and
we both pushed up a chair and I sat back and surveyed
the room.

"I didn't know what beer to get," Phillip said. "I thought
I was going to blow it. The guy said, what can I get you,
and my mind went blank and I panicked for a second.
Then it just came to me. Budweiser. Thank God for all of
the fucking commercials."

Phillip raised his bottle in the gesture of a toast and for
a second I was afraid he was going to do it, drink to my
mother or say her name or tell me how sorry he was about
what had happened, and I braced myself, already uncomfortable and hating him a little bit for doing it now, like this
and here, but instead he just held the bottle up by the neck,
squinted at the label, and set it back down again. I drank
as fast as I could, and hoped that the sooner the bottle was
out of my hand, the less chance there would be for Phillip to make that toast and ruin everything. If he said one
thing, even put her name in his mouth, I was afraid that I
would drop my face to the table and press it to the sticky
residue of the last beer that had been spilled and I would
not be able to sit up again. It wasn't exactly because I was
sad, but maybe just because I had a feeling that even with
my mother dead, there would not be a noticeable difference between the then and the now.

"You mind if we sit with you guys?"

I looked up and there were two women standing next to our table, both of them with beers in each hand, and then Phillip nodded and raised his eyebrows in a silent expression of *why the hell not*, and they reached for chairs and moved in next to us, one beside Phillip and the other beside me, and they each put a bottle in front of them and slid the second bottles toward us, and it took me a few seconds to realize that they had bought us beers. When they were settled in and drinking, they both leaned toward us and asked our names, so we went around the table—Veronica, Phillip, me, and Candy.

Candy leaned closer toward me, and I met her halfway. She asked me what I did for a living and I said that I worked construction, and she thought that was pretty great. I had never worked construction, but I had always been fascinated with the guys who did, with their ragged T-shirts and tank tops and tattoos and dark tans from working in the sun, muscular and dirty and smoking and blasting hard music over the sound of their hammers. Maybe I would work construction if I could.

Candy told me that she waited tables in Battle Creek, but she wanted to move to Humboldt and go to school, but she was getting older and there never seemed to be the chance to go. Veronica was her best friend, and they worked together, and Veronica had a two-year-old daughter whose name I did not catch. After a while, Candy got up and put some money in the jukebox, and after she sat back down the music changed to the Eagles and Candy clapped her hands. "I really love this song," she said. I could picture the album cover in my mind, one from the milk crate by the old stereo in the living room, eagle wings spread over a desert at sunrise or sunset, blue sky fading to white over a yellow band, and not a lick of a hint to give away whether or not the day is looking to start or finish. I had stared at that album cover half of my life, looking for a sign.

Candy and Veronica liked to drink, and they weren't tight with their money, and the drinking led to talking and the conversation was as easily got as the bottles lining up in front of us. Candy had an open face and a wide smile, and when she laughed she had a tendency to bring one hand up and cover her mouth and look away.

The beer eventually got the best of me and when I got up to find the bathroom, Phillip slid his chair back so he could get past Veronica. I waited for him to follow me down the narrow hall, but he lingered at the table, so I kept walking until the smell of bleach and piss and mildew directed me to the right door and I pushed inside and was amazed at just how steady I could be on my feet.

I was pissing in a brown-stained urinal when Phillip came in. "This is the best time," he said. He looked at his reflection in the mirror and let the water run in the sink so that he could wet his fingertips and smooth down the front of his hair. We had been friends for five years, and he knew more things than I wanted him to; he had been around when there had been a steady ride from bad to worse, and sometimes I resented him for that, for the easy way that he could move in and out of my house and my life and stay only long enough to stand witness to some kind of shit going down and maybe eat some of the food out of the cupboards, or an order of takeout, and then he would walk back home to his leather-furniture two-parent slice of existence, and I was the one who had to stay behind and live what he only had to look at.

"I'm a little wasted," he said. Someone had written *asshole* on the wall with one *s*. Part of me wanted to find a pen somewhere and correct it. "What do you think of the girls?" Phillip said.

I turned on the sink and washed my hands. I looked at myself in the mirror and saw the dark circles under my eyes, and my skin had a shine that I had never seen before. "They're nice," I said.

"You like that Candy?"

I shrugged.

"You don't want to trade, do you?"

The water got hot, fast, and I let it run so that it blasted the porcelain and the steam rose toward the mirror. "What do you mean?"

"You know, when we get back to the table, I can swap sides with you if you want. Sit next to Candy. You can take Veronica." Phillip pumped some soap into his cupped hand and lathered up. The soap was a weak green color that looked toxic. "I mean, I'd rather keep Veronica, if it's cool with you, but I figure, hey, your mom just died . . ." He paused for a second. "I mean, you should at least get first choice, you know?" He let the hot water hit his hands and jerked them back so hard that his fingers hit the edge of the sink. "That's fucking burning."

I thought about Christy calling for me, yesterday? The day before? Time had turned soft and minutes and hours felt stretched and pulled. I was no longer sure if it was Thursday or Sunday or if it had just been five minutes ago that Christy had called to me, Roy, come here and there had been no sense of emergency or fear, just a voice even as blacktop, come here, and we had done what we had done so many times before out of habit, the rolling and the looking at what we would find, only this time it was different, more than different, less than different. Maybe this was what indifferent really meant. And then we had been running hot water, so much so that the steam banked against the wall, taking turns soaking towels and cleaning up. There just seemed like so much to clean.

Phillip pulled a couple of stiff paper towels out of the dispenser and rubbed his hands dry. "I mean, they're about equal. Veronica's got the bad skin and mustache, but Candy's a good deuce, so I think it all balances out." He wadded up the paper towels, threw them toward the trash can, and missed. He did not pick them up and try again. "You don't mind a fat girl, do you?"

The room was hot and small and there was still steam in the air, and in my mind I could see Candy laughing with one dimpled hand hovering over her top lip.

"She's nice," I said.

"Yeah, she's great. She's funny, et cetera. It's like that fat girl joke—Hey, why is fucking a fat girl like riding a moped? Because they're fun to ride, but you don't want your friends to see you on one." Phillip laughed and slapped me on the shoulder. I stumbled forward. "But you know I don't care."

Phillip looked in the mirror and smoothed his hair again. "I would settle for a blow job from Veronica. I wouldn't say no to that," he said.

I didn't say anything. I noticed that the floor was cement and there was a drain in the center and everything seemed to slope toward it, but I was drunk, so I wasn't sure.

Phillip scooped some water into his mouth, rinsed, and spit it back into the sink. He squinted one eye closed and picked at a dry whitehead high on his cheek. "If it's all right with you, I want to keep Veronica. I mean, no offense, but I can close my eyes and she'll feel just fine. Fat girls don't work that way."

When we got back to the table, there were more beers and the jukebox was stuck on the Eagles, and judging by the stack of quarters on the table in front of Candy, it would be for a while. The crowd in the bar had thinned and emptied, but when I looked at my watch it was blank-faced and I couldn't read it in the dim light.

"Hey, you know what? Roy's grandparents were Nazis." Phillip leaned back and took a drink from his beer and put an arm around Veronica. "I'm not even kidding. Tell them. Tell them about that time you found the swastika armbands and all that shit in your grandpa's closet."

It was something I thought I had seen once, and maybe I had or I hadn't, I wasn't sure, and when I tried to remember what I had seen in that closet, and I put myself back in that room, all I could smell was talcum powder and see my grandma standing at the window, stiff and straight, staring out at nothing in the weak light, her back to me, the tears streaming because I had said it, I had said names, called her things, told her how my mother would disappear every time that she got off the phone with her, my grandmother with her thick accent and twisted language, harsh, guttural, clipped through the phone and for seventeen years I never once remember my mother asking me how I felt—not once—*how do you feel?* Because feelings, she said, were lies. The only truth was in what you could see.

"Were they really Nazis?" Candy asked. "That's crazy." Her blue eyes were wide and filled her face.

"Did they kill people?" Veronica asked.

"Kill people!" Phillip yelled. His voice put the music to shame. "Probably. Of course. Hey, tell them about that time you had to help your grandma kill all those kittens."

"Oh my God," Candy said. She was staring at me with her mouth open. I could see that her lipstick was cracked around the corners of her lips.

"His grandma made him put them all in this sack. This burlap sack, right?" Phillip didn't want the answer to his question. He just wanted everyone to settle in to what he was saying.

"So he puts them in there—there's like what, ten or something?"

"Seven," I whispered.

"And he has to throw the sack into this pond out on their farm, so he does, you know, puts these baby kittens in this sack and knots the top and throws them out in the pond."

Candy had closed her mouth, but she wouldn't look

at me. She was staring at Phillip and Phillip was smiling as though this was the funniest fucking story he had ever told, and he was taking his time getting to the punch line.

"The only problem is though," Phillip took a swig from his bottle and ran the back of his hand across his mouth, "his grandma didn't tell him that he had to weight the bag down. You know, put some rocks in it or something. So when he throws it out there, it just floats on the surface with all of these kittens screaming and trying to swim, but they're trapped in that bag, you know."

"Screaming?" Candy said.

"Fucking screaming. All ten of them. Roy told me that it was like hearing babies cry."

"But he swam out and got them, right?" Candy asked. She turned toward me at the table and her thigh touched my leg. "You swam out and got them right?"

Veronica had the same look on her face that Phillip did, and I realized that they were meant for each other and it was perfect that she'd found him.

"There was nothing I could do," I said.

"But you could swim out and get them," Candy said.

"My grandma wouldn't let me."

"His grandma wouldn't *let* him. Fucking Nazis." Phillip slammed his bottle down on the table and beer foamed and ran over the top.

"What happened?" Candy asked.

"They died," Phillip said. "What do you think happened? He and his grandma stood there and watched the bag thrash around until they finally drowned."

"God," Candy said. She was looking down at the table, and there was something in her voice that made me want to put my hand over hers and let her know that I was just as sorry as she was. "How long did it take?"

Everyone around the table looked at me. Veronica had her head cocked against Phillip's shoulder.

"Twenty minutes," I whispered.

No one said anything. I could remember watching that brown sack take on water, and I could remember how the pond smelled with all of its black mud and fish and water grass and the summer heat pulling mosquitoes off its surface. I had started to take off my shoes to wade in to get the bag, but Grandma Hannah had put her hand against my arm and stopped me. She didn't say "no," or "stop." She just kept her hand on my arm, not tight, not gripping, just present, and we stood there and watched the sack together and listened to the kittens crying on and on until one by one they tired and drowned and the last one that held the sack above the surface finally gave up and went down with the weight.

Candy's thigh was warm against me. I couldn't remember what she was wearing, if she had on jeans or not. The more I thought about the weight of her thigh, the more I could feel her taking up the space beside me, spilling over the invisible line down the middle until she absorbed me.

Phillip leaned his head toward Veronica's and whispered something in her ear, and she laughed and pulled back and hit him lightly on the chest, but did not move away from him. She stood up slightly so she could lean across the table and cupped her hand around Candy's ear, and

Candy nodded and pulled at the disintegrating label on her bottle, and when Veronica sat back down in her chair, there was a spark of understanding that jumped around the three of them and I was the one breaking the circuit.

I was picking at my bottle label, and trying to peel it off in one piece because I could, and Candy put her hand over mine and I let her, and she squeezed my hand and her palm was cool and damp and soft and so much different from the thigh pressed tight and hot beside me. Phillip and Veronica were kissing; I could see the silhouette of their tongues moving back and forth between them.

"You ready?" Candy asked. "We're first," she said.

I took a swallow of beer and it was warm and hard to get down. The table was covered in bottles and I tried to line them up in rows like fence posts. I didn't look at Candy. "First?"

"Phillip said we can have the car first."

For a moment I was confused, and I was back in my living room and in the corner by the front door were two black garbage bags with the sheets and the towels that we had used to soak up what had come from our mom, Christy and me, before anybody came, and the first thing I had to do was get rid of them, throw away the evidence, everything except the narrow bottle in my front pocket.

Phillip pulled back from Veronica and there was a glazed look in her eyes that threw back the overhead light like the wet road had done up the mountain. He dug the car keys out of his front pocket and slid them across the table toward me. "Thirty minutes," he said. He smiled at me, and then Veronica slipped her hands around his neck and pulled him back toward her and her mouth.

Candy shoved her chair back from the table and stood, waiting for me to follow. The keys were cold and I looked at each of them and knew what they were meant for—the car, the front door, the door to my grandmother's house. I could tell the difference just by touch. Candy took my hand as we walked across the empty floor. When we were outside and the door closed behind us, the Eagles were muffled and the night air hit us. I took a deep breath and swallowed the taste of rain and pine and forest. Underneath it all I could smell a campfire, and I wondered how far away it was and wished that I could sit beside it.

The gravel crunched and shifted under our shoes, and I walked toward the car and led her behind me, leashed with my arm. "It's cold," she said. There were no cars on the highway, no distant drone of a truck coming through. I wanted to run down the white center line as fast as I could, run between the trees and suck down the air until my lungs burned and I had to run with my mouth open just to keep my breath.

When I put the key in the door, Oscar jumped up off the backseat and started barking and lunging at the glass, and Candy screamed and jerked her hand out of my grip, but then Oscar saw that it was me.

"My God that scared the shit out of me," she laughed. "Is that your dog?"

"He was my mom's dog," I said. The past tense had caught up with me. It had only taken a day and a night and already it came second nature.

"He's cute," Candy said. She knocked on the glass and Oscar let out a sharp whine and tried to lick her hand through the closed window.

I opened the door and Oscar jumped over the seat and tried to jump on me. Candy kept holding her hand out toward him and saying things in a singsong voice that I couldn't understand. "He probably has to pee," I said. I hooked my fingers into his collar and pulled him down from the seat, and when he was out of the car, Candy started rubbing his head and scratching behind his ears and he rolled over in the dirt.

"He is so sweet. I love him. What's his name?"

"Oscar," I said. I gave a sharp whistle and Oscar jumped to his feet and tried to sit without touching the gravel. "Go on. Go pee," I said. I pushed at him with my knee and pointed him toward the brush that edged the parking lot in front of the car. From the glow of the lights around the lot, I could see that there was a low scrub of bushes and tree trunks, and then the land sloped up and away from the parking lot and became a hillside and then a mountainside as the ground cover fell away in favor of rocks. Oscar put his nose to the ground and disappeared in the trees.

"Go ahead," I said. I pulled the driver's door wide and swept my arm toward the seat.

She sat down behind the steering wheel and tried to slide to the other side, but there wasn't an inch of slide to be had and she was firmly wedged between the wheel and the seat and to get her to the passenger side from there was going to take a lot of pushing. "We'd be more comfortable in the back," I said quickly, and I reached behind her and pulled the lock on the back door and she stood up and smoothed her shirt front, and then she was able to get herself onto the backseat and with some hard breaths and a few kicks against the floorboard was able to move to the other side and make room for me.

I shut the door, and we were in the quiet, and the car smelled like dog and dog food. The combination reminded me that my stomach was full of nothing but cheap beer and distant handfuls of Doritos, and my stomach did a slow turn that made me swallow hard. I reached for the window crank and then remembered that it was broken off. "Can you roll your window down a little," I said. She turned the crank a couple of times and the air came in and cooled the car and cleaned out the smell in one breath. Outside the car I could hear Oscar's tags rattling and the occasional sound of snapping brush as he walked around in the bushes.

Candy put her hand on the seat between us and in the bright light from the parking lot I could see how white her skin was. I reached out and touched it with my fingertips. It was warm, and I could feel the uneven ridges of veins, but they were soft and rolled away from the pressure of my fingers and I knew that I would have to press hard to find her pulse.

Candy turned toward me, but there was a lot of her that had to come between us and it was going to be hard for me to reach her with my mouth if kissing was the next thing to do. I would have to get up on one knee on the seat and climb up a little, but she seemed okay with that and helped me get into position, and I closed my eyes and fumbled through the best that I could. Her lips were nice, and she was comfortable and slow and when she kissed me I stopped thinking about all of the things that were cluttering my head. She ran her hands down my ribs and pulled at the bottom of my T-shirt, and for a second I thought that I would feel her hands on my skin, but then they dropped my shirt hem and moved down and she fingered the fly on my jeans and her left hand started rubbing at the crease, and then it moved to the right and started squeezing the bottle in my pocket up and down and up and down and I knew the rhythm she was trying to rub and I realized that what she had in her hand was not what she thought she was gripping.

I pulled back from her and she tried to keep me from going but I rolled back enough to get a hand down to my jeans, and she put her hands on my shoulders and pulled me back toward her and said, "It's okay, it's okay."

I fished the pill bottle from my pocket and held it up to her. The light from the pole beside us caught the amber and made it flash like a turn signal. She took it from me and squinted at it to read the label. "OxyContin?" she said. Candy held the bottle up to the shaft of light. "Who's Sharon O'Donnel?"

I leaned my head back against the seat and wished there was no top on the car and I could look up at the stars and find Orion, because he was always there when I needed him. I could always take comfort in the three stars of his belt. "Sometimes my mother," I said.

"Was she sick?"

I remembered the nights of crying in the bedroom, the muffled sound of her pillows taking the brunt of her sobs while Christy and I sat in the living room, inches apart, the TV on in front of us, blank-screened and throwing back light, and the only thing we moved was our eyes.

"Yes," I said.

I nodded and stared out the windshield toward the tree trunks and buckthorn that I knew were somewhere in front of me.

She handed the bottle back to me but I couldn't make my fingers close around it, so we held it between us together. "She's been dead for twenty-six hours," I said.

She was quiet for a minute and when she spoke it was barely a whisper. "Phillip told us," she said. I felt her hand slide up to my wrist. She took the bottle and I let her. "Come here," she said.

She pulled me in toward her and she undressed me in layers and she was so careful and soft that I hardly felt her. I closed my eyes and let her move me, lift my arms one by one, raise the T-shirt, pull it over my head, take the jeans and the socks and the shoes. Every time she took something off me, she pulled me closer to her so that the heat from her body held me like a blanket. I tried to talk to her, tried to apologize, but every time I found my voice, she said *shhhh* against me and lifted a finger to my lips.

When I was undressed, she unbuttoned her shirt and pulled me to her and wrapped the open sides of the shirt around me, and she edged down against the door so that we were both lying across the seat and I wasn't so much against her as settled into her, pressed in below her surface. When I opened my eyes, she was looking up at me, and I could see the creases in her brow, the lines on her face, and I knew that the parking lot light was showing her age. She raised her head a little and kissed both of my eyes and went back to work, moving me, burying me, guiding me, drowning me, and from that height above the seat, rocking and rocking, I could see over the door panel and out onto the hillside, and smell the mountain grape and deer brush leaking in. Far away I could hear a dog barking, faint clips of sound breaking the heavy stillness of the highway and moving away from me. I knew that soon Phillip would be at the car, and he would want inside, and I would have to come to the surface again. I didn't know for just how long I could stay.

CASH OR TRADE

My dad brought her home on Thursday and by Saturday she was out on the lot wearing a pair of cutoffs with the front pockets hanging under the ragged bottoms like rabbit ears. They were short, and when she got hot, she took the bottom of her T-shirt and pulled it up toward the neckline, tucked it under, and pulled it through so the shirt turned into a bikini top with sleeves, and when she was bent over working soap on the tires, there were cars that honked as they turned the corner, not a lot, but quite a few. My dad brought me into the office to file. My job was to wash the cars. He paid me five bucks a car on Saturdays to wash the week's dust off every one, shine the chrome, try to divert the customer's eyes to the glare of the sun off the clean hood and not the ding in the fender or the rust on the bumper.

"How much are you gonna pay me to file?" I asked. "This isn't five bucks a car."

My dad took out his comb and slicked his hair back off his forehead. When he was working he kept it greased up and shiny, but he was on day three of a beard that made him look tired and rough.

"I'll pay you five bucks an hour," he said.

"Five bucks an hour! I can't earn any money on that." Most Saturdays I could walk with sixty bucks in half a day. If I put in four hours filing I'd get twenty. "Washing cars is my job. Why can't she file and I go out there on the lot?"

"Because *she's* good for business," he said. As he finished his sentence a car came around the corner and honked. She raised up from the yellow bucket and waved a soapy hand toward the driver and he honked again, longer than necessary.

"How much are you paying her?" I asked.

Darlene Mason looked up from a stack of finance slips. "Twenty a car." She looked back down, licked her thumb, and started counting the pink papers again.

"Twenty a car?"

"She's good for business," my dad said, and he checked his hair in the round mirror that hung on the wall beside the door and then he pulled the office door open and stepped out on the lot.

"Twenty a car?" I said to Darlene.

She didn't look up. She just picked her cigarette out of the ashtray, took a drag, and went back to adding.

My dad was Big Ed, or Fast Eddie, or just Ed, depending on the commercial. He ran several of them on the local channels—Ed Harvey's Used Cars. *If you can dream it, you can drive it.* He had made a lot of money when I was a kid, and then new cars got less expensive and used cars just seemed cheap and his inventory started gathering dust. He moved a few cars every week, especially if he put on the gorilla suit and did the commercial where the girl in the bikini was stretched out across the hood of the Vette, holding up a sign that said "Make Me An Offer." The girl was Darlene Mason and she was pretty several years ago, I guess, and in the pictures on her desk she was beautiful, but she'd had a couple of kids and everything looked loose in the yellow bikini now, and something had happened to her balance, because she had a hard time holding her position on the hood.

It was June and one o'clock and hotter than hell and there was no way I was going to file a bunch of carbon cop-ies in folders that didn't have any titles that made sense. I didn't have my book with me, just my backpack and noth-ing in it except my best friend Ronnie's story he'd written about Superman killing a hooker. I had started reading Salinger, but switched to Kafka when my algebra teacher made a crack about me and Holden Caulfield being "two peas in a pod," and I couldn't go back to reading the book after that—not because I was mad about the comparison but because I hate the saying "two peas in a pod" and I knew that every time Holden made a decision I would hear that overrated algebra teacher and his comment. Or maybe what he was saying was that I *was* Holden, one step away from being expelled, and I didn't know it yet and probably wouldn't care when I did. I had pulled a hard D in his class all year. I'd ridden the D train right on through the semester before and decided that it was the best that I could do, so I had quit running logarithms weeks ago and started reading about Gregor Samsa, because I figured there was no way that we were two peas in a pod, what with him waking up as a bug.

The office was plastered with The Who posters—"wall-to-wall rock and roll," my dad liked to say. My dad's claim to fame was that he'd been in the crowd at The Who's November 20, 1973, concert at the Cow Palace when Keith Moon OD'd. Moon passed out at the drum kit and was carried off stage—twice—before he disappeared and didn't come back again, and the band couldn't play, so Pete Townshend took the mike and asked the audience if anyone could play the drums—anyone good—and my dad was eighth row to the left of the stage and raised his hand—raised it high because he could play—and he swore that Pete Townshend saw his hand—"Pete was looking right at me"—and was just about to signal to him when Bill Graham pulled some kid out of the crowd two rows in front of my dad and that kid was Scot Halpin and he went on the stage, and sat at Keith Moon's drums, and played three songs with the band, and made history.

When my father drank, which was sometimes often and sometimes more than that, he would tell the story of The Who, and depending on how many beers or vodka and tonics he'd had, he would tell the story with one of two tones—a tone of excitement, of just being there, being part of music history in the making, being so close, or a tone of sadness and a different life where he went up on stage, not Scot Halpin, and he played the three songs and his life changed and he never ended up owning a used-car lot and having two kids and a wife who left him for a pottery teacher. Instead, he went on to tour with The Who, was awarded *Rolling Stone* magazine's "Pick-Up Player of the Year" award, threw televisions out of hotel windows, drank and had women and was a star. When he told the story in that tone, the sad one, he always finished by saying, "I was that close," and he would squint one eye, drain his drink, move his index finger a centimeter from his thumb to mark the distance. "That close."

Out the window I could see my dad was standing next to the Chevy Nova that I wanted him to give me and she was rubbing a sponge in circles on the hood, washing the same spot over and over, and then she took the hose and let the water sheet off the car. She had a good system. It had taken me a lot of Saturdays to learn that water is just as effective as soap and there was no need to overdo the work. She was saying something to my dad and he was laughing and she had this look on her face that told me that she had no idea that she was rinsing a 1969 Nova SS with a 350-horsepower 396 V8 engine and a 4-speed close-ratio transmission, and as I kept watching her, watching her soap and rinse and rinse again and rub the chrome, I forgot a little about the car, too, and just looked at her.

She was Nadine from Bakersfield or Barstow or some town with a *B* and the sound of nothing going on, and from the story Darlene told, Nadine had shown up on the lot on Thursday trying to finance a VW bug that wasn't worth the $1,100 my dad was asking for it. Nadine was on her way to something better, she said, maybe Las Vegas because there were jobs, and that made my dad laugh and when Darlene had told the story she cleared her throat at that part as though there was nothing more to say. My dad wasn't in the habit of bringing people home, but we were living in a big rental house with too little furniture, and Nadine was too young to be a drifter, my dad said, and everybody needed a chance to start on the right foot. Now she was out there washing my cars and making four times my money and I figured that she wasn't only getting the right foot but the whole damn shoe as well.

I turned away from the window and sat down in the swivel chair behind my dad's desk and kicked the filing cabinet closed. Darlene looked up from her adding machine and lit another cigarette. My dad had told her that she didn't have to work Saturdays but she said it gave her a chance to work a half day and tell her husband she was working all day so she could get away from the kids. Usually on Saturdays my dad and Darlene went to Tips bar down the street, where she would finish out her shift.

There was a little TV on the top of a shelf and *The Flintstones* were on. Fred was guiding a dinosaur crane with a giant rock balanced on its head. I wondered why he worked in a quarry, other than because it was the Stone Age, but that seemed like too obvious of a joke to base an entire cartoon on. I thought about calling my brother, but we never had much to say on the phone. The only time I could call him was when I was at the car lot. Me and my dad didn't have a home phone yet—we had the line and the number, but we didn't have anything to plug in and my dad didn't seem like he was in too big of a hurry to get a phone and I didn't really care. Junior year was officially behind me, and I just wanted to make it to the grand finale at the end of one more high school year. I had a girlfriend named April and I had been to her house once and met her parents so that she could go to the movies with me. Her dad was ex-Mafia or something, Big Lou "The Bull" Marino, and he scared me because he had a big ring on his little finger and he drank rum with maraschino cherries while her mom took yellow pills and asked us if we wanted some sandwiches, and when we said no thanks, she nodded and after about twenty minutes she asked us again, and we said no thanks, and this went on for the hour that I was there. Big Lou asked me what my *deal* was, and when I said that I didn't understand what he meant, he put one big hairy arm around my shoulders so that the big ring was just inches from my chin and said, "You know, your *thing*—your *plan*." I just shrugged and hoped that was the right answer and then he leaned in close to me so that I was strangled with alcohol and cherry and Avon '55 Thunderbird cologne, and he said, "Vending machines. That is where the future is."

I leaned back in my dad's chair and put my hands behind my head. I thought about taking a nap for a while. The TV was still running cartoons, but I had gone from the past into the future and George Jetson was yelling at

Jane to get him off that crazy thing. Darlene had her hand in a Cheetos bag and she was alternating Cheeto and ciga- rette and licking the orange off her fingers and digging back through the bag again. "You want some?" she asked and tipped the bag my direction.

"You go ahead," I said. She had a fan running and when it turned toward the wall the papers on the bulletin board lifted up at the edges and fluttered together like insects. The first days of summer vacation were always the worst. Every year I would be excited to turn in my textbooks and run out to the street when the last bell rang, and then the week- end would come and go and Monday would surface and I would realize that I didn't have anything to do and nothing but time to do nothing with. Last summer I read twenty- six novels. I got the suggested reading list for junior English class and went to the Book Barn, and then when I was stand- ing in there I saw all these titles and writers that I wanted to read, so I did, one after the other while the sun came up and went down over and over again and the crabgrass thickened under the constant chopped spray of the Rain Bird sprinkler in the center of the yard. That had been in the old house, and now I was in the new house and I felt tired of words. There was nothing to do and I wasn't even making any money to spend on something I hadn't decided to buy yet.

Nadine was in front of the big office window, rolling up hose slack and moving toward the right side of the lot. She waved at me and smiled, and I lifted my hand in return.

"She's pretty," Darlene said. She picked up one of the framed pictures on her desk, the one where she was riding on the float in the homecoming parade. "I remember those days."

I watched Nadine bend and pull the hose, and I could imagine her muscles jumping under the skin, pulling tight and bunching in little knots. She had tan legs and they were long and narrow and the fringe on her shorts barely dusted the tops of her thighs. She had long dark hair that she had pulled back in a sloppy ponytail, and her shirt was wet and she looked sweaty and shiny with hose water. I knew that April's favorite food was spaghetti and that sad movies made her cry and her first dog's name was Brandy and Brandy had been hit by a car and April wanted to be a teacher someday and work with kids. I didn't know anything about Nadine except that she was nineteen and had all of her belongings in one duffel bag and made me feel something that April never had.

"I guess," I said.

My dad came back into the office and slapped my feet off his desk. "It's hotter than hell out there," he said. His face was red and even though he was in a short-sleeved shirt he still wore a tie and suit pants.

There was a couple walking around and looking at cars, and my dad was excited, I could tell. He called them fish, like fish in a barrel, and he started checking the Peg-Board for keys. "Where in the hell are the keys to that Buick?" he said. He started lifting stacks of papers off his desk and knocking things on the floor.

"Here, here," Darlene said. She took a key fob with a numbered tag out of her in-box.

"What in the hell are they doing in there?"

"That Buick has an oil leak. You wanted to take it down to the Shell station and have Bobby look at it on Monday."

"Yeah, well, wet pavement and gravel don't show much, do they? It still runs like a sewing machine."

He shook the keys in his hand, but there were only two of them and they didn't make much sound. "Floyd, if you see me yawn and stretch my hands above my head, I want you to take the back door out of the office, walk around the parking lot to the side, and then come up through the front. Then walk up to me and say, 'Excuse me, but my mom wants to know if you are still holding that Buick for her.' Got it? No more and no less."

"Are you holding the Buick for my mom."

"No. *That* Buick. Do it right."

"Are you holding that Buick for my mom."

"*Still*."

"Are you holding that Buick for my mom still."

"Jesusfuckingchrist, Floyd. Just do it right. Okay?"

I wanted to say *How much?* How much is it worth to you if I close that sale? But I didn't. I just watched him leave the office and walk across the gravel to the couple, who were peeking through the second row of car windows. They were a young couple, and she may have been pregnant or just fat, but I knew that they would be driving home with a Buick in a couple of hours. Darlene was already typing up the forms.

The office smelled like glue and the carpet had been ripped up under the air conditioner in the window

because the air conditioner leaked and turned the carpet moldy. Now the water just dripped onto the bare cement floor so that there was the constant sound of water
drops marking time and I could hear them ticking off the
seconds under the noise of the adding machine and the
television and the fan on Darlene's desk and the traffic
passing by on the street. I was bored as fuck. I fingered
the stacks of papers on my dad's desk and looked out
the window at my dad cracking the hood on the Buick
and Nadine moving down the rows of cars on the right,
and I thought about staying and doing the work. Then
I thought about having the house to myself and the fact
that Nadine's duffel bag was upstairs in the spare room
and I was suddenly craving to know what was inside. I
didn't care if it was a bunch of old T-shirts and cutoffs. I
didn't care if there were balled-up gym socks and jeans. I
wanted to know something about her—go through her
pockets maybe and dig out her receipts and slips of paper
and gum wrappers so that I could know what she bought
and notes she wrote and the kind of gum that she chewed.
I stood up from my dad's chair and it spun around so that
an armrest hit the edge of the desk and knocked a stack of
papers to the floor.

"Those were in alphabetical order," Darlene said. She
was holding up the bar on the typewriter and blowing on
some Wite-Out so she could get it to dry faster.

"I'm going home," I said. "Can you let my dad know?"

"What about the Buick?"

"He'll manage. He doesn't need me."

Darlene hit the carriage return on the typewriter, spaced the type guide into the next blank, and continued typing. "I guess there's always Nadine," she said.

I slipped out the back door of the office, stepped down the short flight of bare wood stairs, and jogged around the back of the lot until I hit the alley and disappeared down the street.

It had been hot in the office and I knew it was hot outside, but this was furnace-blast heat and I was sweating before I reached the corner of Meadowview and Flower. The pavement was hot, and when the sidewalk broke away and I was forced to walk on the asphalt, I could feel my shoes sinking into the tar and I had to pull hard on them to lift each step and keep stride. I had skipped out on work and didn't have so much as two quarters in my pocket and I was so thirsty that I felt like the act of swallowing would take the last of my spit and make me cough until I puked. I felt a pinch below my ribs and knew I was getting a side ache. I was still a mile from my house and only two blocks from the lot and already I missed the little television on the shelf and the sound of water dripping from the air conditioner and the intermittent flutter from Darlene's fan lifting papers on the board. Maybe five bucks an hour wasn't such a raw deal, especially if it meant a ride home. By skipping out now I was a chickenshit and weak and probably kind of lazy and a disappointment, too, but freedom was freedom and it tasted a hell of a lot better than work.

I turned the corner at Sundance and headed for Coyote Street and the buried suburbs where every street was a credit to the Battle of the Little Bighorn and Coyote Street hit Thunderhead Circle and War Horse and Arrapahoe and Black Hills and Custer Court, but there was no Sitting Bull on the map, no court or way or street, but there were soccer fields and a public pool, and Comanche Park in between them.

A car came up behind me and when it honked it knocked me out of my head and jerked me back to the sidewalk so hard that I screamed like a girl. I had been dreaming about chicken tacos and my ninth-grade German teacher named Fran. I turned around and readied my middle finger for the international gesture of fuck off, but when I turned to the street the Vette was behind me and even though I brought my hand up to shield my eyes against the glare, I could have sworn that it was Nadine behind the wheel, but it all had to be an optical illusion, the beginning of heatstroke. My dad didn't let the Vette off the lot—it was his centerpiece, maybe even his entire center. He kept it parked on a sheet of Astroturf near the front of the office. It was the one car he didn't let me wash because I might scratch it. He had a habit of walking past the car, stopping suddenly, squinting down at the metal, licking his thumb, and rubbing at something on the hood or the windshield or the roof or the door until he was satisfied that it was gone.

The horn went off again and this time I stepped off the sidewalk toward the car and reached out to touch the long front fender to make sure that it was real. I wasn't convinced until I felt hot fiberglass under my hand.

"C'mon," Nadine said. "Let's go."

I leaned in through the open T-top. "Why do you have my dad's car?"

"He took off with some couple and an ugly brown car, so I thought I'd take my own test-drive, you know? I washed all the cars."

I opened the passenger door and slid onto the seat. I had on jeans but even so I could feel the hot leather through my pants and I wondered if Nadine's thighs were burning since they didn't have much cover.

"Why'd you leave?" she asked.

I pushed the button on my window so that it rolled down and I caught a quick puff of exhaust and breeze. "I got bored," I said.

"You want me to take you home or do you want to take a test-drive with me?"

I thought about Nadine's duffel bag upstairs and the hot house or the cool car and her driving, and I hooked the seat belt across my lap.

Nadine drove fast, and she ran through the gears like they were water and she had been driving the car all of her life. The car was dark blue with wide tires and it had enough layers of wax on it to make it look brand-new. My dad had it in the Fourth of July parade a few times, with Darlene Mason driving and him in the gorilla suit and a big banner wrapped around the car advertising the car lot and the deal of the day—in-house financing, zero down, buy now pay later, Ford LTD blue book $2,250—yours for $1,999—but one year it got really hot early and both my dad and the car overheated and there is nothing worse than seeing a sweating man dressed like a gorilla holding his monkey head in his hands, sitting on the nose of a car that is blowing anti-freeze all over the pavement. He stuck to TV ads after that.

Nadine pulled in at a 7-Eleven and told me to sit tight. There was a bunch of guys in dirty orange construction T-shirts sitting in a big truck and Nadine walked over and they were all smiling at her and when she got to the truck one of them opened the door and she leaned against it and looked up at the group while they talked about something that I couldn't hear. The one in the passenger seat shrugged and the rest of them started laughing and he jumped down from the cab and spit a line of chew into the dirt and followed Nadine into the store, and when they came out again he walked her over to the car and handed her a bag and asked if thank you was all he got, and she laughed and said yes, that's it, and he waited a minute and then shrugged and walked back to the truck, where they all watched us back out and leave.

"Here," she said. She put the bag in my lap and shifted into third and hit the turn signal.

I opened the bag and looked in and there was a six-pack of beer, something in green bottles. "Whoa," I said. I wasn't sure what I'd expected, but I'd been thinking about Lay's potato chips and maybe some Gatorade.

"Is there someplace we can go?" Nadine asked. "Someplace with grass and stuff. And shade?" The sun pinned us through the open top and there was no break and I was burning.

"The park," I said. "If you go in through the north entrance and stay on the road it curves around to some trees and a little creek."

"Get me there," Nadine said.

When my mom and dad started dividing up the contents of the old house, they divided up the kids, too, put their names on us like they did with the books and the records so that they could mark their territory and take their ownership. I didn't want to go with my mom. It had all started with a group she joined, and she stopped doing our laundry, and then she went on weekend retreats with these other women who smelled like the Indian mini-mart around the corner from the car lot, and then she stopped cooking. She bought a pottery wheel and took over the garage and she started displaying lopsided vases that didn't hold water and then she took a class at the rec center and figured out that she didn't want to do this anymore and left us all to figure out what exactly *this* was and my dad started sleeping on the sofa bed downstairs. Then he got the house across from Comanche Park and she kept the old house and my brother, Jerry, and we all just divided like a cell.

We took the road that went deep into the park, and Nadine parked at the curb, cut the motor, and the engine ticked and cooled. She took the bag of beers off my lap and dug through her front pockets until she found a quarter. "Watch this," she said. She fitted the edge of the quarter under the bottle cap and tipped the quarter up just a hair so that it pried into the groove, then she pressed it down against the index finger of her right hand, which was wrapped around the neck. There was a pop and the cap flipped off the lip of the bottle and onto the seat.

"That was cool," I said.

"This trucker in Fresno taught me about fulcrums," she said. She passed the bottle to me and then she opened one for herself. "Cheers," she said. We clicked bottle necks and both of us stretched out in our seats. There were tree branches tangled above us and we were circled with shade. I could hear birds moving around in the leaves, but there was no one else parked. Everybody was across the field at the pool.

"Drink up," she said. I watched her tip her bottle and swallow fast over and over again until the bottle was pointed straight at the sky and I could see thin foam slip down the green neck and then nothing at all. She wiped the back of her hand across her lips and closed her mouth on a burp. "Sorry," she said, "but warm beer is no good."

I copied what Nadine had done, and the first few swallows were easy, but then the beer started flowing in faster than down and I thought I was going to choke it up before I could get the bottle drained.

"Good one," Nadine said. She took the empty bottle from me and handed me a full one. I was trying to hear the creek, but there was no sound except for the birds and the traffic on the other side of the park and I wondered if the creek had finally dried up and quit. Jerry and I used to hunt for turtles in the shallow water. Somebody had told us that there were baby red-eared sliders in the creek, and we would spend half the summer trying to track them down. All we ever found was a giant pollywog with two legs and a dead snake.

"Fulcrums and what truckers meant when they offered me twenty to punch the ape," Nadine said. "That's what I learned in Fresno." She laughed but it sounded like a reflex without anything being funny at all.

I took a drink of my beer. In my mind I saw my dad in his gorilla suit jumping out from behind a wall of balloons and Darlene on the hood of the Vette and Nadine dressed in Rocky Balboa trunks and a pair of red Everlast gloves, throwing jabs at my dad. I wanted to ask Nadine if she'd seen my dad's commercials and if maybe she had this vision, too, but I didn't. There were probably other apes and my dad's commercials didn't reach all the way to Fresno.

Nadine was staring out the window, but other than a picnic table under the trees there was nothing to look at for so long. "You have a girlfriend, Floyd?"

April's yearbook picture jumped into my head, and I saw the page and her in the second row on the left side, between Tiffany Small and Aaron Smith. April Smiley. It was the worst name ever. "Sort of," I said.

Nadine nodded and I could see the stray hairs behind her ear where sweat had plastered them to her skin. She had a small beauty mark on her neck just behind her jawline. "You like her?"

We had done an English project together and eaten lunches at the same table for a couple of weeks and then there had been a note passed from April to me, something she had given me between classes when I was on my way to chemistry and it was still cold out and there was a lot of wind blowing garbage against the fences. *Do you like me?*

I had carried the note in my back pocket through the rest of the day, and I took it home with me and spread it out on my desk, unfolded the college-ruled binder paper that still had jagged edges from the spiral binding, and I took my yearbook off the bookcase and opened it to the sophomore *S* pages. April Smiley. The picture was okay. She was a good essay writer. I wrote *yes* on the note, under her question— wrote it in pencil so I could erase it later if I needed to.

"I haven't been home in weeks," Nadine said. "I can't remember anybody there."

"Don't you miss your family?"

Nadine was quiet for a minute but I could see her fingers gripping and releasing around the steering wheel so that her knuckles turned white and went pink and then white again. "Family is kind of a funny thing, don't you think? You don't really know who you are until there's nobody there to make you somebody that you're not."

The engine was still ticking and the six-pack had been reduced to two bottles. I wondered if the water in the swimming pool across the field was cold, so that you had to stretch your towel out on the hot cement in order to warm up after you swam for a while and then your towel never got completely dry—just a tepid damp, and flat, and stuck with pebbles.

Cars started coming into the shade and a family claimed the picnic table, spread it with a cloth and started unpacking bags of food. Out in the grass a guy and a girl were throwing a Frisbee for a white dog. Nadine and I watched the sun spread itself thin through the pollution and turn the sky bright orange and pink and yellow and purple, watched it turn the reflections on the car windows red, and then slip over the edge and pull the colors with it. We didn't leave until the crickets told us to.

My dad's Ford was in the driveway and the lights were on in the house and I remembered that Nadine had taken the Vette and he hadn't really lent it to her. My stomach clenched a little and I got ready to get in trouble. Nadine saw me slump in the seat when she rolled to a stop next to the Ford and she knew what I was ready for without me having to say anything.

"I'll handle this," she said, and then she was out of the car and walking up the steps and pulling the screen door open and there was no rod in her back holding her straight. She was genuinely not afraid at all.

My dad was sitting on the couch with his work shirt on and his tie loosened, and the television was on but there was no sound. He was just staring at the screen.

"Where'd you go?" he asked. His voice was quiet and low and I didn't know if he was talking to me or Nadine. "Darlene said you came into the office, said you wanted to look at the Vette and she gave you the keys to open it up and the next thing she knows you're gone with the car."

Nadine walked over to the couch and stood behind him. She put her hands on his shoulders and started squeezing the muscles to either side of his neck. "It was just a little test-drive, Eddie. Maybe I'm thinking about buying it—it's worth what, about a hundred washed cars? Two hundred?" The only person who ever called my dad Eddie was my mother, and that was only when she was happy with him and I couldn't remember the last time I had heard her say it.

My dad turned around and looked at both of us. "Nadine, that is a 1979 Corvette Stingray L82 with a glass T-top and a 5.7-liter 350 V8 tuned to 220 horsepower. That is a fourteen-thousand-dollar car." His voice was winding tight like an engine, but he downshifted and dropped back to the quiet tone again. "It's my signature car. It's not meant for driving."

Nadine gripped her hands into my dad's shoulders. "It's just a car, Eddie. It's a nice car, but it's not everything." She rubbed his shoulders so that his shirt bunched up under her hands and I was waiting for him to turn on me for being an accomplice, but he didn't. Nadine rubbed the fight out of him.

"Okay," my dad said. He stretched his neck back and stood. "Okay." He picked his glass up off the coffee table and there was a lime rind inside and the glass was full to the brim and I knew he was on vodka and tonics and maybe that was part of the reason he had been soft on our crime. "I sold the Buick," he said. He raised his glass in a toast but me and Nadine were empty-handed. "You need drinks," he said, and Nadine went into the kitchen and came back with beers—one for her and one for me—and I took it and held the bottle like it was a live snake.

"Here's to five hundred over blue book," he said, and we all knocked glass together and when my dad didn't say anything more, I drank.

I had never drank beer in front of my dad—had never really had beers before at all unless I counted the two I shared with Ronnie when his dad left his fishing ice chest in the garage and forgot to unpack it and we sat behind his house drinking them and then pretended to be wasted. My dad took out his Who records—all thirteen of them—and he stacked the turntable and turned up the music and the house was hot, so we opened the front windows and I wondered what our house looked like from the sidewalk, if somebody walking by would look in through the window and see the dining room light shining over the table and hear the music and see us laughing and if that person would envy us and our good time.

"I coulda been the drummer," my dad shouted over the music. "I should have pushed my way to the front of the stage. I keep thinking that—why didn't I just get closer and force my way?"

"I wish you could play for us, Eddie," Nadine said. "I bet you were good."

"I was brilliant," he said.

"I have an idea," she said. Nadine disappeared into the kitchen and when she came out again she had three pots and two wooden spoons and she turned the pots upside down on the table and handed my dad the spoons like they were sticks.

My dad looked down at the kit that most kids start on. "I can't," he said. "This is ridiculous."

But he was smiling like he wanted to and all he needed was a push, so Nadine said, "Please, Eddie," and the next thing I knew he was pounding along to the A-side of the record that was playing.

Nadine only had a couple changes of clothes and nothing much for summer, and she asked to borrow a pair of my boxers and one of my shirts, and the thought of her in a pair of my underwear was more than my mind could wrap around, so I started putting my dad's albums in alphabetical order and tried not to imagine the places in my shorts that Nadine's bare skin was touching. When she came back downstairs she reached out and took my hand and I was too surprised to jerk back or wipe it on my jeans first, and then she was pressed against me and we were dancing, or at least she was dancing and I was shuffling along and trying not to step on her feet. My dad was sweating and his forehead had gone slick and his hair was sticking in points against his skin and his hands were flying, alternating pots, and he was desperately trying to keep rhythm with a kick drum that wasn't there. "The Kids Are Alright" came on and I liked that song and my dad started shouting the words so that Nadine laughed and when she spun me around I wasn't expecting it and I almost fell down, but she pulled me back toward her and kept on taking the lead, and we all decided we liked that song and we let my dad play it over and over again until he got tired of stopping the record and we just let it play through.

When I woke up I was in my bed and my shoes were off but I was still in my clothes. My sheets were in a ball at my feet and my blanket was on the floor in a lump with my pillow. I sat up and my head spun everything to the left so that I had to put my hand out and touch the wall, and then I realized how thirsty I was and all I wanted was a drink, but the very thought of putting something in my mouth made me want to throw up. I waited for the room to center again and then I stood up and went to the door.

The house was shut down and quiet and I stood in the hallway until my eyes adjusted to the dark and I thought I could walk to the bathroom. A streetlight spilled smeary white light through the glazed bathroom window and into the hallway. My dad's bedroom door was shut, but Nadine's was open a crack and I wondered if she had made it upstairs, and when, and if I hadn't been able to walk myself, maybe she had been the one walking me. I went to her door and started to look in through the crack, but I could hear them before I could see them, my dad breathing, and Nadine making quiet sounds that came and went in waves. I could see their shadow on the wall, one shape under the blanket and what light there was marking their movements in negative relief, and I stepped back and went to the bathroom and shut the door and stood over the sink for a while before I tried to drink. I stayed in the dark. Then I held my head under the faucet and let the water run off my face and whatever came close to my mouth I sucked in and drank. I stood up and let the tap run full blast into the sink so that I could feel the tiny spray against my hands, which were gripping the edges and holding me up, and I stood shaking for a minute and I thought the water didn't stand a chance at staying in me, but my head went straight and my thirst retreated and after a few minutes my stomach relaxed and kept the water down. When I left the bathroom Nadine's door was closed, and even though I stood against it as close as I could with my ear almost to the wood, I couldn't hear any more sound on the other side.

I thought I wouldn't be able to fall asleep again, that I was destined to stare at my ceiling, but when I opened my eyes my room was hot and full of light, and I realized it was Sunday and morning. I cranked my window open and a small breeze came in and it was cool and felt good. The neighborhood was quiet except for the sound of a few cars passing through and a lawn mower somewhere down the street. I pulled clothes out of my drawers and went to the bathroom and put my head under the faucet and let the cold water run just like I had during the night, only this time I soaked my hair and drank and washed my face and brushed my teeth. When I was done I almost felt better but there was a taste in my mouth that I couldn't get rid of, something coppery, but more like pennies than blood.

My dad's door was open but the bedroom was empty and I didn't stop to take inventory of the condition of his bed, whether the covers were kicked back, whether it had been slept in or not. I passed Nadine's door and it was cracked again and even though I wanted to keep walking, I stopped and tried to look through the gap. I couldn't hear any noise, so I pushed the door with the palm of my hand and it opened wide and I could see that the curtains were pulled back and the windows were open and the bed had been stripped and the sheets and blanket were folded in a small pile at the foot of the mattress. I looked around the room, and Nadine's bag was gone. I turned back to the bed and then I saw my boxers sticking out from under the stack of bedding. I lifted up the pillow and the boxers were spread out flat as if she were lying there but invisible.

I went downstairs and my dad was sitting on the couch with cartoons on but the sound too low to hear and it didn't matter because he had music playing anyway. He was dressed in a white undershirt and a pair of shorts, and his dark hair was standing up on one side and creased flat on the other. He was drinking a beer and his wallet was on the coffee table and it was unfolded and spread apart and looked empty, and I didn't know if it was empty by accident or on purpose.

"She left," he said. He did not turn to look at me right away, but when he did his beard looked like an eraser had rubbed out pencil on his face and he looked old and hard to recognize.

The needle on the turntable lifted up, moved back and dropped to the beginning of the album. I knew all the words to the song, and so did my dad, and so did Nadine now, I figured, since we had sung it over and over again last night under the hard circle of bright dining room light and the beat of wooden spoons on cheap metal pots.

"I hate this fucking song," I said.

I picked up my backpack from the floor by the front window, and I rolled back the lock on the door and pushed the screen and the air smelled like cut grass and sprinkler water. "Hey, Floyd, wait," my dad said from behind me. "Wait a minute. We can get some breakfast together."

I didn't slow down. The Vette was gone from the driveway and my dad's Ford sat there looking dirty and used. I hit the sidewalk and kept walking, crossed the street and turned right at the corner. Even though it was early there was heat underneath the morning air and I could tell it was waiting to break through and take over for the day. My legs loosened up and warmed to the motion and I felt as if walking had never felt this good before, as if I had never felt it like this with my feet connected to the pavement and me just following along. If I crossed the park I could go back to the old house and see Jerry, but instead I stayed on the sidewalk and followed the street. Ronnie lived a couple miles away and he had my Salinger book. I had lent it to him before I made the switch to Kafka, but now I wanted my book back.

CATCH THE GREY DOG

There had been rain and everything was washed clean, colored knife-sharp and throwing back hard sunshine. There was still the cupboard smell of potatoes—dank and dark—from the dirt that hadn't dried between the yellowed patches of grass that were trying to get a foothold in the gravel. My mother was leaning into the open yawn of the hood of my car, pointing at colored wires with a filed nail, careful to poke without touching so she wouldn't spoil her manicure with sticky grease. I didn't have to look at her to know that she was doing this. There was a man standing beside her, a tall man in dirty jeans, and I knew what kind of show she'd be putting on for his benefit. I knew she was asking questions in her high-fret guitar-string voice, and that she wasn't listening for the answers. What she knew about cars I could fit into the corner of my eye, pick out with my finger, and wipe across my pants, and I was glad that I didn't have to listen to her.

Ruby touched my arm as she spoke. "This is my favorite rabbit," she said.

Ruby had taken it upon herself to tell me her name without asking for mine and walk me over to the sheet-metal garage so she could show me the badly weathered and leaning rabbit hutches that had been built along the outer wall. On this side of the garage I couldn't see the driveway; the sun was blocked and the air was cooler. I could open my eyes without trying to rub the glare out of them. The separated cages were faced with thick, dense wire mesh that was too tightly bunched to squeeze a finger through, but Ruby put her hand up to the front of the third cage and tried to coax the rabbit forward with a weak wiggle of her pinkie through a hole.

"How old are you?" she asked.

"I turned sixteen last month," I said. "What about you?"

"Twelve," she said. "I wish I was thirteen."

"There's nothing great about being thirteen," I said. I could remember being thirteen and in eighth grade, afraid of having to take a shower in PE, but being forced to anyway, standing naked in a group under a shower and trying not to look down.

"I just don't want to be twelve anymore. I feel like I should be older. I look older, don't I?"

She turned to face me and my eyes landed on her chest for a second, on the small bumps under her T-shirt that weren't quite boobs, but were bigger than what my friend Robbie called "mosquito bites." Robbie had told me that he'd had his hand on some mosquito bites once and when he'd tried to rub the nipples between his fingers, he'd gotten lost, slid off the mark without realizing it, and had spent the next several minutes trying to find his way back to second base. "Never again," he'd said. "I could've been pinching at a mole for all I knew."

"Well?" she said.

I leaned down and tried to look through the wire at the rabbit in the corner of the cage. "You could be older, I guess," I said.

Ruby turned toward the cage and pushed in next to me so that our shoulders were touching. She smelled like maple syrup. "Her name is Thumper," she said.

"That's a great name," I said. *Original*, I thought, but I didn't say it. Maybe out here in the middle of Podunk they didn't have a copy of *Bambi*. I looked at Ruby and the bulk of bra under her shirt, and I knew she was too old to really have an attachment to a rabbit's name from a baby's cartoon. Maybe she didn't know that Thumper was a boy rabbit, what with his absence of animated balls and the whine in his voice through the entire movie—it was easy to be confused. Maybe she had hoped for a boy rabbit, mistaken a wad of fur between his legs, and had been strapped with a girl.

"I've had her for over a year now," Ruby said. "She's had a lot of babies. Mostly we sold them, but some of them we kept. These all belong to her. That one right there is her son, Blackie." She pointed at the last cage, where a big black rabbit sat on its haunches and rubbed at its head with its front paws.

"Let me guess," I said, "that one right there is Whitie." I pointed at the white rabbit sleeping in the first cage.

Ruby laughed and pulled her finger free from Thumper's wire. "No, silly. That's Jezebel. She likes to get out of her cage and run around loose. I think her boyfriend is one of the wild rabbits from the field. A jackrabbit, you know."

I grinned and kicked at the damp dirt around the legs of the hutch. There were green pellets spilled on the ground and swollen fat like sow bugs. "Let me guess. Jack, right? You call her boyfriend Jack."

She looked at me and squinted hard, so that wrinkles nearly swallowed her narrowed eyes. "I don't name the wild ones," she said. "That would be dumb." Her eyelashes were dark and long and kissed the tops of her cheeks as she talked. She made a clicking sound with her tongue and Blackie hopped to the side of his cage so he could be closer to her. "Quit begging for food," she said. "He eats way too much."

I looked at Thumper lying on her side against the hay bottom and saw that she was panting despite the cool air in the shadows. Her nose kept up its steady twitch, testing the wind with whiskers stiff as broom straw. She rolled her eyes without lifting her head to watch us. I put my finger up to the wire like Ruby had done, but my finger was too fat to poke through.

"I'd let you hold her," she said, "but she's gonna have babies any day now and it's not a good idea to touch her. Sometimes she bites when she gets like this." There was weak green diarrhea puddled under her and the entire cage smelled like a grass stain. I dropped my hand.

Ruby unclipped the water bottle from the front of the cage and unscrewed the top. "I take care of all the rabbits," she said. "I get up before school and feed them, check their water, and then when I get home, I do it again. Casper says it's my responsibility, taking care of the animals. These are all that are left."

I looked at the small row of cages. The hutches had rope knotted around their legs in places, and the rope was attached to various car parts that lay discarded on the ground—a rusted bumper with a headlight still attached, a red door without a window.

"We used to have a dog," Ruby said. "But Casper had to let him go. He got the taste for chickens." Behind us the grass crept up toward the garage, long grass with tall furry blades that looked like they'd be rough if you tried to roll around in them. "The chickens are gone, too."

I stepped out of the shadow and looked toward the driveway. The man in jeans had straightened up from poking at the engine of my car and now he was leaning sideways against the front fender, lighting a cigarette. My mom had her hip pressed against the driver's side door and was laughing at something the man said. He was smiling, the cigarette pressed into the corner of his mouth, his eyes squinted against the smoke. My mom waved her arm toward me. "Sonny, come here," she called.

Ruby was around the back corner of the garage where a pipe rose out of the ground. She was holding the water bottle under a hose and trying to force a thick stream through the narrow opening without getting back-spray on her pants.

"Gotta go," I said.

She looked up from the hose and smiled at me. Her shoes were shiny with water.

I walked back across the gravel. My mother was telling a story about the time her fan belt broke on the highway and the man who pulled over to help her asked if she was wearing pantyhose stockings, which she was, and she sat in the car and took one off and the man knotted it and used it as a fan belt for her, so that she could drive the rest of the way home without paying for a tow.

"Have you ever heard of anything like that? He saved me at least a hundred dollars," she said. "Maybe more. A three-dollar pair of stockings was well worth the cost, but I never would've thought of doing that. Not in a million years."

The man held his cigarette up and blew ash off the tip so that the cherry glowed. "The heat from the engine binds it together somehow," he said. "Makes it solid and keeps it from tearing. It's an old trick." He watched me walk up from the garage.

My mother threw her arm around my shoulders and pulled me into her even though I tried to step back and get beyond her reach. I could smell the sweat in the underarm of her T-shirt, and her body was all around me so that I felt smothered and short of breath. "And this is my son, Sonny. He's the lucky one I bought the car for—all of this is for him." She pulled me closer to her so she could sweep her hand over the trunk, the dusty blue paint thick with Bondo where the rust had bubbled through.

"Sonny, this is Casper," she said. I looked at the man in jeans. He was younger than my mother, or maybe the same age, it was hard to tell. His face was windburned and peppered with scruff beard, as though he didn't shave often or well. He had long eyelashes, like Ruby, and those sharp eyes, and when he hit his cigarette, he curled back his lips and held the butt with his teeth so that I could see that they were straight, but not very clean. "He's our savior, no doubt about it, we're damn lucky we pulled in here. Of all the driveways we could've turned down, he's the one who happens to be a mechanic. I'm telling you, my luck is always too goddamn good to believe."

"Except for the fact that you bought a car that broke down," I said.

"Oh, you," she laughed. She pushed me away from her so that my tennis shoes kicked up loose gravel. "Always quick to point out every little thing. Mr. Negative. That's what I should call you. Don't you think, Casper? Mr. Negative right here, with his ungratitude and giving his mom a hard time when all she did was buy him a classic car just like he wanted."

Casper looked at me and blew smoke up toward the watery sky. I wanted to tell her that this wasn't the car I wanted. I wanted a '69 Camaro and what I ended up with was a 1970 GTO. It wasn't even the right color. But the worst part about the whole thing was that I didn't care about having a car at all. It had been her idea and I had been forced to go along with it.

"Well, broke down can be fixed," Casper said. "This is one hell of a car. If I was a kid, I'd give up my left nut for one of these." My mother covered her mouth and laughed like she was still in school and had never heard the word "nut" said out loud before. He flicked his cigarette and it landed at the edge of the gravel near a pile of bald tires. I watched the smoke trail and weaken and die. Casper turned back around and leaned over the open hood. "You've got the four-hundred cube engine that should put you at three hundred and fifty horses." He leaned over farther so that his left work boot lifted from the ground and I could see that the laces were untied. "And a sixteen-valve V8." He dropped back down and turned on me. His eyes measured me from my ragged shoes to the too-long hair that touched the collar of my shirt, and I knew the distance came up short. "One hell of a muscle car for a boy."

"But *can* it be fixed?" my mother asked. Her arm was raised against the hardtop and I could see the sweat I'd smelled.

Casper cleared his sinuses and tipped his greasy auto-parts cap back on his head. "To be honest with you, I don't know much about Muncie transmissions. Don't see 'em anymore, and never worked on one. But that's where your grind is. The trannie's dropped and you're running stripped."

Reverse had gone out on us first, and then we were trapped in second gear for somewhere near forty miles, the engine wound high and my mother talking too loud, and me trying to keep my right foot balanced at forty miles per hour. That's when we'd rolled up to Casper's, looking for a phone, and instead we'd found a mechanic with a garage in the middle of acres of farmland, almost like a reverse mirage, the shimmering sheet metal throwing back solid sunshine in lush, green, water-heavy flatland—only to find that he didn't know about my transmission and couldn't fix the car.

"Too good to be true," my mother said. "The catch at last."

"See, I wasn't being negative," I said.

"Now hold up." Casper eased back against the fender again and put a hand in his front pocket so that I could see him fingering loose change or scratching the left nut he was willing to give up for a car like mine. "I said *I* maybe couldn't fix it. I didn't say that it couldn't be fixed. My boy, Boone, he's real good with cars and knows a hell of a lot about these older ones. That's all them guys drive up in Lincoln. I can get him to come over and take a look and maybe between the two of us we can get you back out on the road again."

My mother clapped her hands together and then brought them up to her face in a gesture of prayer. "Thank you, Casper. Thank you and thank you again. I don't care what it costs. I just want the car fixed so we can get home."

"We should be able to get her back on the road," Casper said. "There ain't a reason in hell this car shouldn't make it home."

Fifteen hundred miles to go, I thought. *Not fucking likely.* I seriously doubted that I would see asphalt, streetlights, and the comfort of my bedroom anytime soon.

Ruby came out from the side of the garage and walked to where we were standing. "Thumper's getting close," she said to Casper. "I bet the babies come tonight."

"Babies?" my mother said. "You got a cat out there in the barn?" I looked out at the empty green field behind the garage, at the nothingness.

"Rabbits," I said. "She's got rabbits in cages over there against the garage."

"That is so sweet," my mother said. "Baby bunnies. I just love little bunnies. They make me think of Easter, and all that candy everybody gets, those little chocolate bunnies and those hard candy eggs . . ."

"Why are your shoes all wet?" Casper said. The sharpness in his voice came out of nowhere, like the bottom of a broken bottle overturned in the sand.

Ruby looked down at her shoes and the darkened hem of her pants where the water had crept up the fabric. "Thumper's water was empty so I had to fill it up. I guess I had the hose on too hard."

"I don't pay money for you to wear your good shoes out here to tend the animals," Casper said. He looked at Ruby and she flinched, but only a little.

"I'm sorry," she said. "I'll go take them off."

Casper's hands were gripped around the fender and his knuckles were white. "Go take out some more chicken to thaw for dinner while you're up at the house."

Ruby walked past us. "We don't want to impose on you," my mother said. "Sonny and I can get a taxi and find a room in town." She looked down the driveway toward the road and the fences and the grass that had started to bend in the rising wind. "There is a town here, isn't there?"

Casper loosened his hands from the fender and I half expected to see blue paint on his palms. He shook another cigarette from the crumpled soft pack in the front pocket of his shirt. "It ain't a problem for both of you to stay until my boy can get over here. Me and Ruby could use the company," he said. "It'd be a real good change."

I sat on the porch and watched the light change colors until dinner was ready, and we ate around a big oak table—Casper's fried chicken with too much salt and my mother's mashed potatoes with dirty gravy that Casper had made from the drippings left in the pan. He drank beer while they cooked, and didn't slow down with dinner. My mother joined him, bottle for bottle, and the conversation started to seep like the grease. Casper tried to call Boone several times, but there was no answer. "It's not likely that he's home if it's dark outside," he said. "Him and his buddies are probably on the hunt for girls." He looked over at me while he talked. "You know how boys are. Always sniffing around."

"Sonny'll be at that age someday," my mother said. "Right now he just cares about being in his bedroom. That's it. Just him alone in his room, building things. Isn't that what you do, Sonny? Put things together?" When I was younger, I had put together models, classic cars, and

I wanted to tell her this, remind her that it had been years since then, but she didn't pause for an answer. "I had to buy him something in order to get him to spend time with his own mother." She hiccupped and laughed. "I mean, I found him a car, flew us out to pick it up, and I am paying for the road trip to drive it home. The experience of a lifetime. And look at him. Nothing." She paused while everyone stared at me. "Anyway, you ever seen that cop movie where the bad guys crash that helicopter into the Golden Gate Bridge?" She had both elbows on the table and was leaning forward over her plate so that she could hold her beer with both hands. Her cheeks were pink, as though she had just stepped inside from the cold. "You know, and there's the car that catches on fire and when the people jump from the bridge they don't realize that they're jumping into shark water?" She looked around the table. I picked the dark meat from a small window I had torn in the crisp skin of a thigh. My mother had fucked somebody famous when she was younger. He hadn't been famous then, but he used to hang out at her apartment and drink red wine and talk about foreign films. Whenever she met new people, she couldn't keep from dropping his name, even though it had all happened eighteen years ago—a few weeks in the summer—when he was still in college and she thought his lips were too thin to date him seriously.

She drew out the pause longer than necessary to build the dramatic finish. "The actor who played the cop was my boyfriend," she said.

"Really?" Casper said. "That guy with the dark hair—kinda short, but built real good?" I could tell that he was genuinely impressed, like most people were. "That's something. It's like you're practically famous then."

The pink in my mother's cheeks spread to her ears and brightened like the glow of brake lights on wet pavement. "Well, it was years ago, you know, but we were close." She winked and put her mouth over the rim of the bottle so she could drink from it without lifting her arms. She swallowed and looked over at Casper. "Very close," she said.

He pushed his almost-untouched plate away from him and tipped back in his chair so that the front legs rose off the floor. His shoulders were wide and I could see hard muscle under his shirt. My mother was watching him, and from across the table I saw all the places where her eyes could land. "You want another beer?" he said.

"I'll get them," Ruby said. "I want to go check on Thumper, if it's okay."

"You can clear these plates up first. Put the food away."

My mother stood up and pushed her chair back. She was unsteady on her feet and the top of her thigh knocked against the edge of the table and made the empty bottles rock. We all reached out our hands to hold everything in place, but the table settled and she sat back down. "Why don't we let them go out and check on the bunnies, Casper? Me and you can clear the table and get the dishes done. I'm very good at washing, and you look like a man who knows his way around a dish towel." My mother picked up a boiled carrot with her fork and bit into it, then set it down.

Ruby sucked in her lower lip and started gathering the silverware from around her plate. Casper held his balance backward in the chair and was quiet. Finally he cleared his throat and dropped the chair back to all fours. "I guess that'd be okay for one night," he said. Ruby let go of a deep breath. She piled her wadded napkin onto her plate and pushed back from the table.

"You can take your own plate to the sink," Casper said.

I gathered up my things and followed Ruby to the kitchen. I scraped what was left on my plate into the trash like she had done and set it on the counter. She grabbed a flashlight from a drawer and I followed her out of the kitchen and toward the front door.

"Ruby." Casper's voice caught us. "Did you forget something?"

She turned and looked at me, and I shrugged my shoulders.

"The beers, Ruby. You said you'd bring them."

I could see her wince in the darkness. "Sorry," she yelled. "I'll get them right now." She handed me the flashlight. "Wait for me," she said.

I leaned my weight against the arm of the couch and looked at the bare walls. There were picture hooks but no pictures. Casper's voice carried through the room. "So I see them, you know, five or six of them sittin' on the tailgate of this pickup truck instead of working like I was paying them to do, and they got the engine running, burning up the gas so in case I show up, one of them can jump in the front and act like they were just finishing up with a load.

So I just let them keep sitting there, you know, I don't say nothing. I just creep around to the front and slide onto the seat and I put the truck in gear really gentle, so they can't feel it, and then I hit the gas as hard as I can—I mean hard enough to put my boot through the floorboard almost, and that truck just shoots right out from under them. All of 'em hit the ground, ass over teakettle, you know? Rolling through the dirt. Busted one guy's lip pretty good . . ."

My mother was laughing so hard she could barely catch her breath between words. "You're terrible, Casper, I love it. That's too much."

I didn't have to look at my mother to know that she had her hand gripped to Casper's arm while she was laughing, her fingers pressed into his skin.

We had been around the table for what seemed like hours, long enough for the sun to set and throw the evening into night, and when we were outside, Ruby took the flashlight and aimed the beam toward the garage. The night was cool, but not cold, and I could hear crickets all around us, chirping in different pitches like an orchestra tuning up before a show. I could smell the dampness again, but it was stronger, as though my face was pressed against ground. The sound of the crickets muffled the crisp shift of gravel under our shoes. The weak light from a bulb above the garage shined across the hood of my car, but otherwise it was dark and useless in the driveway.

"I like your car," Ruby said. "Is it really yours?"

I thought about my mother's overexcitement when she told me that she'd bought the car for me and we were going to fly out and pick it up and drive it home—a real road trip, both of us together and on our own. I had been standing in the kitchen with a glass of milk in my hand and she was talking about what to pack and when we were leaving and how this car was like a dream, and I didn't feel anything. I just dug a calendar out of a drawer and tried to figure out how many miles we could cover each day and how long it would take for it to be over with.

"It's okay, I guess," I said. "I just want it fixed so that we can drive it home."

We walked past the car and around the corner of the garage. In the darkness the scrap parts were odd and hard to identify. The stacks of tires were humped shapes pressed against the flat wings of unhinged hoods so that their combined shadows looked like giant insects. Ruby pointed the light at the hutches and I could hear the rabbits change positions inside, shift around and come forward to watch us. We both pressed our faces against Thumper's cage. My eyes strained to see something that hadn't been there before.

"I don't know what I'm looking for," I said.

"Here, take the light."

I held the beam at an angle. Thumper looked at us with wide and wild black eyes, but she did not turn her head away. I ran the light the length of her and we could see her side heaving with her breath, and every now and then it would stop, tense, shudder, and begin again.

"Wait," Ruby whispered. "Move the light forward a little."

I pointed the flashlight at the alfalfa hay that was threaded with tufts of light fur, and we saw darkness and something thick like snot. "She's doing it," Ruby whispered. "Look at that."

I pushed my face closer and then I saw it, something wet moving the green stalks, a tiny paw with nails so thin I could see through them. The newborn rolled and writhed like a worm pulled from under a rock. It looked like a fat severed finger under the light. Its head seemed too big for its body and its eyes were shut tight with its tiny ears flat against its head. It was hairless, naked, pink, bloody, and blind.

"What's wrong with it?" I said.

"Shhhh, I think there's another one coming," she said.

Thumper's side heaved and strained and tightened. There was more blood, and the mucus. I looked away. "They're deformed," I said. "There's something wrong."

Ruby stood up. She was smiling. "That's what they look like," she said. "They get hair later, and their eyes open, too. Haven't you ever seen something get born before?"

I pointed the flashlight at the ground and we stepped back from the cages. "No, I guess not," I said.

"Well, all babies are different when they come out, just like us. They change as they get older."

I started walking around the edge of the garage back toward the house, but Ruby took my arm and pulled me toward the tall sheet-metal door that was open wide enough for us to step through sideways. "I don't want to go back yet," she said. "I want to wait until Thumper is done." The breeze caught stride and I shivered. "We can sit in there for a while." She pulled me through the opening in the garage door and what little light there had been was suddenly cut to nothing.

Ruby took the flashlight from me and pointed it at a couple of milk crates that were turned upside down on the floor. We walked over and sat on them. I could smell oil and grease and sweet gasoline. There was a window in the wall and after a few minutes my eyes adjusted and I could see shapes in the darkness. Ruby turned off the flashlight.

"Casper is out here most days," she said. "This is where he spends all his time." Her voice echoed in the small building.

"He works on a lot of cars, I bet. Stays pretty busy, huh?"

Ruby cleared her throat and I could hear her shoes scrape on the cement floor as she shifted her weight. "He hasn't worked on a car in a long time," she said. "A really long time."

I waited for her to say something to change that statement, but when she stayed quiet I shook my head a little and turned so that I could try to see her. "Wait a second. I thought he was a mechanic. That's what he said."

"Oh, he *was* a mechanic. Now he just works on this." She pushed the button on the flashlight and suddenly I could see a lawn mower in front of us, its engine split open, the parts pulled free and dangling like guts. The light went off again and my eyes could still see the negative image of the lawn mower in the dark.

"I don't get it," I said.

"Well, it's not the whole lawn mower that he works on. It's just the carburetor. He keeps it over there on the workbench under the window, and he sits out here with a stopwatch so he can time how fast he can take it apart and put it back together again." I could hear her thumb rattling the switch on the flashlight but she didn't push it hard enough to turn on. "When he was in Vietnam, they used to do it with a gun, you know, take it apart, lay out the pieces, and see how fast they could put it back together. Now he does it with a carburetor."

I tried to imagine Casper out here in his dirty jeans and unlaced work boots, clicking the button on a stopwatch so he could beat his best time.

"He was in Vietnam?" I said.

"That's where he got his name. He says he was like a ghost." Ruby set the flashlight in her lap. "He is still like a ghost, I think," she said. "Sometimes I wake up at night and he's standing in my room, against the wall by the door, and I never heard him. Even when he walks up to the bed, I don't hear him, and I even try to hold my breath, but there's nothing."

I tried to picture Casper's dark shape in my bedroom, and I could feel the hairs on the back of my neck stand up a little. "Can I ask you something?" I said. "Where's your mother?"

Ruby was quiet for a minute. Through the window I could see thin clouds cross the moon. "She left," Ruby said. "About six months ago."

"Where'd she go?"

"She never told me."

"Really?" I said. "Don't you miss her?"

"A lot," she said. "But if I need to, I think I can find her. She once told me that if something bad happens, I should walk down the road toward town and find the bus." Ruby paused and in the half darkness I could see her tuck her hair behind her ear. "She showed me a picture of the bus, the one with the grey dog on the side. And she told me I should catch the grey dog and ride until I got to the first town that starts with an *L*." She looked straight at my face without blinking.

"Wait a second," I said. "So you take a bus and get off at a town that starts with the letter *L*, and you think you're going to find her? I mean, you don't know which bus or which direction to go. That's impossible."

I felt Ruby's hand on my jeans, just above my knee. She leaned in close to me so that I could smell her breath, buttery with dinner's potatoes. "The point is to leave, Sonny. First I leave here as fast as I can, and then I can be free to start looking."

"So why did your mother leave you in the first place?" The hand felt warm on my leg.

"Because maybe something bad happened, and she had to go."

I thought about that for a second, but her hand was distracting me. "Did something happen with her and your dad?" My own father had left years ago to be with a dark-haired woman he'd met on a layover in Vegas.

"Casper is my stepdad," she said. "My real dad died when I was a baby."

We were both quiet for a while. I listened to the wind outside as it tried to force its way in. "Can I ask you something?" she said. "Have you ever done it?"

I laughed suddenly and choked on my own spit so that I couldn't answer until the coughing stopped. "No," I said. "I've never done it."

"Casper thinks that I've done it," she said. "I haven't, but he doesn't believe me. He's always looking at me funny, you know, watching me. And I get in trouble for everything. I can't help it. I'm worse than Boone, but he won't ever come back anyway."

"Your brother? I thought he was coming out here to fix my car? That's what Casper told us."

"Boone won't speak to Casper. He hates him."

"Then how is somebody going to fix my car? Your dad . . . Casper, whatever, he said he can't fix it, but Boone can, and he was calling him all night and he said that Boone would probably be here in the morning." I realized my voice had risen to a whine and I forced myself to stop talking.

"It's not true," Ruby said. "Boone won't ever come back. Casper says that Boone is weak and that's why my mom always favored him. Casper says that maybe Boone is queer, you know, and that's why he ran off." I could hear the sound of metal rubbing metal outside in the wind. "Boone put a lock on the inside of my bedroom door before he left. I don't use it, but Boone told me maybe sometime I should."

I took three deep breaths of fumes and closed my eyes. All I could see was a dark blank wall and changing shadows and my broken car outside. "If Boone really isn't coming, I guess we'll have to figure something else out tomorrow," I said. "We can get a tow into town."

Ruby's hand moved higher on my thigh. "It's been kind of nice to have you and your mom here, though. It's been really good." Her small bony fingers squeezed at my jeans.

I wanted to tell her that when I was eleven, I heard my parents having sex in the middle of the night, and it was a terrible sound that I will never forget—worse than crying, and empty, and sad. I went into the kitchen and opened the cupboard and started throwing our dinner plates against the floor, as hard as I could.

"Maybe we should go check on Thumper," I said. I stood up and her hand slid from my leg. "It's getting late."

I waited near the entrance to the garage while Ruby took the flashlight and went to check the rabbits. I stood against the door to block the wind, half of me in the darkness and half of me in the yellow light from above. There were bugs swarming the bulb, and every now and then I could hear one hit the glass with a solid-sounding ping.

When she came back, she was swinging the light and smiling. "There's four," she said. "Maybe more will come, but right now there's four. Thumper's got them all lined up against her."

We went back to the house, where everything was dark and quiet, but after being outside our eyes were adjusted and we didn't bother turning on the lights. I thought that I could hear voices somewhere in the back, but Ruby said it was probably Casper's television, which he liked to run late into the night. They had made a bed for my mother in one of the extra rooms, but I didn't try to find her. Ruby brought me blankets for the couch, crocheted afghans and a quilt that someone had sewn together from pieces of the clothes she had worn as a baby. She took my finger and ran it over the corduroy from her first pair of overalls. She covered the couch with a sheet and spread the blankets out while I sat and watched her and undid the laces on my shoes. When she was finished, I thought she might sit down and keep talking, or maybe I was afraid that she might, and I realized that we were alone and out of the wind with blankets and a place to lie down. Instead she fluffed up a pillow and put it on the make-shift bed, and then she touched my arm gently, almost like my mother would, and told me that she hoped I would sleep well. When she was gone, I slipped off my socks and pulled the covers around me, suddenly conscious that I hadn't brushed my teeth, but too tired to do anything about it.

It was the screaming that woke me up before the sunshine did. At first I was unsure about where I was, the strange smell of the pillow under my head and the heavy bulk of blankets did not belong to me. I sat up and everything clicked back into place, except for the screaming outside, which was high-pitched and very loud.

I walked out the front door and held my arm across my face to block out the too-bright light. My mother was leaning against my car with a mug in her hand. She turned around when the door slammed behind me. "It's about time you decided to get up," she said. "I thought you were going for one of your noon wake-up calls."

I stepped off the porch and walked across the drive-way. The gravel was sharp and I tried not to put all of my weight on my bare feet. "What's going on?" I said.

When I got closer to my mother, I could see that the mug was chipped and had the name *Susan* written in flowered script across the front. She was wearing a button-down men's shirt that did not belong to her. "Casper says that sometimes this happens." She pointed the mug in the direction of the garage and I saw that the door was pulled open. Inside, Ruby was crying hard, her face red and smeared, and Casper had a beer in one hand, and with the other hand he was pulling on an end of rope and yelling something about a hammer. Ruby stepped back and I could see a rabbit noosed by its hind legs to the end of a rope that went up toward the dark ceiling of the garage. I could tell it was Thumper. She was trying to kick her back legs free, and every time she did, her body would spin and make the rope jump like a pit bull was giving it a good shake. And when the kicking slowed down, she would open her mouth and scream like nothing I had ever heard before, like a girl, or maybe ten girls, something human and too afraid to feel pain.

"Jesus Christ," I said. "What in the hell is going on?"

My mother sipped at the coffee and shifted her weight back against the car. "I guess she ate her babies, mostly all of them, anyway. Ruby has one of them wrapped in a towel over there, but it won't live past tonight without a mother. Casper says that once a rabbit gets a taste for something like that, it's no good anymore. It'll never be right again."

"So he's hanging her for it?" I asked. I couldn't take my eyes off the body spinning at the end of the rope, all of her stretched out long while her ears hung down toward the floor, and her front legs pawed at the air around her head while she screamed.

Suddenly Casper swung something and there was a soft sound that I could not describe, but would probably remember for the rest of my life, and then there was quiet in the yard. Even Ruby's crying had scaled down to something like a whimper between breaths.

"I can't stay here," I said. "We need to get the car towed and go."

My mother turned on me then, and she was smiling but there was nothing light in her eyes. "We can't judge what they do here, Sonny. This is farm life, something we know nothing about."

I looked around at the garage with the tires and car parts and dented sheet-metal sides, and beyond that a wire fence with leaning posts, and then grass and more grass and empty sky that was too blue to consider. "This is not a farm," I said. "*He* isn't even a mechanic. Do you know that? He can't even fix the car, and no one is coming to help him. Ruby told me." I turned to walk back to the house but my mother caught my arm and her fingers sank into the place between the muscle and the bone.

"Ruby told you that? I wouldn't believe anything she says if I were you. Casper told me that ever since his wife left him, she's gotten into trouble at school, started telling lies and running around with boys that are almost twice her age. He says it started even before his wife left, all this troublemaking, but now she's out of control and it's all he can do to keep her in line anymore."

I could see Ruby crying in the garage. She looked as though she was miles away from the age of thirteen. "I don't believe him," I said. "And I can't believe that you do."

Her hand tightened on my arm and I knew that when she let go there would be marks. "I like it here, Sonny. I like Casper. I haven't met a man in a long time who makes me laugh and feel good inside. And I'm not in any hurry to lose that feeling. We're gonna stay here awhile and see what happens. So get used to it." She loosened her grip on my arm and I pulled away from her. She let me go, but when I looked back at her, she was staring at me, trying to swallow me with her eyes.

Casper set a bucket under the swinging rabbit and I saw him take a knife from his back pocket and open it to the longest blade. I turned away from the garage and scanned down the drive toward the road. My mother once had a boyfriend who could play the drums and when he was drinking he'd hit them hard. He used to call it "Jake Brake"—the sound of a semi on a steep grade, and if I closed my eyes I could hear the sound again coming up from my chest in a solid beat. For a minute I lost my sense of direction, but I knew which way I had to turn. The grass was high, but I thought that I could see the black strip of asphalt rising up through the green.

FIELD DRESSING

At first I thought maybe it was me, some dark cloud of dying that was hanging over my head, but when Shirley and I sat there on the embankment and I tried to convince her of things before the sun went down, she told me that there was never any rhyme or reason for death coming, and she didn't believe in any god or fate or destiny or bigger plan. Shit happens, she said, and as it was we both figured we'd probably freeze to death once night came, and we were in about the deepest shit there could be.

My father went out for cigarettes and orange juice one Tuesday morning when I was five years old and never came back, and it had been my mother and me together since as long as I could almost remember, except for a hazy image of him tying my shoes, explaining to me again how the rabbit ears go in and out of the hole. My mother burned all the pictures and remnants of him in the weeks after he left, and there was nothing to anchor me to him.

When I was eight my babysitter was a ten-foot piece of rope knotted around my wrist and the other end tied tight to a leg of the couch. I could watch TV, sleep, get in the refrigerator, have access to two cupboards, and pee in a bucket—the bathroom was twenty-two feet away and we had only one length of rope. By the time I was thirteen my mother had four DUIs and a way of walking slumped over like she was carrying something heavy on her back. She had a boyfriend named Tyler and he had been in and out of "the program" for years—AA, NA, AA again—he went back and forth every time he failed, so she quit vodka and announced that she was off the drink, for me, for Tyler, for the sake of a normal life, but then the plastic bottles of Listerine started showing up around the house in places where they didn't belong—under the couch, behind the TV. It was the original kind, which burns so bad you can't swish it around in your mouth for a full thirty seconds, but she could do more than swish it; she could drain half a liter bottle in a day, empty three in a week, and smelled like medicine but not bad breath. She and Tyler pulled the blinds, drew the curtains, and decided to see whose liver would kick out first. My mother won.

She spent most of a Friday on the bathroom floor, and I called 9-1-1, but by then it was Sunday, and then Tyler said he had a warrant and went out the back door as soon as the flashing lights and sirens came down the gravel road. Uncle Nick was the one who picked me up from the hospital, my mother's older brother and only next of kin, and he took me back to the trailer to pack a bag and then he drove me four hours north to what he kept calling my *new home* as we went up the interstate, as in *I think you're gonna like your new home* and *We've got a new bed set up for you in your new home.* His was a deep voice of reassurance, but I was whipped and dog-tired and I stared out the passenger window without talking so I could watch the mile markers tick by without counting them.

For the next three weeks I went limp. Uncle Nick drove me places, bought me things, signed me up here and here and here, and I just went with him, stood quietly, filled out forms to the best of my ability: *father's name, date of your last tetanus shot.* I spent two Saturdays sitting on a folding chair in a portable building behind the VFW hall, taking a hunter's safety course—trigger, safety, barrel, butt—and then the test, and then I had a junior hunting license and my Uncle Nick was more proud of me than if I had won an award at school, which I was not attending yet because my mother was not big on organizing or saving things or filing papers, and I didn't have a birth certificate or any proof that I was fifteen and a California resident and really who I said I was. Uncle Nick could smooth that over with Bob, the hunter's safety teacher and Uncle Nick's trout-fishing buddy, but the school couldn't be smoothed over and they put me in a holding pattern until proof could be shown. I couldn't say that I was sorry for the delay, but then I found myself wandering around the house with Uncle Nick's wife, Shirley, home during the day, telling me not to put my feet on the coffee table, put my cereal bowl in the dishwasher, take a shower, don't watch so much TV—*don't you read?* —and after three weeks of avoiding her and her bird hands that liked to snatch at me and my things, I was in the backseat of the truck, climbing in elevation, facing five days with them in the mountains—or until Uncle Nick and Shirley took their deer—whichever came first. *Bucks*, Uncle Nick reminded me. *Buck hunting—there's a big difference.*

Uncle Nick was a big man, not particularly tall, but with a stomach that hid his belt buckle and rubbed the steering wheel as he drove. He used to smoke, but was determined to quit, so he would put a cigarette in his mouth without lighting it. He would just suck on it, hold it between his fingers, put it back between his lips again. He was a talker—didn't take a break, could hold a conversation about anything, jumped from subject to subject, and covered everything once a subject stuck. Shirley was a clock-watcher and a speed monitor, a passenger-seat driver who told Uncle Nick we weren't making good time, it was taking forever, slow down, you're following too close, you're back too far, you're swerving.

Just past noon we pulled off the freeway and stopped at a chipped and faded burger stand near the two-lane junction between highways and ordered lunch. Shirley was disgusted with the picnic tables because they were splintered and carved up with names and dates and misspelled bad words that told Joey B. to *fuk off*, but we took a seat anyway because Shirley didn't want spills in the truck, so we sat outside in the sunshine eating.

"Me and Shirley have been married . . . let's see . . . five"—I could see him mentally ticking off numbers and changing his mind—"no, six years. Six years in August." He picked up a fistful of fries and put them all in his mouth.

An El Camino full of teenagers pulled into the gravel parking lot and I turned to watch the girls get out while the driver gunned it once, twice, turned the stereo louder for a minute to blast the chorus on a song I didn't know, and then cut the car to silence with the turn of the key. The girls were tall and long-legged and there were three of them and the driver looked as though he either really didn't care that he was chauffeuring three girls or was doing a good job at pretending not to. I had never ridden in a car with that many girls. I could've had my learner's permit last month but I had never taken the class for the certificate or the test for the paper and we didn't have a car anyway because my mom was busy dying. I sometimes thought about what it would be like to drive, have my own car, maybe chauffeur three girls out to burgers on the way home from school, but I couldn't even see that desire as more than a dream because from where I stood now that reality was not even in the distance.

"So Shirley, she's taken a deer every damn year that we've been together," Uncle Nick said. "Me? I've taken zero. No deer in six years. I call that shit luck." He had a piece of lettuce stuck to the front of his teeth but neither of us pointed it out to him.

"Buck fever," Shirley said. She was a skinny woman without a defined age—she could've been thirty or fifty—and she had wiry blond hair that she kept pulled back off her face with a black headband. I don't know if she had ten headbands or just the one, but she was always wearing it no matter what time of the day it was. She had faint freckles on her face, like splatter from a flicked brush, and she chewed slowly, took forever to get through half a burger, and had one breast—the other one had been cut off because of cancer the year before she met Uncle Nick. When I came in the house and met her for the first time, she had walked to the doorway and given me a stiff and lopsided hug and when she stepped back to look at me, she held out her arms and said, "I've only got one boob," and glanced down toward her chest where her T-shirt rose and fell like a hill butted up against a valley. "But I'm a survivor, so you better think twice before cracking a joke," she said, then picked up my bag and walked it to the back bedroom of what my Uncle Nick had been busy convincing me was *my new home*. That was all she said to me.

"Tough as nails," Uncle Nick had said and shook a ciga-rette from the soft pack in the breast pocket of his denim work shirt.

The wind made a halfhearted gust and tried to pick our grease-stained burger wrappers from the table. We all reached for them, but Shirley had those bird hands that could dive out of nowhere and managed to shove them all under her soda cup before I could get my hand down. She gave me a sideways glance out of the corner of her eye and said something under her breath, something at me, but the wind was rattling the bent rain gutter on the burger stand and I couldn't hear her. It looked like her mouth said *you suck*, but maybe I was wrong.

Uncle Nick didn't notice anything. He just kept forklifting fries to his mouth, five or ten at a time so that he had to chew while he talked. "Buck fever, my ass," he said. "Bad luck is more like it. I never get a clean shot."

"He always misses," Shirley said, and she didn't smile as she said it.

Uncle Nick and Shirley had deer tags for zone X-4, which Uncle Nick informed me contained the prime spots—Crater Lake, Eagle Lake, Antelope Peak, Harvey Mountains, Upper Hat Creek Rim, Butte Creek Rim, Ladder Butte, Negro Camp Mountain, Black's Ridge—and was one of the most sought-after zones in the state. Deer tags for X-4 were only awarded by a drawing in June after all interested hunters applied, but Uncle Nick called it a lottery, as in he and Shirley had won it along with 413 others, and they were determined to both take deer this year, *bucks*, and Uncle Nick had already been scouting the zone, had decided on where to camp and where to hike and where to hunt, and he thought himself crafty because he had found an area that was hard to get to, out of the way, and went against the grain of deer-hunting success tips, which suggest that deer are more dense in less forest, and not the other way around. We rose in elevation and small green signs by the roadside announced the change—2,240 feet, 3,180, 3,540. Shirley turned in her seat and told me to stop chewing my gum like a cow—she could hear me chewing over the sound of the truck—and when we finally stopped climbing we went down a dirt road, and another dirt road, and the truck bounced over rocks, gullies, washouts, and Uncle

Nick turned the hubs to four-wheel drive so we could climb out of mud tracks and low spots until the ground evened out again. The trees came up thick and tall and crowded the road that wasn't really one until the road faded out altogether and Uncle Nick rolled to a stop and said, "We're here."

We got out, one by one, and I tried to shake the pins and needles from my legs. Uncle Nick put his hands on his lower back, stretched and belched. Shirley dusted off her hands even though they were clean, and walked around the back of the truck so she could lift the latch on the cabover camper and open the door to make camp.

I had never been in the mountains before, and I had not realized that there was so much quiet. It was a quiet that wasn't without noise, but the noise was a hushing sound, the wind up high bending the pine trees, and there were the sounds of birds, but a different sound than in the city, not a call of warning and near misses, but maybe real communication and happiness, and somewhere above us I could hear a woodpecker. The air was clean, but I could not describe what I meant by that, only recognize that it was.

Shirley set up chairs and Uncle Nick had me find big rocks so we could make a fire pit. He said we were lucky that it wasn't fire season or we'd be freezing our asses off at night, and we made a makeshift circle, stacked the rocks and then gathered dead wood and made a pile. By the time we were done with that, Uncle Nick was huffing and puffing and said we'd done enough manual labor for one day and it was time to drink beer. He got comfortable in a chair and talked me through how to build a fire—pine needles, bark, and scraps, a lot of blowing, stack the wood in a tepee to let the air circulate and don't let the flames get too high. He drank and pointed. When I was done he handed me a Coors and we sat in the last patch of light, drinking.

"You excited about tomorrow?" he asked. He had already folded and crushed three empty cans and was cracking open a fourth. He put a cigarette in the crease of the corner of his mouth and tilted his head back to look at the clear sky between the trees.

"I'm nervous," I said.

"Well, you're gonna be the spotter, keep your eyes peeled, but if you get a clear shot I want you to take it and we'll just put my tag on it and take it home. What the hell—it might be the closest I get to taking a deer this year anyways." He tried to sound hopeful but did a bad job at it. He would be disappointed if I got the deer. He pulled the cigarette from his mouth and held it between the first two fingers of his right hand, against the side of his beer, and it was hard to remember that it wasn't lit. "Just remember that we're looking for forks—forks and bigger—no rack, no shot, right?"

I opened the ice chest and reached for a Pepsi, then decided to test it and took another Coors instead. Uncle Nick didn't notice, or didn't care, and he raised up out of his chair and tossed a mossy chunk of wood onto the fire so that there was a whole lot of smoke until the fire could stutter back again. Shirley came out of the camper and I sat down and hugged the beer can between my thighs so she couldn't see the label. She handed us bowls of spaghetti and pulled up a chair of her own.

"Goddamn this fire is smoking, Nick." She coughed and waved her hand back and forth in front of her. "Robbie, you got dish duty and cleanup tonight." She said it without looking at me. "Four tomorrow?" she said to Uncle Nick.

"Sounds good. Up at four. Up the trail by four thirty. Take the early movers."

"You think you can get up that early, Robbie, or should we leave you in camp?" Shirley asked. I didn't know if it was the beer and a half in my head or just the way the wind carried, but it sounded like a dare.

"I'll be ready," I said.

"Jesus, I can't eat out here. Fix this fire, Nick."

Uncle Nick took down a six-pack and I managed three more by drinking fast and staying in the shadows. Shirley was either a messy cook or she did it on purpose, but the tiny kitchen in the camper looked like a pipe bomb had gone off, and when I started trying to wash things Shirley told me that water wasn't free up here, what we had had to last us, and she made me heat water a little at a time, wash everything first, rinse fast, and then she told me that the dishes weren't clean enough and maybe I could do a better job tomorrow. She reached for a bag of marshmallows and a box of graham crackers and began stepping down out of the camper.

"Whatever," I said low and under my breath—it seemed like it was the way she and I communicated—and she turned fast and grabbed my arm up high, dug her bony fingers between the bicep and bone.

"What did you say to me?"

"Nothing."

"You know, I am no dummy. I know how teenage boys are—lazy, mouthy, dumb. Nick has a big heart and when the phone rang, he couldn't say no. Me, I said why in the hell do you need to rescue your sister's boy when she couldn't take care of her own? And she sure as hell couldn't, could she? But Nick thought he could do something for you. Make things better. I told him that he couldn't. So watch it. I have a lot of leverage around here and all I have to do is tell Nick three words—*I am done*."

I didn't sleep that night. I tried, but the makeshift table bed was too short and unless I kept my knees slightly bent or slept with my legs at an angle so they hung over the side, I couldn't fit. I felt claustrophobic and smothered. I could hear Uncle Nick breathing, falling in and out of snoring like a lawn mower that's sputtering on fumes, and I could hear Shirley, her sounds of sleep quieter but sharp, and the air in the camper was too hot and there was not enough oxygen to go around. I stared out the little window and watched the oval piece of sky where the stars were bright white and there were too many to count and wondered if this was my life. When I was sitting in the hospital after they wheeled my mom away, the county people came and asked questions, made the call to Uncle Nick. They asked how long my mother had been dead and I had to explain to them that I really didn't know for sure. I turned over on the too-short bed and tried to remember how my old house looked when I used to walk in the front door. I was forgetting things. When the alarm went off I was relieved because my eyes were already open and I had been waiting for a long time.

Shirley made coffee in the percolator on the tiny stove, and I stepped outside to dress. It was cold and the cold was an edge against my skin whenever a section was exposed. I dressed fast, dressed in layers, the way that Uncle Nick had said I should. We filled canteens from the water jugs, put a few granola bars and sandwiches in a small pack that Shirley carried, and then the three of us slipped on bright orange vests and took our oiled rifles, one by one, from the rack in the truck—Shirley's Browning A-Bolt and two Remington 700s, one for me and one for Uncle Nick—his a brand-new one he bought so he could pass me down his old. I looked out at the forest around us and tried to adjust my vision, but there was no hint of morning in the sky and we struck out in a darkness like full night.

"Keep your muzzle down," Uncle Nick said, and we formed a line behind him, Shirley in the middle and me in the rear, and the cold in my fingers crept up my arm and I was a little bit sorry that my pride was too big to let me stay in camp, where I could be warm, try to sleep, be alone.

We walked in silence, Uncle Nick holding a short Coleman flashlight to spot the ground, the only noises the snap of sticks under our boots and the sound of fabric rubbing. I was wide awake for a while, breathing through my nose, and my eyes feeling too big for my head, and then I started sleeping on my feet and followed along while time passed without much notice. Uncle Nick had found an area of thick scrub that he wanted to get to when the sun came up so we could be waiting if a herd came down to nose at the dew. We wound around the thick brush, climbed over boulders, and slid over the backs of dead logs, and suddenly morning came like the flick of a switch so that what was impossible to see before was now in sharp relief, and the sky lightened from black to gray and we moved faster up the mountain. In the dark we had gone slow and stayed on the flat ground, moving between trees and turning sideways to slide through bushes. I could smell the green of broken branches and split leaves, but in the darkness I could not see them as we passed, and I was careful to look down a lot and watch my feet in the back splash of light.

When the sky was bright enough to define distance, Uncle Nick came to a stop and we stood beside him and looked out at the forest in front of us. "Let's divide up," he said. He was breathing hard and it was difficult for him to whisper. "Shirley, you head out to the left, not too far, but so that you can cover some ground between us. Robbie, you go right. Remember—no rack, no shot. And try to be quiet. There's a clearing about an hour and a half up from here, wide open for about two hundred yards, so just keep moving east and when you get to the clearing, we'll come back together and take the north trail."

We each took a sip of water and then fanned out, left, center, and right. I found a thin break in the weeds and thought it might be a game trail, and I watched for signs that I was moving in the right direction. I wanted a deer. The feeling came on me all at once—ten minutes ago I didn't give a shit if I shot a deer or got blisters on my feet or walked off the edge of a cliff. I had gone limp, and I was just dragging along at the end of their lead. They moved the flashlight, and I took the direction. But now I wanted one. I wanted to be the first one, beat Shirley, make Uncle Nick proud, be somebody different than I was. I liked it in the woods—I liked the smells and the sounds and the sharp ends of sticks poking into me whenever I tried to pass through. I tried to remember everything that I hadn't paid attention to during hunter's safety when we learned about game hunting. Deer, pheasants, ducks, dove, quail. I closed my eyes and tried to relax my eyelids so that my eyeballs wouldn't jump around behind them.

Bitterbrush, mountain mahogany, tall sagebrush. I didn't know what any of it looked like, but I knew it grew dense and the deer would gather there and these were good places to wait and watch. I kept moving east, or what I guessed was east based on where the light was thickening. I walked quietly, tried to make my boots light and my steps weak so I didn't step all the way through to the ground, break the pinecones, crush the things that might make noise. I imagined myself depending on the kill. My hands started to sweat against the gun and I thought I heard something and my heart stopped. I froze in place and waited. There was something to my right and I followed it and raised the rifle so that it was closer to my body and closer to my chin so that if I lifted my arms the barrel would be in a straight line with my sight. I tried to slow my breathing down, concentrated, and walked on slowly, waiting for the brush to part.

In the mountains, sound echoes and travels at strange angles. I heard the gunshot but could not tell the direction—for a second I thought that it was in front of me, but then the reverberation bounced back and I knew it came from my left, somewhere ahead. It was a strange sound—a sharp crack and then a hushing sound afterward, like the sound running water makes when it moves fast, and then the sound trickled out and died. I waited for a second shot, but there was nothing. I waited for my deer in the brush, but there was no more movement, and I realized that whatever had been there had been small and close to the ground and for the past ten minutes I had probably been tracking a squirrel. Then I thought that maybe the gunshot had come from Uncle Nick or Shirley—probably Uncle Nick more than Shirley, based on what she had accused him of—buck fever—not a sickness, but a weakness, she said. A jumpy hunter whose excitement got the better of him when the game stepped out from the trees.

I started walking toward the sound of the shot and figured that even if I came up on other hunters I was moving in the right direction instead of ranging wider to the right. I didn't want to be the last one to the clearing, make Shirley wait, take the accusation of her glare for the rest of the day. I needed the first kill and I hoped if another group had taken a deer it meant that a herd was moving down the mountain, that maybe there were more and they were coming my way.

I kept moving left and forward, walking over downed limbs and rotten wood. The sunrise had brought smell back to the forest as the air warmed, and everything was rich and deep like broken dirt. Ahead of me I could see a flash of orange between the thick trees, and then I saw more orange and I kept moving forward until the orange took shape and I could see two vests, one up and one down. I started walking faster and thought that maybe Uncle Nick had finally taken his deer and I almost yelled out but then I thought maybe I was coming up on other hunters that I didn't know and yelling might startle them and get me shot or scare something important or just make me look like an idiot.

I pushed through another tangle of brush and saw that Shirley was standing on the edge of a gully—the ground dropped off in front of her and didn't reappear again until it was a good eight feet away—and Uncle Nick was on the other side but half out of view because only the top of him was out of the gully.

Shirley heard me coming and turned to me and her face was white. I had heard about faces going white—white as a sheet, white as a ghost, but I had never truly seen it happen. One time my friend Eddie drank half a bottle of Strawberry Hill and turned waxy yellow, but this color wasn't the same. Shirley was white, and I stopped where I was as if her face had froze me.

"It's bad," she said and she turned back toward the gully and I waited for Uncle Nick to gain the high ground on the other side, but he wasn't moving. His arms were above him and his rifle was over the edge of the gully, out of reach. He looked like he had stretched out and gone to sleep in the sun.

Shirley slid down our side of the gully and I realized that it wasn't that deep, maybe three or four feet, and then she was crouched next to Uncle Nick, touching him, rocking him from side to side. I stepped all the way out from the trees and went to the edge of the gully, dipped to the bottom, came up the embankment on the other side and looked down at

Uncle Nick. His right cheek was pressed to the ground but his left eye was open and looking at me and around me, but he did not blink. "He's dead," Shirley said, and she started rocking him again, pushing his arm with the palm of her hand so that he tipped up a little on his side and came down flat again.

"What do you mean?" I asked.

"He's dead. That's it. I don't mean anything else."

She wasn't crying and I'm not sure what I expected, but I watched a lot of TV and I knew that sudden death was tragic and full of hysteria and women had a tendency to scream, oftentimes in some sort of disbelief, and there was crying and a lot of shouting of the dead person's name and a demand that he wake up. Wake up right now.

But Shirley just rocked him with her hand, and then I knew what she was doing and I didn't want her to do it, but she was faster than me and just as I reached down to make her stop, she put her weight into the rocking and got enough leverage to roll him over and then he was staring straight up at the sky and there was still only one eye that was trying for focus. The right side of his face was no longer a face, and I needed only a quick glance down to know that he had been shot and it had taken the right side of his face and the back of his skull and he was like a monster in a B horror movie, divided down the center of his head, left side normal, right side bad—corn syrup and food coloring everywhere.

"What happened?" I don't know why I asked it. There was only one answer with no mystery behind it.

"He got shot," Shirley said. We both stood there trying to find someplace else to look. Shirley was staring back over her shoulder at the bank behind us, and I was looking out at the forest, at the trees and the grass and the rocks.

"Did you shoot him?" I asked.

Shirley didn't say anything for a minute, but she did not turn to look at me. "He shot himself," she said.

A squirrel came out of the underbrush up ahead, and then another one followed it and they both scrambled up a tree in chase. Uncle Nick's friend Bob hadn't been a bad hunter's safety teacher. He was funny and told us jokes about Helen Keller that made me ashamed for laughing, and he was patient mostly, able to go over the same material again and again until there were no more questions and he was satisfied that we understood it, would remember it, could maybe even recall it later when the time came that we needed it—The Ten Commandments of Firearms Safety, number seven: Never climb a fence or tree or jump a ditch with a loaded gun. All of us repeating it in unison and then Bob pausing for a minute and already smiling before he could finish: *So, why did Helen Keller's dog try to kill itself?*

There was blood. The dirt was dark and the blood didn't stand out in contrast to the ground, but there was a thickness under him, under his head, and when I could look closer I saw that there were pine needles stuck to the side of his face, or what wasn't his face anymore, and the blood held them like glue. Nothing moved around us; the squirrels were gone and there were no birds. There was real silence now and nothing broke it.

I stood on the edge of the gully and watched a small breeze shift the tops of the trees. My legs were tired and my feet felt like blocks in my boots. I was suddenly aware of my rifle and I didn't want to hold it anymore. I bent over and set it on the dirt beside me.

"You should unload it," Shirley said without looking at me. I ignored her.

Despite the circumstances my stomach started growling and I wondered what time it was. Uncle Nick had a watch but I didn't want to know the time that badly.

"Well," Shirley said, "this isn't good."

I almost wanted to laugh. We were in a forest on a mountain, miles from the truck and even more miles from a town, and it didn't much matter the distance because I had no idea of the direction. But laughing would've been a bad thing and I didn't want her to think that I didn't care, because I did.

"We're gonna have to pack him out," I said.

Now Shirley did laugh and I was startled enough to jump and loosen the dirt under my boots and send a tiny avalanche toward Uncle Nick's left hand. "You want to try lifting him?" she said. "Because you weigh what, one sixty? One seventy?"

"One sixty-six," I said.

"Okay, one sixty-six. Me, I'm pretty much pegged at one ten—I used to be closer to one twenty before the cancer, but Nick," she looked down at him and her voice softened a little. "At Nick's last doctor's appointment he came in at two eighty. Now that was about a month ago and if anything he's gone up because the doctor said he shouldn't, so he's pretty much me and you added together, plus change. You want to try to lift him?"

"You could take his legs and I could take him under the arms," I said. "We could take a lot of breaks."

"Robbie, we couldn't get him to the other side of this ditch even if we took a week of breaks. You ever heard of the term 'dead weight'?" She was still staring off into the distance, at the gaps in the trees, at everything that was nothing. I shook my head but she didn't see me. "It means that when a person dies they really weigh more—maybe not on the scale, but in the fact that when the life goes out of them, everything settles. What you could've maybe lifted before becomes impossible after."

"So one of us goes for help. One of us stays with him and one of us goes back."

"Do you have the map?" she asked.

"Map?" I hadn't seen so much as a state park brochure since we left the house.

"The map in Nick's head."

I started cracking my knuckles. It was a bad habit, and I had been told to stop a hundred times but I could not quit.

"You see, it's kind of funny," she said. "Directions were Nick's thing. I was in charge of food."

I finished up with my left hand and started on my right, folding each finger over and pushing the joint with my thumb. "We came from that way," I said. I jerked my head toward the trees.

"And then?"

"I came from the right, followed the gunshot to my left. So if I go to the left I should find my way down."

"To where exactly?"

"I guess to where we split up."

"And then which way do you go from there? We spent over an hour in the dark, following Nick and a goddamn Coleman light."

I was quiet for a minute. "Maybe things would look familiar."

"Maybe," she said.

There was dirt in Uncle Nick's hair and on his scalp. "How were we going to get a deer back then, if we couldn't carry one?"

Shirley finally turned and looked at me and I realized that she had an age and it was older than I had figured, and there were lines in her face that I had never seen before. I knew that under her vest she was wearing a pullover sweatshirt, and under that was probably a T-shirt, and under that was a long-john shirt, and under that was where cancer had left its mark, and I wondered what her chest looked like, if she was scarred badly.

"We field dress a deer," she said. "Cuts its weight down and two of us could trade off packing it."

I didn't want to think what I thought, but I did and I couldn't help it, and I hated it when my mind made me see things that were not right to see—Shirley's cancer chest, my mother and Tyler doing it in the back bedroom, Uncle Nick gutted and hog-tied to a pine pole so me and Shirley could hike him out.

Shirley bent down and unzipped the pack around Uncle Nick's waist. Inside were a coiled and knotted piece of clothesline, a Hefty bag, a Ziploc freezer bag, a bundle of twine, and a blue rag. She pulled the things out one by one and set them on the dirt beside him. When she was finished she unsnapped the sheath on his belt and laid the knife with everything else.

"There's what we have," she said.

We both looked down at the collection of things we couldn't use.

"And a flashlight," I said. "And three guns."

Shirley turned and sat down on the embankment, drew her knees up to her chest and wrapped them with her arms. "I went to nursing school," she said.

I hadn't given much thought to what Shirley did or had done before. All I knew was that she was home a lot and kept a strict watch for fingerprints on glass, shoe scuffs on coffee tables, dishes in the sink. She had followed me around for days, correcting where I put things, which towels I used. Most days I tried to pick a place and sit still.

"I dropped out," she said.

"Was it the blood?" I asked. "Looking at things cut open?"

Shirley smoothed her hair back from her headband and looked up at the sky. While we had been standing and sitting and waiting for an idea, the sun had been moving and it was on the west side now, and weaker than before.

"I never minded the blood, and looking at the insides of people never bothered me. I quit because I didn't see the point. Why do we go to so much effort to save people from dying? My mother died of cancer when I was seventeen and there wasn't a team of doctors or nurses that could do a thing for her even though they tried for weeks,

pumped her full of drugs so that by the end she kept calling me Julie, and that was her sister's name. People die. It's
the wrong kind of thinking to believe that we've gotta pay
somebody to hold a bandage and stop the blood if the
bleeding is going to happen anyway."

My mother had been dead before the ambulance came
and they did not do CPR, or use a stethoscope, or hook up
oxygen, or let the sirens loose, or roll back her eyelids and
call her by name. She was dead and now Uncle Nick was
dead and it was me who had touched both of them.

Shirley picked up some loose dirt and let it fall through
her fingers. "There is no plan for us and no God and no
matter what drug they invent there ain't nobody who is
gonna live forever. We're just these things that work without most of us knowing how and we're just thin skin and
blood and everything has to work at the same time without us thinking about it. It's amazing that we live at all.
So I quit because things happen and I didn't want to be
somebody who tried to make somebody else believe that
what I did for them was gonna keep them alive."

She had never said that many words to me before.

The wind came up as the sun began its descent and we
ate the sandwiches in silence and took small sips from the
canteens. "There are other hunters up here," she reminded
me. "Somebody else is bound to come through."

It was too late in the year for mosquitoes or flies, but
bugs found Uncle Nick anyway, and there wasn't much we
could do to shake their attention. It got colder but I tried
not to notice, and I ignored the fact that October nights

could slip to twenty-five degrees up here and Uncle Nick had been the one to tell me that fact as we built the campfire the night before.

"I think I could make it back to the truck," I said. There was cold creeping down the back of my neck and I was tired of sitting and waiting and brushing back bugs and biting small corners off my sandwich and hoping for somebody to find us. I had a strong feeling that we were the ones who were going to have to find somebody else, and we weren't doing that by sitting beside the ditch.

"You know this is black bear country?" Shirley said. "Mountain lions. Bobcats."

"I'll take a gun," I said.

"And you'll what, leave me alone? Let me sit here in the dark with the smell of blood coming off Nick?"

I tried to imagine Shirley sitting scared with the rifle raised, trying to sight in a bobcat that just kept circling and circling like a shark in the water.

"Then maybe you should go," I said.

"Right. Be a moving target? Fall off a cliff? Trip and break my ankle and lie someplace else dying so that by the time the forest service comes to rescue us there's two dead bodies and you?"

"I just think we're not doing anything good by not doing anything at all."

Shirley picked up her rifle, pulled back the bolt, shot into the air, spit the shell out to the ground, pulled back and did it again and then again. The shots came so fast that I screamed a little and put my hands to my ears.

"That was something," she said. She opened the flaps on her vest and dug through her pockets. "Well, now I'm out of shells."

The sun had finally crossed over the tops of trees and slid past the edge of the horizon and I knew that there would be seven minutes of light left because it took seven minutes for the sun's light to reach the earth in the morning and seven minutes before it slipped back at night. I was cold. To the west there were clouds banking together, joining up, and they were dark despite the light.

"It's getting cold," Shirley said. She blew into her hands and went back to hugging her knees to her chest. "You know, Nick got shot in the head. There's nothing wrong with his clothes."

As the evening had settled in it got easier to look at him and I started measuring up what Shirley had said.

"This is wilderness survival. You have to do what you got to do," she said.

I knew she was right in a way, but I didn't know just how far she would take it and I prepared myself for what might come—Uncle Nick stripped down to jockey shorts and tied up to a pole and hanging like a spitted pig.

"I don't know if I can," I said.

"You'd be surprised," she said.

I didn't want to help her but she made me, and while she unbuttoned and unzipped, I rolled him up and to his side as need dictated so Shirley could remove his layers. She set the vest aside and divided up the rest. I got his long-john shirt, his socks, and his jeans. Shirley took his long underwear and his denim work shirt. She wrapped his undershirt around his face and I think it made us both feel a little better.

"All the clothes are cold," she said, and I was glad that she stopped there and did not remind me that it wasn't just the clothes that were cold.

Darkness brought things to the bushes and we took turns swinging the flashlight at noise. There were a few times when the light reflected back the flat glow of an animal's eyes, and then we'd yell and shout *get out of here* and sometimes the eyes would turn and fade back to the bushes, and sometimes they wouldn't. The one who didn't hold the flashlight was the one who held a rifle and when it was my turn my nerves hummed like telephone wires. I was afraid I'd shoot Shirley, shoot myself, or, worse yet, shoot Uncle Nick again and have to know that I shot a man who was dead.

The rain came late but with as little force as spit from the sky, and although we both wanted to slide down to the bottom of the gully and out of the wind, we were afraid that animals would sense our retreat and we wouldn't be able to see them coming. Shirley took Uncle Nick's vest and wrapped it around our shoulders, and even though it didn't cover us well it made me feel warmer.

"Tell me about your mother," Shirley said. We had been sitting in quiet, breathing steadily, and I thought she was asleep sitting up because I almost was and when she spoke I jerked the rifle forward and shoved a wad of dirt up the barrel.

My eyes were heavy and there were no memories stuck in my head, which was wispy as cotton candy, nothing

more than spun sugar for thoughts and nothing of substance I could hold on to.

"Do you miss her?" she asked.

Sometimes at night my mother would stretch out on
the couch in front of the television, and during the times
when Tyler had a job and worked nights, she would hold
out her arm and tell me to *come here* and I would stretch
out next to her so that she was behind me, holding me
on to the couch, keeping me from falling, and we would
watch television together and if I was quiet, I would feel us
breathe together, both of us keeping the same pace, and I
wouldn't pay attention to the television because I'd be too
busy trying to match the rise and fall of her chest.

"Sometimes," I said.

"Missing is like a toothache," she said.

At some point in the night, maybe after the last of the
rain had dried up, or maybe just before when the ground
turned damp around us, I let my eyes close all the way
and did not try to catch myself when I slid toward sleep. I
let myself fall down the chute. I don't think it was a deep
sleep because I thought I could remember surfacing a
couple of times, once to realize that I had pulled myself
into the fetal position and the dirt was warm underneath
me, and once to notice that Shirley had given in too, and
she was next to me, asleep, and Uncle Nick's vest was over
the top of us and she was close, both of us facing the same
direction, and I knew the cold would force her against me,
so she could share more of my heat, hold me to her so that
my back was her front. But when I woke up just before

sunrise, when there was mist and very little light near the ground, I saw that she had turned away in the night, was far away from me, had taken the vest for herself.

I was starving. My neck hurt, my sides ached. I couldn't tell if my clothes were wet or just cold but either way they were no longer holding in warmth. Shirley sat up and started rubbing at her left shoulder, which had been pressed against the ground, and neither of us said anything. Uncle Nick was blue white and his veins looked close to the surface and covered him in thin lines. Birds started checking in with each other and the sun broke through the fog around us.

Shirley stood up, stretched, handed me a granola bar. "We made it," she said.

In the early light of a new day I felt like I could find the truck. I looked out toward the stand of trees that we had come through and tried to see past them to the broken grass I had trampled trying to move quietly in one direction. And then it came to me that we had been thinking too small, trying to hit a small target with a rock—get back to the truck—when actually we could hike toward the roads. There were highways that cut through the mountains and forest service roads were bound to come out somewhere. If we came down from where we were, we might be able to hear big rigs on the steep grades and we could walk toward the sound.

"We could find a road," I said. I was excited suddenly. "If we went down and that way"—I pointed to my left—"I think we could get back to a highway." I was chewing my granola bar fast, as if there was another one after this, and I had to remind myself that there wasn't.

Shirley looked off toward the direction I had pointed. She raised her hand and shielded her eyes as if she was cutting out the glare, but the sun was still weak and there wasn't much light bouncing back.

"I think you should go," she said.

I hadn't really thought of just myself going. I had thought of the plan as *we* and I had pictured both of us walking, both of us sharing the relief of finding a road.

"What about you?" I wadded the empty granola bar wrapper into a ball and set it on the ground, then thought better of it and put it in the pocket of my jeans. Even though I had Uncle Nick's pair over the top of mine there was plenty of gap at the waistband to get at my own.

"I'd like to stay with Nick."

The trees were full of birds now and I could see a squirrel jumping branch to branch on a short pine. I gave Shirley all the extra clothes, and when I handed her the jeans she reached into the back pocket and took out Uncle Nick's wallet and opened it. She handed me the money that was inside, forty-two dollars, and apologized that there wasn't more. Nick didn't like to carry too much cash, she said.

She gave me the knife but kept the guns and when I was ready she gave me a stiff hug and it was hard to feel her under all her clothes. "Don't send help, Robbie," she said.

I stepped back from her. "What are you talking about?"

"You heard what I said last night and I meant it. I know my cancer is back but I didn't have the heart to tell Nick and I like it up here. Nick's here. I don't want to go back and spend six months with people forcing me to live."

"That's just crazy talk," I said. "You're dehydrated and your blood sugar is probably low. You need to sit here and drink some water and eat your granola bar and wait for help to come."

"Okay, Robbie," she said. "You're probably right."

When I left the gully and passed back through the trees, she was sitting on the embankment and adjusting her headband. She looked small. Uncle Nick was no longer a person, more like an unearthed rock that was rising out of the ground. It hadn't rained hard and the grass had not bent with the weight of the water. It didn't take me long to find the trampled weeds of my trail. I imagined what it would be like to come out on the highway, jump down out of the woods and walk the gravel shoulder with my thumb out. Maybe a trucker would pick me up, and he would ask me where to and I would tell him Los Angeles and he would say he wasn't going that far, but he could drop me at the next city where the interstate connected. And maybe he would be playing old country music like my mom used to listen to—Conway Twitty or Dolly Parton—and he'd have a thermos of coffee and offer me a cup from the lid. I knew that sound had a strange way of traveling in the forest, and the shot could've come from anywhere—there were 413 other hunters taking down deer this week. There was the pop and the hush, but I did not flinch like I had before.

GAME-BRED

If I concentrated really hard, clamped my mind down and squeezed it tight as a fist, I could remember what it was like to be nine years old and getting my leg torn to shit by a rock-headed pit bull named Geraldine. She was a thick brown dog who liked the taste of kid skin and her owner was a fat old lady who thought maple-walnut ice milk on a cone was a treat I loved. Everything about her house was hell, and for seven months I was sent there on Tuesdays when my mom worked late. I went through a lot of socks in that time, and I learned to take it, learned to let my leg go limp so Geraldine could square her shoulders and shake it like a rag, because if I ran, she was like a fire that would gain strength from the air. With Geraldine I learned the true meaning of stop, drop, and roll, and so now I tried to remember that feeling of being bitten—the smell of sweat and fear and maple-walnut spit and knowing that

I wouldn't run—because I owed Richie Dobkins a hell of a lot of money and if I couldn't come up with the cash by kickoff tomorrow, Richie was going to do a whole lot more than just chew up the skin on my legs and send me home with a wad of shredded socks in my pocket.

Richie's Uncle Dave had a house up in Northern California, somewhere near the town of Trinidad, on the isosceles side of the great white breeding ground triangle, and the last guy who'd owed Richie a hell of a lot of money got taken for a boat ride and dropped in the water, about a mile from shore, in nothing but his clothes and a life jacket. That thought kept me awake at night—being dropped in the ocean with a life jacket on, so my head was high enough out of the water to see the first dorsal fin coming—or not see it, which would be about ten times worse, to just be waiting and waiting and not know what was underneath me, bobbing around, stone-cold alive and waiting for the shark to hit like a freight train. I was a weak swimmer who was six months from graduating with a 1430 on the SATs. I had fifteen hours until kickoff and my mom was in Reno. I took her Plymouth Suburban and her Wusthof, parked down the block from the Tri-County cash machine, and waited.

I had practiced in my bedroom. I needed a good voice and a quick arm with the knife, so I stirred together equal parts Johnny Cash and Norman Bates and turned "Give me your money" into Folsom Prison Blues behind a shower curtain. I didn't want to hurt anybody, but there was a fine line between threat and circumstances, and put under pressure, even a lump of coal can turn to diamond, hard and clear. I just needed one good minute at somebody's back and come tomorrow I could tell Richie that I wasn't gonna fuckin' fish *or* cut bait.

I was thinking about that, fishing and the Discovery Channel and what it looks like when one of those big-ass sharks comes out of the water and takes forty pounds of chum off the end of a stick some idiot is holding out over the side of the boat, and I almost missed her, the girl at the cash machine with her purse under her arm and her card in her hand. She was a tall girl, and from where I sat I could see that she was alone—even the passenger seat of her car looked empty—and the street was quiet and soft with fog. I cracked the window and took a deep breath and it felt cold and good in my lungs and I was snapped clean and awake. The storefronts were dark and the sidewalk was lit with the staggered row of street lamps that were having a hard time muscling their light through the thick air. The sound of cars was distorted—they could've been streets away or miles away, I couldn't tell. I wiped my hands across my jeans and pushed at the Wusthof and thought about taking this first pitch—letting this one go and waiting for the next—but this was a sucker pitch, a lob, a girl all alone, and this might be my only chance to swing for the fences.

I eased the door open and slid off the bench seat, dragging the knife with me. The girl didn't turn around. I hugged the car until I hit the sidewalk, and then I stood in a shadow and caught my breath. I was sucking air like I'd just run from my house and it was hard to get my lungs full again. My heart was tapping out a code and I had to lock my jaw to keep my teeth from chattering. It had been easier in my bedroom in front of the mirror. I knew that this was how it would feel when I hit the water up north— shaky, cold, and in over my head. I got myself walking and I stayed quiet and didn't stop.

She was looking at the receipt in her hand, and she had her finger on the button by the screen and then I was behind her and I cleared my throat so I could touch bass, and she turned on me before I could get the words out. I had the knife handle white-knuckled and locked in my right hand and I wouldn't be able to drop it and run even if I wanted to. The blade was solid against my thigh and I got to "Give me . . ." before she shifted her weight forward and said my name.

"Nolan?"

I turned the blade on its edge and if I'd pushed it a little harder I could've made it bite through my jeans. There was no more air in my lungs—what little I'd managed to hold since standing in the shadow had evaporated like the fog under the streetlights. I tried to finish my sentence but all that came out was a long squeak, like a balloon at the end of a neck-pinched release.

"I know it's you. Nolan from Andrew Jackson Junior High."

I nodded and tried to breathe through my eyes because they were the only things open.

"It's me, Ivy. Ivy Greenway. You have to remember me." She smiled at me and I did remember her. She was my girl-friend in eighth grade. Ivy—my friends used to groan and grab their nuts, tell me how badly they wanted to climb her, ask me if she was poison. She was the first girl to put her tongue in my mouth and to take mine even before I was sure that I was ready to give it.

"I remember you," I said. I cleared my throat and swallowed something thick that I would've rather spit.

She tucked her hair behind her ear. "You're not smiling," she said. "Was I that bad?"

A car rolled to the curb behind us and two guys in heavy jackets got out. They both pulled wallets from their back pockets and stood near us, lined up and waiting their turn. Ivy pushed her receipt into her purse and I saw the white edge of twenties go with it. "Go ahead," she said to me.

"What?"

"I'm done. You can have the machine."

I shifted my weight and moved my feet a little bit, as though I was caught between stepping forward and turning to leave. The two guys looked at me. Over their shoulders I could see my mom's Plymouth down the street waiting for me. I could hit it at a dead run and I might be able to get past the guys if I swung wide, but it would be impossible to run without raising my arms, and as soon as the knife came up for its first slice of air, I had a feeling that I would be kissing asphalt and getting to know these guys a lot better. There was sweat on the back of my neck, under the hood of my sweatshirt, and I was cold.

"I left my wallet in the car," I said. I nodded toward the street and both of the guys turned to look at the Plymouth. Then they turned back and looked at me. "Go ahead," I said.

They each gave me a hard stare and I felt their eyes drop and slide down the front of me. I didn't flinch. I exhaled through my nose and the air came out in puffs of steam like stallion snorts. I paced the breaths—easy in and easy out. Their eyes touched off me and skipped around but they didn't land for very long. The shorter one stepped past me and then they were both past me, and I could hear them settling up with the machine.

"You taking two?" the shorter one asked.

"Three," the tall one said. "Might as well."

My mouth watered and I thought about what it would take to drop both of them and double down, and I realized that it would probably take a .38 and I didn't have a gun.

In the time it took for me to fantasize taking the guys down with a knife, doing some kind of karate move, they had settled up and were gone and Ivy had dug a cigarette out of her purse. "You don't happen to have a lighter, do you?" she asked.

I shook my head.

"Damn. I should've asked those guys. They totally smelled like weed. Did you smell them? Jesus."

I shook my head again. All I could smell was the dirty paper scent of money.

"We probably could've got a dime bag off of them," Ivy said. "I don't know why I just stood here and passed that up. Damn." She pinched her cigarette between her front teeth and started digging through her purse again. "You don't happen to have any weed, do you?" she asked.

I shook my head. The knife handle was getting sweaty, and I hadn't realized how heavy it would get after holding it awhile. The longest that I had ever had one in my hand was when I was helping my mother chop vegetables in the kitchen.

"Does your car have a lighter?" she asked.

I shrugged. "I guess so," I said.

"Can I use it?" She held up her cigarette. She started walking down the sidewalk toward the Plymouth. I heard a siren but could not tell which direction the sound came from, or how close it might be. I wondered what kind of emergency was happening while I stood there with my mom's knife squeezed tight to my leg. Ivy stopped and looked back. "Are you coming?" she asked.

She waited for me to catch up to her, but I hung back a few steps so that she would be less likely to notice my knife-handed lockstep. "It's freezing," she said. "I hope your heater works."

I imagined us sitting in the Plymouth, parked at the curb with the engine going so the heater could run and Ivy's window cracked so she could ash her cigarette over the glass while I watched busloads of old women stop in front of the cash machine so they could all take a turn at the money.

There were Christmas lights in some of the store windows, and the sidewalk reflected back reds and greens and blues. I wished that Christmas lights never had to come down, but there was something naked about strings of bulbs left exposed in the daytime, and their only good moment was when the sun set and the light left the sky and they came on, strand after strand, blinking quietly. Ivy tripped on a crack in the sidewalk that I didn't see—the concrete had been splintered and raised in an odd angle so that the two panels were no longer flush, and she hit it just right, her left foot going first, and her ankle rolled and instead of going down, palms out and ready, she grabbed for me, took two handfuls of sweat-shirt, and I did what came naturally and reached out to catch her. My hand had gone numb from the elbow down and I didn't know that I had dropped the knife until I heard its dull thud on the cement, handle and then blade, a muted clatter that didn't sound metal at all. Ivy looked down but I didn't.

"Jesus," she said.

We stood there for a minute, most of her weight pressed against me, her left ankle still on its side and my sweatshirt knotted in her fists. We were clouded in the steam from our breath, and when it finally cleared and she was able to stand upright, shake me loose, I moved the knife a little with my foot, poked at it as though I were checking a snake for life.

Ivy reached down and picked it up. She held it out toward the light in the window next to us so that the blade glowed weak blue. "This is a big knife," she said. She kept it in her hand and walked the rest of the way to the car, and when she was beside it, she waited for me to unlock and open her door as though this was prom night and the dance was over and instead of the table centerpiece or a mint tin stamped with *Dream a Little Dream*, our party favor was a twelve-inch Wusthof, the handle black with a red trident, our school colors and the weapon of our mascot—Home of the Tritons.

When I shut her door and I could see her through the window, the cigarette that she'd dropped when she stumbled, wrinkled but not crushed, the knife on the dashboard, I thought about running. My legs ached with the urge. A car passed on the street and I wanted to raise my hand and block my face from its headlights, but I looked into them instead, full force with both eyes open until they passed.

I swung my door open and folded myself into the seat. Ivy had the lighter pushed in and was waiting for the pop. "It works without the engine on," she said.

I drummed my fingers on the steering wheel and stared at the lighter, too.

"Any second now," she said.

The car smelled like mildew from where the rear power window leaked. I tried keeping a towel below it, but when the rain came, there wasn't much that I could do. By December it was a water trap and created a constant smell of wet and damp that I got used to. The lighter popped and Ivy pulled it from the dash, sucked her cigarette to life, and the smell of mildew faded in favor of smoke.

Ivy exhaled loudly. "Perfect. Sometimes you get to the point where you want this taste so badly, you know? I mean, maybe people who don't smoke just don't get it—the way these just taste good—that first puff when you know you're finally getting a cigarette you've been waiting for. I can't explain it."

I could feel the sharp edges of keys in my front pocket and I was reminded of the sharp edge of knife on my thigh, and I fished the keys out and set the ring in my lap but didn't move to start the car.

"I only smoke Lucky Strikes," Ivy said. She held up her cigarette and squinted one eye against the smoke so she could admire it. "Back in the twenties they used to advertise Lucky Strikes as a way to lose weight—you know, have a cigarette instead of a cookie. Women were chain-smoking them to their filters." She exhaled and reached for the window crank but there was nothing but the armrest and the button.

"They're electric," I said.

She cupped her hand under the tip of her cigarette and waited.

"Sorry," I said. I fumbled the key to the ignition and turned it so that the window could come down. Ivy tipped her cigarette over the edge and I watched the ash fall and stick to the drops of moisture on the glass. I knew that by the time she finished her cigarette the passenger side of the car would be peppered with gray.

"So women were smoking these things like crazy and staying skinny and Lucky Strike's sales went up something like three hundred percent. You gotta admire that. That's why I smoke them."

I could hear the soft click of the keys as they dangled from the ignition, and the sound became quieter and quieter as the motion ran out of them. Outside of the car the street was empty and the cash machine was nothing more than a strip of light under an awning. It was getting later.

Ivy pinched her cigarette between her lips, squinted an eye, and picked the knife up from the dashboard. "So, is this for personal protection, or are you just paranoid?"

I reached for the knife but she held it back and out of my reach. I would've had to slide across the seat to take it and it seemed like too much distance to cross. There was an entire section of brown vinyl between us, and a third seat belt, and so I dropped my hand and let her keep it.

"It's my mom's," I said. I folded my hands in my lap and looked down at them.

"So, you're taking it out for a ride? Getting it some air?"

I felt hot and confined. "It's a long story," I said.

"Well, considering you don't have a radio in here, we don't have much else to kill the time with." There was a hole in the dash where the radio had been—a decent aftermarket that one of my mom's boyfriends had installed as a birthday present. I told her that it had gotten stolen when I was at school; somebody popped the lock and yanked it. She had been disappointed and angry and told me that it wasn't safe to drive her car to school and afterward I found myself freezing my ass off and walking in the half dark to get to first period on time, but I got forty bucks to pawn it outright, and I had managed to roll that forty into about two hundred, on a streak, until last weekend and a bad Sunday.

"Do you know what point spreads are?" I said.

Ivy held her cigarette out and poked at the paper with the tip of the knife. "Maybe," she said. "Something about sports, right?"

"Betting sports. Basically it evens out the chances of either team winning by adjusting the score. But that's not important."

"But it's important enough for you to have your mom's knife."

"Okay, last Sunday I put everything I had on the Patriots game against the Jets—took the spread at plus 8.5 with the Patriots as the favorite—I mean, playing at home, on a roll—and with the Jets out a starting running back and Pennington throwing like shit, they'd have to put the ball on the ground and New England's defense against the run was going to shut the Jets down. It was a sure thing." I unlocked my fingers and flexed them. I had been squeezing them together so tightly that my wrists were numb.

"It *was* a sure thing? I take it that it wasn't."

"I also bet the under."

"You lost me," she said.

"What it comes down to is that I bet on one game and I lost two ways, and now I owe this guy Richie Dobkins a hell of a lot of money and he's going to serve me up a lot of pain when I can't pay him in the morning." My voice almost cracked but I cleared my throat and caught the waver.

Ivy's cigarette was impaled like a bug on the tip of the knife and she raised the blade up so she could take a drag like she was smoking a roach. She held it for a second and then exhaled toward the window, and the window steamed over until the smoke rose and cleared. "So this is personal defense in case the guy jumps you, right? Get him before he gets you and all that."

I looked out my window at the street and saw a small dog walking down the sidewalk on the opposite side. It was a wiry dog with dark hair and it sniffed at the doorways and posts but did not linger. I couldn't see a collar on him, but the way that he walked made me think that he knew where he was going.

"I just need some money," I whispered. The dog lifted his leg against a parking meter and then kept moving west.

I felt something sharp in my thigh. Ivy was pushing the knife into my jeans.

"You were going to fucking rob me," she said. "You were gonna what . . . take my money? Stab me?" She pushed on the blade and I thought I could feel my jeans open up to let the point through.

"It wasn't like that," I said. I tried to edge away from her but I was pinned against the door. "I didn't know it was you."

She pushed the knife again and this time I felt it go beneath my jeans. "So if it hadn't been me—say it was some other woman—you were gonna wave this knife at her and scare the shit out of her and take her money? Because you lost a fucking bet?"

She pushed the knife again but there wasn't much pain. "I guess so," I whispered.

Ivy pulled the knife back and tapped the blade against the dashboard. "That is fucking ballsy," she said. "I mean, totally insane, but absolutely Clint Eastwood. I love it."

My lungs felt like two tiny sacs that couldn't hold more than a puff.

"Oh my God, I had no idea that you were this kind of guy. I mean, where was all this when we were going out in eighth grade?"

I shook my head.

"Remember that time we made out in your bedroom when your mom was gone and you got all freaked out?"

"I didn't freak out," I said. I wanted to rub my leg. I needed to feel for a puncture mark through my jeans, broken skin, blood.

"You freaked out. We were kissing, tongues and every-thing—and you got a total hard-on and when I reached down and touched it you jumped up and went downstairs and turned on the TV."

I remembered kissing Ivy, and there had been a lot of hard-ons, and I couldn't imagine that if she'd offered to touch it I would've turned her down.

"I was totally willing to have sex with you that day," she said.

I touched my thigh with the tips of my fingers but I couldn't feel a break in the fabric. My leg was not warm with blood.

"You missed your chance." She smiled at me and I wasn't sure if she winked or if she had something in her eye, but I was suddenly tired. I leaned my head back against the seat and closed my eyes. "I have an idea," she said. "You know where the Loaf 'n' Jug is on Twin Oaks? Out there past the three-way signal?"

I nodded.

"Take me there. I have a really good idea."

I looked at her but didn't move. I had thirty-six bucks and that would get me enough gas to drive three hours in any direction. I tried to imagine all of the possible ways the radius might extend if I were at the center of the circle.

"Come on. I'm not kidding. You'll be so happy, I swear." She reached over and patted me on the leg and I tried to measure if there was any pain. Just because I couldn't feel my leg bleeding, didn't mean that it wasn't. I turned the key and the ignition caught and the engine turned twice and fired. Ivy pulled the control on the heater to high. "I have to be honest, though." She had to raise her voice to be heard over the noise of the fan. "Before, when I said that stuff about getting weed from those guys—I was just kidding." She smiled and rubbed her hands together in front of the vent. "I've never gotten high—I don't even know for sure what pot smells like. I don't know why I said that I did."

The Loaf 'n' Jug sat on a weed patch of yellowed grass about a mile past the last trailer park and fifty yards from sheet-metaled wrecking yards, chain-link fences, and a Pick-n-Pull that offered a free yard shuttle on a flatbed trailer behind a GMC dually on Saturdays and Sundays so you didn't have to walk the lot. The asphalt was potholed and littered with crushed cans and bottles and chip bags and candy wrappers and cardboard beer cases and enough plastic six-pack rings to strangle a hundred seagulls at the dump. When we were parked and the engine was off and ticking, Ivy turned toward me and put her hand on mine, and even though it was warm and dry as paper, I had to stop myself from sliding out from under it and folding my hands in my lap, where they belonged.

"I'm gonna do this for you, okay? So don't worry about it. This place keeps their entire day of sales in the register—they don't even drop the cash until they close out at night. There's hundreds in there. Maybe thousands." Her hand squeezed mine and I could feel the bones in her fingers. "It's the easiest money in town. I swear."

I shifted in the seat and the springs under the vinyl squeaked. Ivy dropped my hand and then she moved out of my reach and took the knife and the dome light came on before I could say anything, and then she was out of the car and pushing the door of the Loaf 'n' Jug open. It opened without sound. I watched her walk to the counter, but it was hard to see her behind the warning signs and ID laws and MasterCard logos and beer ads and Shoes Required stickers on the door. I tipped my head at an angle, but I could see only segments of her—the bottom of her jacket, the back of her left leg, an elbow. I tried to piece them all together to make a picture of her inside at the counter, but I couldn't remember if she was right-handed or left-handed and the knife kept switching position. She was in there for a long time.

I looked over my shoulder at the empty road behind us and I waited to see flashing lights in the distance, red on blue, but there was nothing but Christmas lights at the wrecking yards and pinpoints of white sodium globes peppering front lots like low-hanging stars. There was fog in the fields, suspended above the patchy weeds, and it shifted and broke up as bursts of breeze blew through it.

Ivy came out through the swinging door and as it opened I saw the height marker on the frame, which tagged her at five feet seven. She was carrying a small brown bag and I felt my stomach cramp at the thought of how much might be inside. A fine line of sweat ran from under my armpit and I felt it slide down my ribs and veer to my back and soak into the waistband of my underwear. And then Ivy was back in the car and she set the knife on the seat between us and I waited for another drop of sweat to run because it was a feeling that I could count on.

"That was fucking great," she said. Her cheeks were flushed and her lips were bruise-blue under the light from the store awning.

I realized that we weren't moving yet and I reached to turn on the car because we were far from a getaway, but Ivy stopped me. "We're not in a hurry," she said. "Just wait a minute."

I could see the guy behind the counter, and it was the first time that I realized that there was another part to all of this. I saw his hand rise above the register, a bare arm, and I half expected to see a phone cord anchoring it to the counter, but there was nothing, just the flash of his white skin like a fish moving under water.

Ivy opened the bag and tipped it upside down and my stomach dropped into my knees and I couldn't breathe and I was counting what came out before it hit the seat and then I realized it was packs of cigarettes, Lucky Strikes, and there was no rubber-banded green mixed in with the hard shapes of red, white, and black.

"This is great, huh?" Ivy said. She picked up one of the boxes, smacked it against the heel of her hand and folded back the top. "I always turn two lucky cigarettes," she said. "You know, you are really only supposed to turn one, but I figure if one is lucky, two should be double. Hedge my bets, right?" She pulled two cigarettes from the pack and flipped them tobacco-end up so that they stood out in contrast to the filters around them. "I could've gotten a carton, but these were the last of the Luckies and I won't even switch brands for free, you know?" She pushed in the cigarette lighter on the dash and we both watched it and waited for it to pop.

I picked up the crumpled bag from the seat and shook it but nothing more fell out. My stomach climbed off my knees and decided to rise to my throat and I couldn't swallow the taste of puke away.

When the lighter popped, Ivy pulled it and hit the cigarette and there was smoke again and I was no closer to the money I needed than I had been an hour ago when I sat in the Plymouth down the street from the cash machine.

"I used to work here," Ivy said. "I got fired for giving blow jobs in the beer cooler, but I guess that's another story." She exhaled toward the window, but I had closed it when I shut the car down and now the smoke banked and could not escape. "You know, that's how I got kicked out of school. You remember Mr. Montgomery?"

Mr. Montgomery wore tight shorts even though he didn't teach gym. "I remember him," I said.

"I did it with him. One time. It wasn't a big deal or anything, but I guess his wife found out and things got kind of bad from there."

Ivy and I had gone to junior high together, but she wasn't at school freshman year and I figured she had moved over the summer, and then I forgot about her because six months is a long time when you're fourteen and things have a way of changing and people have a way of moving on.

"I have this condition, you know?" she said. "I'm a nymphomaniac. There's nothing I can do about it. My mom's tried therapy and doctors and pills and one time I almost had shock treatment, but nothing works."

"You're a what?"

"You know—a nymphomaniac."

"You light fires?"

"Oh my God, you're joking, right? I'm a nympho. I love sex. It's like a compulsive thing. I can't help it." Ash fell off the end of her cigarette and landed on her pants but she didn't seem to notice. I wanted to reach over and wipe it off, but it was close to the inside of her thigh and I was afraid of that short distance.

There was a knock on my window and I jumped so badly that I hit the horn with my hand and the noise made Ivy scream and then I screamed. All I could see was a bare hand against the window, with its knuckles pressed against the glass. They were scabbed and scraped with what looked like teeth marks. I looked at Ivy.

"Put the window down," she said.

I turned the key and the window slid out from under the knuckles and then a face bent down and filled the gap and it was a young guy with shaggy blond hair combed forward over his eyes. "I'm on break," he said. He held up a box of Rolling Rocks and Ivy started clapping and then he reached through my window and hit the button for the back door lock, and then he was in the car—a smell of leather and Big Red—and Ivy was turned around and slapping the headrest.

"Nolan, this is Dean. Dean, this is Nolan." He stuck his palm over the seat and I shook it left-handed and then he dropped his hand and replaced it with a bottle of beer while Ivy passed her cigarettes back and the car filled with smoke again.

"That's one big-ass knife," Dean said. He gestured with his cigarette but I didn't have to look. I knew the length. "Ivy said you owe Richie Dobkins money. That's some shit luck, huh? I know that bastard. I heard he fed some guy to the sharks."

I tasted the burn of puke in my throat again and I was grateful that the beer was opened so I could drink right away. I rinsed my mouth and swallowed the foam. "I know," I said.

"I'd help you out if I could and all, but I have a hard enough time covering for my skim, you know, and the owner's a nice guy. I don't want to screw him over or anything. He's got a little boy who has to wear these leg braces—can't even bend his knees to ride in the car. So I don't take more than he can miss, you know—he doesn't give raises and I don't ask for one, but I'm not driving that piece of shit for the rest of my life." He pointed forward over my shoulder but there was no car in front of us, just the storefront, Budweiser banners, and a muddy BMX bike leaning on a bent kickstand. "This ain't a bad set of wheels. What is this? A '75?"

"Seventy-one," I said.

"Plymouth, right? Damn." He drained his beer in two swallows and pulled another one out, twisted the cap, and kept talking. "Look at the room in here. It's got the fold-down third seat, right?" He looked over his shoulder at the empty space where the seat could've been. "Plenty of room to stretch out back there, huh? You know what I mean." He laughed and hit my shoulder with the bottom of his bottle and beer foamed over the lip and ran down the neck to his hand. "If I had this, I'd drop a performance cam in here and pull all the torque I could get. What is this, about a 360? V8?" He leaned back in the seat and stretched out his arms.

"Yeah," I said. "Dual exhaust, Edelbrock intake, disc brakes, 6x9 speakers . . ."

"No stereo, though."

"Yeah, no stereo, but it's got the boxes. Power steering, Progressive rims. Fifteen-inch tires." As I ticked off the specs Dean kept leaning forward until his face was on the edge of the front seat and I could smell the beer on his breath.

"Damn," he said. "You want to sell this?"

I knew the NADA guide value on the car—had looked it up a hundred times and bet that money a hundred times over in a hundred different ways—divided it over every game on a weekend or just pushed it all at one game and went for the money shot. I had spent afternoons digging through every fucking envelope in every fucking drawer in every fucking room of our house looking for the pink slip, and I could not find it. At night I stared at the ceiling and saw myself placing that one good bet. I could feel how I'd feel if I won and it felt so good that I wanted to feel it for real.

"I can't," I said.

"You guys are boring me," Ivy said. "I hate listening about cars." She waved her empty bottle at Dean and he replaced it with a fresh one. "I gotta go use the bathroom."

While Ivy was inside, Dean offered me a piece of jerky and we sat there chewing and drinking without talking. I hadn't eaten since I'd left the house and my stomach was running on cold beer. I drank fast and my head felt warm even though the heat had long since left the car.

"Ivy is a cool girl," Dean said. "I really like her."

I wondered if Dean was one of the receivers of her beer-cooler blow jobs, but I didn't want to ask.

"It sucks about her mom, you know. All that shit Ivy went through. I couldn't even imagine."

I listened without turning around. I didn't know what he meant.

"Her mom starts dying of cancer and Ivy quits school so she can work and pay the bills. I mean, that's some serious commitment. I don't think I could do it. I hate fucking working and my mom isn't close to being dead, but if I could help her take a few steps toward it, I sure as hell would." Dean laughed and we drank for a while without talking. "Everybody was in love with Ivy and she wouldn't go out with any of us. Drove us crazy, man. When her mom died and she quit, I stopped looking forward to coming to work, you know."

I imagined Ivy on her knees in the cold walk-in, tucked behind the cases of Miller Genuine Draft, blowing Mr. Montgomery in his tight red shorts, and then Mr. Montgomery changed to Dean, with his hair hanging in his eyes and his leather jacket zipped to his chin, and then I saw Debra Winger in a hospital bed, waiting for her kids to come in, and I closed my eyes until the pictures drained and I could taste salt in my mouth and hear the waves and the boat and the sound of things cutting the water.

Light rolled across the side of the car and I heard an engine gun and drop before the driver cut it and I opened my eyes and saw a bunch of guys step out of a Chevy truck beside us and walk toward the door.

"Well," Dean said, "I guess break time is over. Gotta go ring up beer and smokes and porn and make sure those assholes don't graze the chip racks or pocket shit when my back is turned. Never a dull moment, you know?" He patted me on the shoulder and opened his door. "I'm gonna leave you the beer. I bet you can use it." He gave me a thumbs-up and if he had made a joke about swimming or keeping my head above water, I probably would've thrown a bottle at him. I watched him give Ivy a hug as he went inside and she whispered something in his ear and then she was back again, inside the car, and smelling like smoke and soap.

"It's all taken care of," she said.

I watched Dean round the counter and stand behind the register. "Good," I said.

She picked her beer up from the floorboard. "So let's go," she said. "You know how to get there, right?"

"Back to your car?" I said. "Sure."

Ivy rested her beer between her thighs and dug a tube of ChapStick out of her purse. "Not my car, Nolan. Richie's house. You know how to get there?"

The fluorescent lights turned the knife a sick yellow color and every now and then the shadow of a small bug crossed the blade. "Very funny," I said.

"I just got off the phone with him. We had a nice little talk and came up with a deal."

I turned in my seat and my elbow cracked the steering wheel but I didn't care. It was a good pain. "What are you talking about?"

"I told you. I made him a deal. But we have to get over there before his mom gets home from work. She does graveyard at the mill, so we're running out of time."

My hands were shaking and I wanted to squeeze them together, but one of them was choking the life out of a green glass bottle and the other one was pulling uselessly at my jeans. "I don't have the money," I said.

"It's okay. I worked out a trade with Richie."

"You don't know him," I said. "You didn't talk to him."

"Don't be so paranoid, Nolan. I talked to Dean when I was in there getting the Luckies. He used to do some collecting for Richie and had his number, so he gave it to me. I called him while you guys were out here. Everything is fine."

I didn't believe her but I wanted to.

"If you don't believe me, go ask Dean."

I looked through the windows and Dean was blocked by the squared shoulders of the men from the truck, who were pointing at things behind the counter.

"I don't understand," I said.

"Look Nolan, I like you. I don't know if it's something left over from junior high or if there's something about you now that is working on me, but the point is that maybe you're thinking in too much of a straight line, you know? You owe Richie some money, so you think you have to pay him with money, but you haven't given too much thought to trade. Get it?"

"No," I said.

"I offered him something of value. That's it. So take me over to his house and let's get this settled before sunrise, okay?"

I looked at the six boxes of cigarettes on the seat between us and I did the math and their grand total came up way short of the figures Richie had added up for me. "This isn't enough," I said.

Ivy looked at the cigarettes and then she looked at me and she smiled. "You really don't get it, do you?" She exhaled and pushed the hair off her forehead. "I told him that I'd fuck him if he washed what you owed him—cleared the books, whatever—and he said I'd better be good, and I told him that I am, and he said he'd be the judge of that and so there—you're off the hook."

I didn't know what to say to her so I said nothing.

"It's easy money," she said. "I can take anything for five minutes, and there's no way he can last. Maybe I'll just blow him and get this whole thing done in two minutes like a fucking drive-thru. You'll come in two-minutes-or-less or it's free." She laughed but I couldn't see her face. She was staring out her window at the dark field and waves of trash in the weeds.

"You didn't get fired from here," I said. "Dean told me."

Ivy took a drink from her beer but didn't turn to look at me. "Dean is crazy," she said. "He's a good guy, but he's fucking nuts. You know why Dean works the night shift here on the weekends? Because the owner, Gary, keeps this big wooden baseball bat behind the counter—one of those slugger ones, you know, and this one time these two guys came in and tried to muscle Dean for the money in the till, and you know what Dean does? He grabs that bat and beats the shit out of both of them. *Both* of them. He beat one of them so badly that they didn't think he was going to live, and the other one didn't get out of the hospital for three days." She turned to look at me and I realized that she had nice eyes and that was something about her that I remembered from junior high. "And the funny thing is that Dean didn't think about it like he was a hero or he saved Gary's store or something like that. Dean got a taste for it after that. Every time a customer walks in Dean has one hand hovering over that bat and he's just waiting for somebody to look at him sideways, you know? Next time somebody tries to take the cash or a pack of chewing gum, they're not gonna get lucky with a coma. They're gonna get killed. All Dean wants is that one shot." Ivy finished her beer and set the empty on the floor. "The fog's getting thin. We better get going to Richie's, but I gotta get some candy first," Ivy said. "Something hard. You want something?"

I shook my head. Ivy leaned over and kissed my cheek and I let her. Her lips were sticky with ChapStick wax, but I didn't wipe the smear away until after she was inside the store.

The Chevy truck of men reloaded and backfired to life and I could hear the blast of their music until they rolled backward and turned toward the road. There was a dead rat in the place where the truck had been, a dead river rat stretched to its full length and stiff on the asphalt. It was un-touched and whole despite all of the wheels that had rolled across that spot, and it was on its side, in its entirety, tail extended, and I couldn't help but stare at it. In the light I could see the way its gray hair blended to white on its belly, peppered like a squirrel, and its tiny claws were curled into fists and tucked beneath it. The only thing that I couldn't see was its head because of the angle I was sitting and the shadow of a Little Debbie wrapper that covered it.

I reached over the seat to take another beer while I wait-ed for Ivy and I grabbed her open pack of cigarettes, which Dean had left behind. All the cigarettes were the same, fil-ters facing up, and the two lucky ones were gone. I set the pack on the dash and picked up the knife. The handle was cold and heavy. Ivy's purse was on the seat next to me, so I poked at it. It was open and if I sat forward I could look inside. I could see shadows and shapes of things that looked familiar, pieces of paper, sheets and wads. I dug the knife in and tried to find the cash.

When I was a kid, the old lady who owned Geraldine was married to a guy named Charles and on Saturday nights my dad would go next door and stand in his ga-rage and drink with him, and when it got dark and late and they were drunk, they'd take me to the backyard and let Geraldine off her chain. Charles would give me ten bucks to go five minutes with the dog, and he'd hold her by the collar, jerk her around, and lift her off her feet un-til she was whining and spitting and there was foam on her mouth even though she was old and white-muzzled, and then I'd take off running and he'd let the dog loose. There'd be a lot of noise after that from my dad and Charles shouting drunk encouragement until the money changed hands and they backed their pick—but in the yard me and Geraldine were silent and the only sound we made was contact.

I got two of Ivy's twenties on the end of the knife, and I fished them up the side and over the zipper and out. Inside the store I could see glimpses of her walking the aisle and Dean at the register, but behind the cluttered glass I could not see them completely.

When we hit the middle of the yard, I'd let Geraldine take me down, but I was double her weight and had a lot of kick in my Chucks, and I could take the shaking a lot longer than she could give it, and in time I would wear her down, take her fight, and she would turn. Even when her teeth dug in and took a piece of me, and my ankle went warm and I knew there was blood, I had that ten bucks in my pocket that kept me dead to pain, made me want to win, and she might take me for a minute, bring us close to even, but on those Saturdays they were right to put their money on me, because I didn't know how to give up, and probably wouldn't have even if I could.

GAP

Bobby paid eighty bucks for a handful of Scarlet Pussy—
fifteen seeds of Afghani hybrid that the ad in the magazine
said "could blow your mind"—and when the first green
shoots came up out of the peat moss, me and Bobby started thinking about how much we could sell an eighth for,
and what exactly an eighth was—grams or ounces—and
we started seeing dollar signs and '71 Pontiacs with dual
exhausts and 455 V8s and 400 Turbo-Hydramatic transmissions. I was six months away from getting my driver's
license, but in my mind I already saw myself behind the
wheel, right foot on the gas and everybody wanting me or
wanting to be me. The car meant everything. The license
was just paperwork.

"They look like tomato plants," I said. I had Bobby's
closet door open and inside the light was bright and
white and hot. There was a tarp on the floor and a pair

of Bobby's dress shoes, and we had the pots lined up in front of a plastic pink fan I'd taken from my sister's room. I picked up a spray bottle and shot a mist of water across the naked stalks.

"They're not tomatoes," Bobby said. "No way. If I find out that I paid eighty bucks for a bunch of cherry tomato plants, I'll fucking sue the company."

"Oh yeah," I said. "What're you gonna do? Ask your mom to get you a lawyer? Take it to *The People's Court* and explain how you paid money for some marijuana seeds and what you got were tomato seeds, a total rip-off, and all you want is your eighty bucks back, and maybe some money for your pain and suffering because if your mom knew that you were growing these in your closet, she'd kick the shit out of you and it would all be for nothing if the most you could do was harvest these plants and then go downstairs and make a salad?"

"If you keep opening the closet and looking at them, they're gonna die and it won't matter if they're fucking daisies," he said.

I shut the door and picked up the January 1980 issue of *Playboy* that Bobby had on his desk. He'd found a box of *Playboy*s in the shed out back—eleven issues, January through November, that one of his mom's boyfriends had left behind, along with a broken Coleman lantern and a half-empty box of .22 shells—and now they were under his bed, and the box of shells was in his desk drawer, and we spent a lot of quiet time after school in his room, licking our thumbs and turning pages. We knew the name of every centerfold and her stats, and what her favorite food or color or thing to wear was, and I mostly liked to spend time with the May issue because the centerfold's name was Martha Thomsen and when she was looking at me over her shoulder, pink satin panties cut like half-moons, I didn't give a shit if there were two hundred and twenty-six other pages in the magazine—that full-color tri-fold glossy was all that mattered.

"You haven't told anybody about the plants, have you?" Bobby asked. Me and Bobby had been friends since fourth grade, and while the rest of us grew and got older, Bobby just got wider and had to wear glasses and the best thing he had going for him was the fact that he was a fucking genius, but as far as I knew, being smart never got anybody laid. I tried to help him out the best that I could—got him on protein shakes and free weights for an entire summer, but Bobby was the worst kind of fat, a deceitful soft, like a cucumber that has been left in the refrigerator drawer too long and looks okay until you grab it and your fingers punch right through. Underneath his clothes I knew that he was held together with the same unreliability as pudding skin, and it was that thought that stayed with me the most—seeing his dents and dimples, and his chest, white and hairless. I heard the calls of "fatass" in the locker room and "wide load" in the halls, but Bobby would just give the assholes the finger and load his tray at lunch as though piles of food were a way to say "fuck you."

"She's got great tits," Bobby said. He held up the picture of Lisa Welch, even though I'd seen it so many times that

I knew her fingernail polish was red and there was a tiny scar just above her left collarbone. "I mean, all of these girls are fucking great," he said. "Everything about them—their skin and their hair and their tits and those stomachs so flat you could rest a drink on them. They're perfect."

Outside it was raining hard and we had walked to Bobby's from the bus stop. My T-shirt hadn't dried all the way through and now it stuck to me in places. I had forgotten my jacket in my gym locker and my walk home was going to blow. My backpack wasn't waterproof and the last thing I needed was a stack of swollen notebooks ink-blurred and stuck together on the night before a biology test when me and a C were just kissing distance apart. Bobby lifted the curtain above his bed and slid his window open so that we could smell the wet trees, smell the dirt and the street, and the sound of the rain ran together so that it was a solid noise without the definition of drops.

"I can name about fourteen girls at school who look like that," I said. "You get them out of their clothes—any girl—and she's got everything that these centerfolds do. I'm serious. They ALL look like that." I pointed to Amy Miller and Michele Drake on the cover of the January issue, both of them in tiaras with their legs wrapped around Steve Martin, who was in a diaper.

"Wesley, Wesley, Wesley," Bobby said. He set the magazine on the bed in front of him, but did not close it. Outside there were sirens in the distance, but the sound faded as they moved away from us. "I hear what you're saying, and part of me totally agrees that naked girls all look hot, but I think even you can admit that any girl looks like a prom queen when she has your dick in her mouth."

He gave me a smirk and I cocked my arm back to throw Miss January at him, but then I decided I didn't want to wrinkle the pages. He thumbed his glasses up the bridge of his nose, but did not flinch. "One time," I said. "I got a blow job one time." She had told me she was a freshman, but I found out later that she was really in seventh grade and the only person I could admit that truth to was Bobby. I knew that for my other friends, head was head and the only shame was in getting none at all.

"You never answered my question," Bobby said.

"Yes, you're a fag," I said. I unzipped the pocket of my backpack and started digging around for cigarettes.

"Have you told anybody about our plants—that we've got this plan and everything?"

I pulled out a Bic pen without a cap, a wad of gum with lint with hairs that didn't belong to me, and a paper clip I had unrolled and straightened for some reason that I couldn't remember now. "Why would I tell anybody?" I said.

Bobby looked out the window, but it had turned blank with fog. "Because maybe I think that you'd rather do this with somebody else. Like Joe Ross or one of those guys."

I gave up on finding cigarettes and started poking the paper clip into the carpet. "I want to do this deal with you. I mean, you're the one who got this all figured out. I just know how to turn Ziplocs into cool little baggies with a lighter."

Bobby ran the edge of his closed fist against the window and wiped away the film but there was still nothing outside to look at.

"I need a cigarette," I said.

"My mom's got a carton on top of the fridge. Go get a pack. She'll never know the difference."

"Your mom smokes lights. I fucking hate lights."

"This isn't Circle K, Wesley. You get what you get."

I stood up and walked over to Bobby's turntable, flipped *Road to Ruin* to the B-side, and as soon as "I Wanna Be Sedated" started, I cranked the volume and stepped into the hallway. Bobby lifted his magazine and unfolded the pages. I knew that he had been with only eleven women in his life—January through November—and there wasn't much chance that he'd have another one unless December showed up in one of the other boxes in the shed. I pulled his door shut behind me and all that I could hear was the muted sound of Marky on drums and the rain sheeting the roof.

My Chucks were drying on Bobby's floor, so I walked the hallway in my dirty socks, and just before I rounded the banister to head downstairs, I caught movement out of the corner of my eye and I stopped. Bobby's mom's bedroom was at the top of the stairs, next to the bathroom, and when I turned I saw that her door was cracked and there was someone inside. I took two quiet steps backward and slid against the wall so that the stucco snagged my T-shirt and I held my breath without thinking about it. It was too early for Bobby's mom to be home, and I knew she changed boyfriends more often than Bobby changed his sheets. I took a step away from the wall and moved toward the space in the door so that I could get one eye focused inside.

What I had seen was her reflection in the mirror, her white skin moving past like a cloud passing in front of the sun. Bobby's mom, Rose, was naked, with her back toward me, and I stood there looking at her, with my socks stuck to the carpet and my lungs screaming for air. Rose Harris was big in a way that I wouldn't know how to describe until The Fabulous Moolah took the WWF title from Wendi Richter in 1985 by pulling a screwjob, and I was half in the bag at the time and watched it all go down on TV. It was Rose Harris I saw in the ring that night, all five foot five of her thick and solid and sixty years old, coming back to me, and it was Rose Harris that I watched in that bedroom, watched her so that even though her back was to me, her front was caught in the mirror and I could see everything— the purple grooves of stretch marks that ran over her hips and around to the middle of her back, and the skin on her stomach, white and puckered and loose. Her nipples soft and dark at the ends of her breasts, which hung so far down her chest the skin beneath them was folded and creased. She was putting powder on, dusting it into her palms and rubbing her body, and in the reflection I could see a pink towel on the bed behind her, and I noticed that her hair was wet and stringy from what I guessed was rain.

And then I saw her face in the mirror, and she smiled— not all the way, but enough that I knew that she saw me, had probably seen me the entire time. I tried to make myself smaller so that I could disappear into the wood of the door, but she knew that I knew that she saw me—this was between us now, and her hands did not stop filling with powder, her cratered thighs lifted and exposed, dusting and rubbing, so that her body was glossy and shined.

I could've stepped away then and come clean from her, traced my way back to Bobby's room and lied about the cigarettes, put on my shoes and ran, but instead I kept that moment for myself, with nothing but a gap between us, and I watched her for as long as she let me, until I had memorized her and there was nothing more to see.

THE DIVING REFLEX

One-Legged Ed had moved in last year, three houses down from Hurley Gatz, but it wasn't until summer that me and Hurley caught on to what One-Legged Ed was doing. It was late July and nothing moved, and the thermometer had locked its grip above the ninety-degree mark ever since June and didn't show any sign of tiring. The neighborhood hummed with the constant noise of air conditioners that kicked on early and stayed on late, and me and Hurley Gatz holed up in his living room, drew the curtains, and flipped through channels. We might have stayed that way—burnt the whole summer in his house—but his mom started coming home from work for lunch and kicking us out, locking the door behind her, and Hurley didn't have a key. She said that fresh air was good for us and we should be out doing something, something that she called "playing," when in fact Hurley and I hadn't played in years. Hurley knew that she didn't give a shit if we lost ten pounds sweating in the shade or ate the last can of Pringles and rubbed our greasy fingers on her couch—what it came down to was the fact that the mechanic was back with Hurley's mom and the mechanic was pitching in for bills and he had started making a lot of noise about the cost of the electricity we were blowing through with our thermostat control and nonstop television. We didn't thank Hurley's mom on the first day for kicking us out, but later I would realize that if she hadn't, we would not have found the dead girl—and cable television couldn't compete with that.

Harrison Creek was more of a slough than a creek—backwater that had been brought on by the Fish and Game's construction of fish ladders off the river to move the migrating salmon upstream while still keeping a count. The slough was slow moving and prone to stagnation when the season was dry and there was no rain to fill the mud cut of puddles or its banks. In lucky summers the slough was wide and thick, and we would challenge each other to swim across it because the opposite shore was just far enough away to make you feel winded when you hit the midpoint and there was always a moment far from shore when you made the decision to flip over, go belly up, and hope you could backstroke the distance. It would start out as a race, but at that midpoint it always became a shared struggle to keep above the surface and not drown.

The slough was across the road from where we lived, and when Hurley had motorcycles that ran, we would ride them across the road and down to the banks—tear through the trails that flattened the brittle and high yellow grass. Hurley Gatz's motorcycles were prone to breakdown, and their only chance at repair was when his mom was dating the mechanic, so whenever she kicked him out, we'd be without them, and even though he had been back in Hurley's house since late June, the motorcycles wouldn't run, constantly smelled flooded with gas, and the mechanic wouldn't do shit because of the electricity bill and the fact that he considered us freeloading. If he knew that the cops had come knocking a couple of times because we didn't have licenses and weren't supposed to be riding on the street, he would have just sold them off to his drinking buddies at the Palomino Room, and mostly he was just looking for an excuse to do it anyway.

It was hotter than fuck, but next to the slough it was cooler and we had decided to stop kicking around in Hurley's backyard, waiting for something to do, and walk down there and swim. We both took our shirts off and shoved them into our back pockets. The water had a smell—thin black bottom mud, frog, and cattail all competing for the same heavy air. It was a familiar smell and it made me feel good. I sat down on the bank and watched the bugs swarm in shifting clouds that hung over the surface. It was even too hot for the fish to take bait, so we hadn't bothered to bring poles even though it would pass the time. I knew the fish were at the bottom, beneath the layer of water that the sun still warmed, and that was the best part of swimming out there—diving down to the point where the water went cold.

Hurley was lecturing me about *The Flintstones* and pol-lywogs and God, and smoking cigarettes he'd stolen from the mechanic, and I was sleepy and warm and loosened my laces, slipped out of my shoes and jeans, and waded out into the water until the bottom switched to soft mud and small waves knocked against the tops of my knees. I could smell cigarette and pond mud and wet grass and I wished I had something to float around on like at a pool. I waded into the blond grass without looking down, just felt it touch my legs and wrap around and then my shin hit something stiff and narrow that bobbed and moved and it took me a minute to realize that the blond grass was hair and the tree branch was an arm and I was wading through a person.

"There's a girl in the water," I said to Hurley, but he wasn't listening to me. He was preaching about good and evil and Bugs Bunny, and putting his stolen Zippo to a Lucky Strike.

Hurley Gatz and I had lived on the same street for the last seven years. He and his mom had moved in during a rainy November, right before Thanksgiving. Most people liked his mom—she was pretty and young and laughed easily, and she liked to drink and dance, and people liked that about her, too. My dad worked up in Susanville a lot and wasn't home much, so my mom started hanging out across the street at Hurley's and they would sometimes go out and leave us behind and that meant we could do what we wanted to do. Lately what we wanted to do was spy on One-Legged Ed down the street, and we had stashed binoculars up in Hurley Gatz's bedroom and we would cut the lights on the house, open the window in his room, slide his bed up to the sill, and pop the screen off so we could lie there and look out on the neighborhood.

Usually we just spied on Missy Lingenfelter making out in a blue Ford with someone who looked way too old to be in high school, who had a beard and a way of leaning his head back on his seat when Missy was no longer in hers. We both knew Missy. The blue Ford came around a lot late at night, and sometimes Missy was already inside and sometimes she wasn't. Sometimes we watched her crawl out a downstairs window, and then she'd get in the car and they wouldn't go anywhere, just stay at the curb and we would watch the flat bottoms of her feet press against one of the rolled-up back windows and we'd spend the next four minutes trying to dial in the focus on the binoculars and fight over whose turn to watch was next.

But then One-Legged Ed had moved into our neighborhood and Hurley Gatz and I had kept our eyes on him ever since. He was missing one leg below the knee and there were a lot of rumors as to how and why it was gone, and he was gray-bearded and long-haired and he kept his hair pulled back and sometimes he wore glasses with thin wire frames like a doctor's. He went around on crutches, and he had a tendency to crutch up to the corner of Placer and Karel, and he'd sit on the dirt patch that had been left behind by a hundred restless pairs of tennis shoes waiting for the school bus over the years, and sooner or later a car would pull up and One-Legged Ed would struggle up from the dirt, crutch over to the driver's side window, lean in, reach in, reach out, and crutch away back to his house. He sometimes did this two or three times in a day, or sometimes more, and sometimes not at all, but he did it more than he didn't do it, and me and Hurley took notice of it, because no matter how much we tightened the focus, the binoculars couldn't dial in what happened between One-Legged Ed and the cars.

In the past few weeks there had been guys coming and going from One-Legged Ed's, guys with jackets and patches that said things like "Harley-Davidson," "MIA-POW," "In Memory of Tanks 4-27-77," "These Are My Church Clothes." Me and Hurley kept a list on a sheet of paper in his room. The guys drank and smoked and blared the Stones' *Emotional Rescue* for days and days from speakers they set up on One-Legged Ed's back porch, so that the entire street was forced to keep time with Charlie Watts. From Hurley's bedroom window we could look across two houses and into the small window on the side of One-Legged Ed's garage—a window high up that looked out at the night sky for him and was a hole inside of him for us.

Yesterday I had put the binoculars up to my eyes while Hurley read *Swank*, and Ed and the guys were all crowded around the table in Ed's garage and they had some crazy shit in there. The Stones told me that I need money so much I need money so bad and I turned to Hurley Gatz, who was reading out loud from an article on Gail Palmer doing porn, and I told Hurley what I saw. There were beakers and flasks and tubing and burners throwing small flames. "One-Legged Ed is making a fucking bomb," I said.

I had thought about it all night, what One-Legged Ed might want to blow up, but as we both stood looking down at the girl—Hurley from the shore and me from the water, I forgot about everything that I had seen in that garage. The girl was facedown and we couldn't recognize her from the back. I thought about flipping her over, and maybe Hurley thought about wading in and doing it, too, but neither of us said it out loud or reached to do it. In fact, neither of us touched her, and on the one occasion when I was close enough to her outstretched left hand that a small wave sent her fingertips to lap against my knee, it was all that I could do to keep from making the heavy slow-motion run from the water to the ground, and maybe not stopping until I came up from the underbrush, crossed the road, ran to my house, and scrubbed my knee clean.

"You really think she's dead?" Hurley asked.

I looked up at him and his face was blank. There was no color in him at all. Even his body was a strange shade of white, as though he had been drawn in as a pencil outline on paper and left that way.

"How long do you think we've been looking at her?" I asked. "How long do you think we've been talking here and she's been facedown?"

Hurley still had the cigarette in his hand and he suddenly seemed to remember it, took a drag that didn't burn, and dropped his hand to his side again. He exhaled but no smoke came out. "She could've been sneaking breaths," he said.

"Okay, yeah, maybe," I said. "Let's count. Let's see how many seconds go by and see if she breathes."

We both started counting in unison. Our voices were the only sounds except for distant traffic and the faint familiar whine of a lawn mower, and it seemed strange to hear ourselves ticking off numbers—one, two, twenty, one hundred seventeen. I kept my eyes focused on her back so that if there was the slightest bit of movement I would catch it.

At five hundred thirty I quit counting. Hurley went ahead for ten more, and then he stopped, too. "Did you see anything?" he asked.

A small hot wind kicked up and the waves shifted her back and forth and back and forth against the thinning weeds from the shallow shore. She moved in unison— arms and legs and body all together. I knew it was hard to pull that off in the water. Part of you always wanted to dip below the surface and get out of sync with the rest. "Nothing," I said.

"Jesus," Hurley said.

"Fuck," I said.

A large soot-colored bird jumped down from an overhead tree branch behind Hurley and came up to the water near us. His eyes were hard black and sharp and there was a yellow line on his beak. He hopped up to the edge of the water, stuck his face into it, and then rubbed it under his wings. We were both hypnotized by the process and we watched him repeat it over and over until his feathers were fluffed and he glistened wet in the sun.

"I don't recognize her," Hurley said.

I looked down at her and tried to put her into some kind of familiar perspective. She was wearing a pair of jean cutoffs that were frayed and loose around the tops of her legs. Her legs were thin, and even though they were below the surface of the water I could tell that they were tan. The skin looked as if it had been pulled tight and there were creases set deep in the backs of both of her knees. She was wearing a gold anklet, and it was shiny, and one of her shoes was missing and her foot was bare. Her pale heel stuck out of the water. The other foot was strapped into a thin brown sandal with thick soles.

Her T-shirt was dark blue, but maybe would've been light blue if she was dry. It stuck to her skin, and I knew that if I put my face into the water next to her and opened my eyes, I could look over at her and see that she had boobs. I could tell from the way her back was shaped even though there weren't any bra straps. Both of her arms were drifting—the left one moving out a little ways from her body, the right one reaching out past the top of her head. There was chipped orange polish on her nails.

"Look," Hurley said. He had a stick in his hand and he was using it like a pointer. "Look at her hand." He leveled the end of the stick over the hand that waved above her head. Her nails were broken and jagged. "She was scratching at something," Hurley said.

"Or she bites her nails," I said.

"Not anymore." Hurley pushed the end of the stick against the back of her right hand and the stick dented her skin before it popped her hand below the surface of the water with a small splash.

"Don't," I said. "Not with a stick, okay?"

Hurley went back to shore, sat in the grass, and tucked his knees up to his chin, pushed his hair back. He put the stub of a cigarette in his mouth and found his lighter and went to work on it. I waded back to shore and sat on the ground and pulled the laces from my shoes. When I had both of them, I tied them together to make one long string.

I walked the short distance to where the body was floating and I looped one end of the string around the girl's left wrist, knotted it, and looped the other end around a broken piece of branch, knotted it, and stuck the branch into the soft mud. "There," I said.

"What do you want to do with her?" Hurley asked.

"Keep her, I guess."

For the rest of the afternoon we sat on the bank and flipped through mental pictures of girls we knew, said their names out loud to each other, gave descriptions when we didn't know the names, tried to figure out who she was. By late afternoon we had run out of names and faces, and Hurley was out of the mechanic's cigarettes, and the mosquitoes were thick and biting and we decided to go home because there was nothing else to do.

I didn't eat and went to bed early. I took my sheets off so I could run them under the bathroom sink and get them wet so I could put them back and lay on them to try and break the heat. I dreamed without sleeping and the faces of girls kept repeating their images every time I tried to close my eyes. I could hear my parents eating in the other room, hear the sound of their silverware clicking, the sound of plates stacked in the sink. I heard the TV come on and I heard my father's voice, and I thought I was asleep but I wasn't. I finally gave up, took the phone in my room, and called Hurley. His mom said he'd gone to bed, but he took the phone from her and told me that he'd been just as unasleep as me. It was a suck way to waste a summer night, so I pulled on some clothes and walked over to Hurley's and the mechanic and his mom had gone out, so we took a can of Pringles up to his room and dug the binoculars out of his sock drawer, popped the screen, and took our place at the window. It wasn't even dark yet; there was still sunlight in a bright line on the horizon, and the sky was deep orange and made me think of the girl and her nails. I wondered if she was okay there on the shoreline, tied to the branch. I wondered if anybody would find her—I hadn't thought about it before, the fact that we weren't the only ones who used that strip of swimming space—and I wondered if maybe we should've covered her with something but I couldn't think of what.

"Do you think she's okay?" I asked Hurley.

Hurley was on his stomach with the binoculars pointed out the window toward the rows of houses and the street beneath us. "Who? Missy?" He shifted his weight and started fine-tuning the focus.

"You know who I'm talking about."

"I think I've seen her before."

I sat up and accidentally kicked Hurley's stack of magazines. The new world sex record issue—eighty-three men in one night—slid into erotic cookies—bet you can't eat just one—slid into sex and alcohol (how to get it up when booze brings it down) slid into the Q and A on junk food making you a limp lover—take our remedy. The mechanic had great reads. I had secretly taken home the Cheryl Tiegs issue, had her safe between my mattress and springs, and if Hurley got blamed for that one disappearing, I would be sorry, but not very.

"Who is she?" I said. "Is she from school? It's that girl from my algebra class, isn't it? That one girl who used to sit in the back and then she got moved to remedial, right?"

"No, that's Diane Kenyon, and she is very much alive. I saw her at Holiday Market today, bagging groceries."

"Then who is she?"

"I don't know exactly. I know I've seen her, though. Look at this—Mrs. Irwin is out in her yard in her robe again. Disgusting." He tightened the focus on the binoculars.

I read articles I'd already read in the mechanic's magazines, and eventually the sun disappeared and we were shut into darkness. It was Thursday and the streets were quiet. One-Legged Ed's driveway was lined with motorcycles and big guys smoking cigarettes and talking loud, but his garage was dark and there wasn't much to look at. Sometimes we would see someone pass by the windows in his house and we would follow his movement for a while, watch him step out on the back porch, light a cigarette, stand out there and smoke until someone else came out, joined him, took a hit, passed it back.

"I wanna go see her," I said.

Hurley was quiet for a while. He set the binoculars on his bed and rubbed at his eyes. "What are we going to do with her, Reece? I think we should tell somebody."

"I don't want to tell anybody." I could feel my heart under my shirt. I felt hot. "Not until we figure out who she is and we can report it. Maybe there will be some kind of reward." I wasn't sure why, but I wasn't ready to lose her and I had to go see her and I would go with or without Hurley. We heard a motorcycle fire up and I closed the magazine. "Nothing in the garage?" I asked.

"Nah, it's quiet. Just the usual." Hurley lifted the binoculars and looked out on One-Legged Ed's house. "There's girls there tonight." He handed me the binoculars and I moved forward on the bed beside him. I could feel his bare arm against my shoulder, and I could feel the heat on his body, and I could smell him beside me—soap and sweat and laundry detergent. I looked into the darkness and tried to pick out faces in One-Legged Ed's crowd. The girls were young, but older than us, and they stayed close to each other and to the men, and sometimes they reached out and grabbed one or another by the arm and there would be laughter and we could hear it over the rooftops.

"I count five," I said.

"What are they doing?"

"Nothing. Laughing. Drinking beer. Smoking. One is putting on lipstick. You want the binoculars back?"

Hurley rolled onto his back and shut his eyes. "No. Just keep telling me. Where's Ed?"

"I don't see him," I said. Then the light flicked on in the garage and I waited and finally someone passed in front of the window and I could see it was One-Legged Ed and he had a girl with him. In the light I could see her better than the others, and she was small with long brown hair and skinny legs and she was wearing a skirt and she looked bored.

"He's in the garage. With one of the girls."

Hurley opened his eyes for a second. "What are they doing?"

"Nothing. I can't tell."

"Does he still have the bomb?"

"Wait, she's fucking kissing him. I swear to God, she has her tongue in his mouth."

Hurley sat up. "Give me the binoculars."

We sat on his bed and watched the girl kiss One-Legged Ed and I was turned on and disgusted and couldn't seem to stop watching, and Hurley pulled his shirt off and I took the binoculars back and smelled Hurley and watched the girl and didn't want to stop doing any of it. Hurley was whispering song lyrics, and he kept his eyes closed and he pushed at the front of his jeans with his palm. When he was asleep I left his house and walked out into the street and I could hear the music from One-Legged Ed's and I wondered what would happen if I just went over there, knocked on the door, and invited myself in. I wondered if they would let me stay, or if they would beat the shit out of me and drag me home by my laceless shoes.

I went home but did not sleep. I lay on my bed and didn't fold the covers back, just waited for the light to come back to the sky and for another day to start. The heat did not break in the night and I was slicked with sweat by the time I heard my dad start the shower and my mother start the coffee and both of them move toward work. My parents liked to fight in low whispers and there was a lot of that lately, but I couldn't decipher any of it and tried to forget it anyway.

When there was less than light, and only the promise of it, I left my house and went back to the slough and cut through the grass and the trails and found the path to the shore where the girl was tied. I expected her to be gone, cut loose, and was just as scared as I was hopeful that I would find a broken stick, dirty laces, and nothing but green water, but of course she was there, just as we'd left her, facedown and not breathing and flexing with the small ripples of water. When I got close enough to the shore to see her, I heard a frog jump and there was a big splash and I screamed a little and then laughed at screaming and that sound scared me, too.

I sat on the grass in front of her and saw the remnants of where we'd been the day before—the crushed cigarettes and stamped weeds. The shoelace was still tight on her wrist and the stick was still upright and anchoring her to the shore. Her hair covered her head in all directions and there was no chance even to see the profile of her face.

"I wish I knew who you were," I whispered. "I wish I knew you."

I stretched out on the grass and the ground was cool beneath me. Moisture crept up and dampened my shirt and it felt good and I closed my eyes for a second and when I dreamed, she was with me, in my dreams, and we were on our way to the prom, and I was in a tux with a pale blue shirt, and she was in a blue dress and I had a car that I had never seen before, but it was mine and instead of going to the dance, without saying anything, we decided to park out by the river, the real river and not the slough with its warm slow algae and green bullfrogs and smell, but by the river that moved and ran and went deep and stayed cold. We sat in my car and I played the Stones and she started kissing on me, on my neck, and I let her and she was beautiful. When I looked at her, it was as if I couldn't see her exactly, but I could tell that she was beautiful, and I kissed her back and then it was as if I was watching it all from a window and I could see my silhouette in the car, through the rear window, and I was sitting up in my seat and she wasn't, and I could feel her next to me, and also watching all of this from the window was Hurley, and he had his hand on the front of my jeans and he was pressing me, and I could feel him, too.

When I woke up the ground was dry and the sun was already hot and I was thirsty and there were yellow weeds pressed into my cheek and a short trail of ants on my arm. The girl was still in the water and everything was the same. I heard a plane overhead but could not see it, just the trail of white it left behind as it split the blue down the middle like a seam. I kicked off my shoes and pulled off my jeans. I waded into the water next to her. There were places on her body where the water did not reach and she looked dry and hot and exposed, so I splashed water over her, slowly, cupped it in my hand and sprinkled it over her like rain. I stood close enough to her that I could feel her fingers touch me when the water shifted the right direction and she knocked against me and I let her. Her fingers did not feel like fingers, but I knew that they were and I knew that they were hers and even though I wanted to, even though I almost did, I could not put my hand around her arm and lift her enough to see her face, roll her onto her back and turn her to the sky.

I went to Hurley's but he didn't open the door. His mom finally did and said that he didn't feel well, was still sleeping, but she was having a party that night and I should tell my parents and I was welcome to come over and keep Hurley company. As I was walking back to my house, I heard an upstairs window slide open and I turned around just in time to take a Hot Tamale to the head. "Get back here, fucker," Hurley shouted. The noise set off a string of dogs barking and old Mrs. Irwin in her robe looked up from her front flower bed. Hurley gave a shrill whistle and then slammed the window shut. Mrs. Irwin looked at me and smiled.

The mechanic was already at work and Hurley's mom had called in sick so she could pick up the liquor and food and she was in such a good mood that she let me and Hurley eat Pringles and watch cable and let the air conditioner rip all morning. We repaid her kindness by tapping the keg for her and getting chairs out of the garage and hosing things down and putting out plates and bowls of peanuts and testing the beer to make sure that it was fresh and testing the cups by filling some with beer to make sure they'd hold the liquid and tasting the beer to make sure that it wasn't lite beer because nobody drank that shit we said and by the time she sent us out of the living room and back to Hurley's room, we were about half drunk. We took full cups with us and decided to try to keep them full for the rest of the night.

By nine o'clock there wasn't one person in the house who wasn't holding on to someone else for balance, and the volume had reached its peak and Hurley's Uncle Walt had put on *Frampton Comes Alive* and there were too many voices who thought they knew most of the words and were trying to join in on the choruses. At a quarter to ten, Hurley and I were sipping warm beer from the bottoms of our red cups, and we had the binoculars pegged on the street below, but all of the action in his house had moved to the backyard and all we could see were the cars parked nose to tail on the street. At eleven, One-Legged Ed left his front door and started crutching his way down the sidewalk, toward the Gatz house and the party that it had become.

"You won't believe this," I said. "One-Legged Ed is coming up your driveway."

I passed Hurley the binoculars and he climbed up beside me and I watched him swing them onto One-Legged Ed, who had a brown bag pressed tight to the crutches as one blue tennis shoe traded places with nothing, step after step.

"I don't fucking believe it," Hurley said.

"Let's go answer the door."

The front door wasn't even closed, so it was stupid to answer it and we found ourselves standing there like a couple of jackasses when he finally made the turn at the end of the walk and started up toward the porch. In the background I could hear my mom's voice and she was saying something about chicken and then One-Legged Ed was right in front of us, gap-toothed, bomb-making, and spit-shined in what looked like a new shirt.

"Howdy, boys," he said.

And then he did something that neither of us expected. He winked one eye closed, touched it with an index finger, and then pointed at us, separately, one by one. And then he was crutching past us toward the noise in the kitchen and somebody yelled, *Gary, you old son of a bitch, good of you to come* and it sounded like the mechanic, and maybe it was, but neither me nor Hurley turned around to watch the greeting or the greeter or the moment when the crowd broke and swallowed him in.

"I want to go see her," I said.

We went back to Hurley's bed and listened to the music pound through the floor. "Forget about her," Hurley said. "Give me the binoculars." Downstairs, someone screamed laughter and there was the sound of glass breaking, and then more laughter, and a car door slammed, somebody coming or going, and then the music stopped and a few minutes passed before something else came on again.

Hurley leaned forward, half out the window, knocked his cup off the sill, and let it roll down the roof to the gutter below. "You won't believe this," he said.

He passed me the binoculars and I tried to figure out what I was looking for, and then he pointed right and down and I followed his finger, and I landed on One-Legged Ed's house and bounced around from window to window looking for something to catch. There was nothing, and there was nothing strange about that, One-Legged Ed was here, and then I realized that there was more than nothing, too, and it hit me that the side window of the garage was gone. It just wasn't there anymore. I spun the wheel between the lenses, tightened focus and tightened again, and then I saw that the window was there but it wasn't a window anymore—it was and it wasn't. Someone had painted it black, and it was impossible to see through—there was the hint of light behind it, the black wasn't completely dark, but there was nothing to see through to anymore. Our sight ended at the window now, and there was nothing to see—just light and the absence of what was once there, and over the rest of the house the curtains had been drawn and that was it. The hole inside to One-Legged Ed was closed.

"That son of a bitch," I said.

"You ain't kidding."

I tossed the binoculars onto the bed and stared at them for a second. They were worthless. Missy was moving to Southern California for college and nobody wanted a close-up of old Mrs. Irwin in her robe in her front yard.

Hurley exhaled hard enough to lift the hair off his forehead but he didn't say anything for a while. "It's all over, Reece. This summer is officially done and gone."

"It's not even August, Hurley. Why are you being like this?"

"It's August in a week. School in a month. Summer is done. This is boring. I want to do something else."

"I thought we were having fun," I said.

"We were. But now I'm not. C'mon, Reece. It's time."

Downstairs, somebody had plugged in an electric guitar and was trying to play along to the music. Finally they gave up and went into the intro for "You Really Got Me."

"Time for what?" I said.

Hurley looked out the window at his cup in the gutter and the row of cars at the curb, and then he shut his window and the room changed its quality of sound. "Time to tell somebody, okay?"

The guitar made a seamless rift into "Louie Louie" and everybody cheered. Hurley stood up and opened the bedroom door, and the party moved upstairs, if only in volume, and then he stepped out of his room and I thought he might stop for a second, look back at me, wait, but he didn't. He just kept his back to me and closed the door.

After a while, I went downstairs, but I didn't look for Hurley as I walked through the crowd that filled the living room. When I hit the sidewalk in front of his house, I just kept walking, and then I was on asphalt, and then I crossed over onto dead grass and dirt. I knew my way without light, and I didn't need sunshine to call the corners, dips, potholes, and uneven places in the ground. I could find my way to the slough with my eyes closed, and I walked part of the trail that way, eyes closed, and when I came out on the open bank beside the water, I smelled the slough before I ever touched it and felt the quality of the air change into a coolness that made goose bumps break out on my skin. There were frogs calling on all sides, back and forth so that the noises blended together into one long harmony of sound with crickets and the last remaining whine of insects that had become lost after dusk. I slipped my shoes off and went in with my jeans on. The mud felt good under my feet, a reminder that I wasn't sober, but I wasn't drunk either, and I had had enough by then to know the difference. I found the anchor stick and pulled it out of the mud so I could get the shoelace free. Then I took the loop and put it over my own wrist, felt the wet heaviness of the thin lace, and slid my hand the distance until I found the other end around hers, and I spun her slowly, so that her right hand turned toward the opposite shore and I turned with her. There wasn't enough room between us to make a full stroke, but I could half dog-paddle and keep her alongside me, both of us treading together toward the open water of the middle and the opposite shore beyond.

I would be sixteen before fall, maybe get my driver's license, start the high school year that counted for college, and probably be a better swimmer to take on crossing the slough by next summer. Across the water beyond the far shore was the freeway, and I could see the steady roll of lights and hear the drone of trucks shifting gears as they prepared to make the long turn toward north and the distant edge of the state beyond. I put my face in the water and held my breath, and even when I thought that I could hear voices on the near shore behind me, see the narrow fingers of flashlight beams pointing in my direction and over my head, I kept my face down and stayed on course, felt the temperature change in the water below me, the shallow warmth giving way to deeper cold, pulled her weight and didn't think too much about where we were going—only that I could stay this way if she wanted me to.

THE LAST MILE

My parents had bottomed out just about six months ago, divided and split, and I told each of them that I was staying with the other, but really I was somewhere in between. My father said he and my mother were bare-knuckled boxers who once beat each other down in three rounds in a gravel parking lot outside of a bar at the edge of some mill town they were passing through. He said he came out the winner despite the fact that he had a scar across his forehead, and he would not look me in the eye when he lifted his hair to reveal the jagged raised skin. My mother said that my father had crossed a line. That there are some lines that cannot be crossed and once they are, nothing is ever the same inside a person or out. She told me that someday I would cross that line, too, because it was unavoidable, genetic, a part of my blood, and I waited to see that line, to recognize when I had crossed it, because maybe then I would be free from the pressure of knowing that it was coming toward me like a freight train or a car with its headlights off that hits you on an open road out of nowhere in the dark. Leeanne's father had given me a check for a thousand dollars to leave her alone. He told me as much—"Walk away," he said—and I only half heard him because the other half of me had already walked right into his house when he was no more than a sleeping threat upstairs and I had had his daughter as much and as often as I wanted. I probably got her pregnant on purpose and she probably let me get her pregnant on purpose, and we both did it for the same reasons—because the line was somewhere and there was a before and an after and we both wanted to know on which side we stood.

It had been sprinkling earlier, nothing more than spit on the windshield, but we hit committed rain thirteen miles out of Mad River, and the first time that the four bald tires kissed themselves free from the asphalt and slid us out of our lane on a tight sheet of water, Leeanne called me a motherfucker and cinched the seat belt tighter around her pregnant stomach. The second time they did it she let out a scream, something like the small noises she made when we were in darkness—backseat, bedroom, her daddy's couch—when I was closest to her mouth, her lips on my shoulder and one eye toward the door, and as we fishtailed I knew that we would not see fourteen more miles to the next city. I slowed the Ford to a crawl on the broken shoulder of the two-lane highway and looked out at the dirty gray that had become our Sunday, and I waited for Leeanne to say something hopeful that would let me know that if I went ahead and put us back on the road heading west, it would be the right decision even if the traction failed. But Leeanne just sat beside me on the split bench seat with both of her hands folded over the lap belt and her stomach where the T-shirt pulled as tight as the skin beneath it to cover the swell. The right turn signal was a hollow clicking that reminded me that time was wasting—even while we sat hidden in the rain—and down deep, underneath my fear and my hunger and the ragged edge of worry for everything I had done and was about to do, I was impatient to move and make distance.

"We can either wait or try to go back to that town," I said. The last road sign had promised a new city in fourteen miles, Poker Flat, but we'd never make the ride over miles of downpour, bad tires, and not enough money.

"I saw a sign not too far back, off the road where some buildings were," she said. "It might be a motel. Maybe we could stay there for a little while until the rain quits. I'm tired of being on the road." She kept rubbing at her stomach. It was a movement that I had grown familiar with over the past couple hundred miles—one hand tucked under the top of her pants and the other hand smoothing down the shirt over the skin, one long stride, ribs to waistband, over and over again without sound.

"You sure it was a motel?" I said. My stomach made a noise that reminded me that motels and restaurants liked to take up space in the same parking lots, and where there was a bed for rent, there was bound to be food, and the last time I'd had more than coffee in my mouth had been a lot of hours ago when there was still sunshine and flat clouds that were whiter than dinner plates. That was before I knew her father had offered her money, too, had threatened me dead, had done everything but yank a hanger out of Leeanne's closet and taken care of the whole situation himself.

"I saw buildings and lights," she said. She did not look at me as she talked. Her hand was still moving in its steady arc over the hump of her stomach.

I rolled down my window so that I could see the road in both directions, and the rain came into the car for a minute; needled at my bare arms, put dark spreading stains on my short sleeves. The sky was heavy murk above us, bruised and black, and I knew that if I kept my head out the window for a while longer somewhere out there I would see lightning splinter toward the ground. The air had the smell of brine even though we were miles from any hope of water that didn't come from the sky. I switched on the left turn signal and then swung the car into a wide U and headed back.

I had hoped we could just keep driving on a loaf of bread and a package of lunch meat, fulfill my plan to just roll to a stop when the last of the gas gave out and call everything good and just start out wherever the car came to rest, and maybe we might have if Leeanne hadn't been six months pregnant. But plans have about as much substance as daydreams, and every time you are two steps away from everything coming true, somebody slaps you between your shoulder blades and knocks the reality back into you. It doesn't help much that money goes half as far as you think it will.

We took the cheapest motel room and went straight to bed and wrapped the blanket around us. While Leeanne flipped through the television channels, I cracked sunflower seeds and spit the shells into one of the short glasses from the bathroom.

"You smell good," I said. I reached out to touch her, to maybe pull her toward me and kiss her and feel the weight of her body against mine, but she was as firm as a cement freeway divider and she didn't turn or kiss me or touch me back at all. She just smiled and dropped her hand to her belly and she started her rub. It was a habit, like cracking knuckles, and I hated it. I rolled onto my side away from her and spit some sunflower seeds into the glass without cracking them. My lips felt chapped on the inside.

"The baby's sleeping," she said. "I don't want to wake her."

"You want me to rub your feet?" I said. "I can use a hot washcloth and make you feel better."

Leeanne bit at her bottom lip and for a second I thought that she might start crying, but then she exhaled hard so that her bangs lifted off her forehead and then she turned to me and gave me a half smile. "I'm tired, that's all. Maybe you could just talk to me so I can fall asleep."

I rolled over and put my hand over the top of hers while she rubbed her stomach even though I wanted her to stop. After a few rounds, she moved her hand out from under mine and I took over and I decided that I would move my hand the length of her twenty more times and then I would stop. "Tomorrow I'm going to put some better tires on the car." I rested my head against her so that I could listen to her breathe. Leeanne's eyes were closed and her inhales came slow and deep. I dropped my voice to a whisper. On the television a tiny lizard erupted from a leathery egg, blinked at the too-bright light, and slipped away into deep dark grass.

The motel was on Bond Road, just off the highway, and there was an intersection with a Flying J gas station and a few low buildings on gravel lots. Monday came up without sun, and I left Leeanne sleeping and went out to find food and tires that would get us the hell out of there.

The second building I walked up on had the sound of air gun and the smell of grease, and I could see a stack of radials twenty deep behind a chain-link fence. I walked the distance to the open double sliding doors and waited for the man working the gun to notice me. He finally looked up from the car he was bent against and I shot my hand up in a weak wave.

He flipped a switch on the back of the compressor and the garage was suddenly quiet, except for the sound of a radio playing old country turned low. "You need something?" he asked. He pulled a cigarette from the front pocket of his work shirt and pinched the butt between his lips so he could bite the filter off. There were flecks of tobacco in his teeth that I could see from where I stood.

"I need tires. Maybe one, maybe two. Probably four," I said. "Two-thirty-fives. Used, if you have them."

The man rubbed at his cheek and left a smear of grease where his finger had touched. He was not a tall man, but his shoulders were broad, and both of his sleeves were rolled tight over hard muscle in his arms despite the fact that his hair had crept back from his forehead. "You a mechanic?" he asked.

I cleared my throat and wiped at my lips. "Shade tree mostly," I said. "But I've done some things. Brakes and shocks, carburetors. I did most of the work on my own car."

He spit a mouthful of thick saliva at the ground. "Must not have done such a good job if you're walking around instead of driving."

"I've got my car," I said. I pointed behind me, back toward the motel. "It's parked over where we're staying."

He smiled and held his hand out toward mine. "I'm just giving you a hard time," he said. "I'm Chuck."

The chipped and faded sign that faced the road said *Deacon's Auto*.

"You're not Deacon?" I asked.

"Nope," he said. "That's an old sign."

"You think I can get a deal on some tires?" I asked.

"You ever changed out a 406 V8 for a 427 side oiler with twin four-barrel Edelbrock carbs?"

I scuffed my tennis shoe into the gravel. "No," I said. "I never have."

Chuck laughed and hit me hard on the shoulder. "Me neither," he said. "But I always wanted to. Might still do it someday." He led me into the garage and under the car on the lift. He looked up and pointed with a stained finger. "This one needs new rotors. Probably everything on the front and the rear. I don't do anything fancy around here. Just patch them up and send them back."

I could smell oil and gas and hot metal, new rubber and old tools. There was something about the smell of a gutted car that made me feel like I wasn't afraid of anything I had done. "I just need tires for a Ford," I said.

"You want to earn some money?" Chuck asked me.

I looked up into the open underbelly of the car and saw things that were familiar and I could hold on to them and get a sense that was steadier than the road west and Leeanne's constant fucking stomach rub.

I reached out and shook Chuck's hand.

"I know," he said, "you've got nothing to lose. I was you once. You just don't want to someday be me." He laughed, but it didn't sound like much.

I bought breakfast and had them box it up so that I could take it back to Leeanne. She was still curled in the middle of the bed when I got back to the room, but then she rolled onto her back and opened her eyes.

"That smells good," she said. "I'm starving."

"I got a job," I said.

She picked a piece of bacon out of the box and started eating it. "What am I gonna do while you're working? Am I just going to sit here?" Her eyes were still puffy, but they shrunk down quick and sharp. "I can't just sit here," she said. "I want to do something, too."

I rubbed her leg underneath the sheet. "You can relax and take care of the baby and watch television and rest. You're supposed to be resting anyway."

Leeanne started eating scrambled eggs with her fingers. "I wish we hadn't left. I wish I was still home so I could go to school and see my friends. I miss my friends."

I wanted to tighten my hand around her leg and jerk her out of the bed, pull her onto the carpet so I could lie next to her, and hold her down and put my mouth right up to her ear and she'd have no choice but to listen to me. Instead I lifted my hand from her leg and held my tongue. "If we would've stayed, your dad would've made you give up the baby," I said. "And he would've done something bad to me. Remember, Leeanne?" I had told her about what happened when I turned her daddy's money down, what he had offered me next—something along the lines of *how much do you think your life is worth*, and after that it had been harder to get off with Leeanne when we were doing it on her daddy's couch.

"I had a dream last night that my father said that we could get married and we had a big church wedding and all my friends were there."

"We'll have a wedding someday," I said. I said it mechanically, with about as much hope as the second hand on a clock has of changing the pace of the next minute.

Leeanne dropped the chunks of egg into her mouth like a bird. "I wasn't pregnant in the dream," she said. "And there wasn't a baby at the wedding. Don't you think that's weird?"

I thought about how her daddy had grabbed me by the arm and pulled me against his face so that little drops of spit flew off his lips when he spoke, and each word was harsh and forced and full of his bad breath. He had said things that I didn't think a man would say about his pregnant daughter, and things I didn't think anyone would say at all, but that hand biting into my arm and separating my bicep from bone was enough to convince me that he knew the meaning of his words. "Maybe you were pregnant in the dream, but you weren't showing yet. Maybe this was earlier," I said.

She looked at me and licked her breakfast from her fingers. "Maybe," she said, "but I don't think so. I don't think there was a baby at all."

I started picking up hours at the garage, and Chuck asked me questions while we worked, asked me about my life, and I told him a story that sounded good out loud— everything approved and honored and whole. The work was not hard, and I liked the feel of grease under my fingernails and the scratches on my hands and the cuts from stripped bolts and slipped tools.

On Thursday I was welding a rust patch into the rocker panel of a '66 Ford when Chuck yelled at me to turn the radio up, and I shut the iron off and did what he asked. I picked up the air hose to blast the dust off the piece I was working on, and Chuck grabbed my arm and his fingers tightened into my coveralls.

"Hold off on that for a minute," he said.

We stood there in the silence, with nothing but the radio playing too loud and Chuck's hand on my arm, and when the song was finished, Chuck walked over and snapped the radio off and the silence between us deepened an inch, and then he walked out to the gravel lot and pulled a cigarette from his pocket and smoked with his back to me. I didn't know whether to work or stand still, so I cleared my throat and walked out to the sunlight and gravel, facing the road.

"You want a cigarette?" Chuck asked.

I shook my head. I could hear the cars on the highway, everybody accelerating to someplace farther than there.

"It's that one goddamn song that does it to me," Chuck said suddenly. "I've gotten good about most things, but that's the one I can't get past." He dropped ash from his cigarette and stared out toward the road. "Deacon used to play that song all the time—had the whole record, but only played that song. About drove me crazy. He knew all the words, used to sing it at the top of his lungs just to piss me off, I think." Chuck smiled and spit onto the gravel, rubbed at it with the toe of his boot. "Deacon was my son. Only kid. Used to work out here with me—bitched about it a lot, but he did good work. He had the patience that I didn't have, like you do."

I shoved my hands into my coveralls and fingered the quarters I was saving to buy lunch with. "He move away?" I asked.

Chuck laughed and pushed his greased and grooved hat back. "No, he went off and got himself killed. Coming home from drinking one night, and he was seeing this girl that I guess he was fighting with." Chuck blew a double lung of smoke toward the blank sky. "So on his way home he rolled his car, for whatever reason, ass over teakettle on the road, took out about fifty feet of a neighbor's fence."

I waited for him to finish, to say just a little bit more, because it seemed like something had to come next, a "but" or a "so," except Chuck was quiet and just stood there with his cigarette pinched in his lips while the ash grew at the tip. "I'm sorry," I said. I moved the quarters against each other, squeezed them because I did not know if I should pull my hand free and reach out and touch Chuck on the arm or the shoulder or the back, like I had seen people do in the movies. I had never touched a man who was older than me, other than my father, and those were times that I could count on one hand.

"Yeah, well, it happens, right? Boys die all the time." Chuck tossed his cigarette and we both watched the smoke rise from the dry rocks. "You gonna sand that piece flush, or are you gonna just leave it thick and hope that nobody notices?" He walked back into the garage and did not wait for me to answer.

On Friday Chuck came to me and said that he and his wife had been talking and they had an extra room above the garage at their house, and maybe Leeanne and I wanted to move into it, save ourselves a few dollars. I had spun some lies to him, and I felt bad about it sometimes—told him we were married, told him she was pregnant and we were excited and had been heading to the ocean because her doctor said babies who live in the salt air thrive more than babies who don't. He had asked about our families, but I had gone vague and quiet as if I hadn't heard him ask at all.

Leeanne was glad to be moving because moving gave the hope of change. She was restless most days, angry and sad, her moods shifting like wind. I never knew which way I might catch her when I came home from Chuck's, smelling like lube and sweat and brake dust and gasoline. At the motel I didn't pay for long distance in our room because I was afraid that she would get weak during a long afternoon when there was a lull between shows, and she might miss her mother because she saw a mother and daughter on TV, reunited or working through their troubles. I was afraid of telephones, kept my nickels and dimes hidden so she wouldn't be tempted to walk to the pay phone by the road. Sometimes when I was running a dipstick into an oil pan or rotating a set of tires, I'd wonder if she was thinking about home, and if she was, how hard was she thinking?

Chuck's wife, Vivian, came out and met us in their driveway, and we all stood around for introductions. Behind her was a shaggy black-and-white dog that barked twice and then shut up at the sound of our voices. Vivian was a small woman, young-looking in a way that might have been influenced by the quality of the light. She had blond hair that she wore piled on her head, and her voice had all the flavor of the old country lyrics that poured out of the radio in the shop, and for a second I thought about Deacon and his favorite song. Something about long limousines and a shiny car. Her voice carried loss, and when she smiled at me and asked me if Tyler was my given name or was it just something I fell into, I almost told her the truth, that on paper my first name was Martin and the only thing I'd ever fallen into was bad luck. I almost told her about the line in my blood and that I was fairly sure

I had crossed it, or was about to very soon, in a matter of months, but truth is hard to rope in once it gets loose. I knew that it was much easier to breed lies, because they are like rabbits and multiply in the wild on their own.

"You told them about the grange hall tonight, didn't you, Chuck?" she said. "Did he tell you that we want to take you out tonight and buy you a good dinner?" She looked at Leeanne's swollen stomach and winked at her. Leanne did not look at her in return.

The room above the garage smelled like new paint and there were clean curtains on the rod. Chuck opened the window to air out the fumes, and he pointed out the dresser and the bed and the small bathroom with a toilet and a sink. I kept thanking him, and Leeanne sat down in the middle of the bed, and Vivian pulled her into conversation that I should've been paying close attention to so that I knew the lies being born, but mostly the talk stayed safe—*How far along are you*, and *Is it a boy or a girl*, and *Do you have any names yet?* Vivian did not ask us where we were from or where we were going or if our folks were anxious for the baby to come. When they were satisfied that we were settled, they went back down the narrow flight of stairs and left us to rest before dinner.

"How long are we gonna stay here?" Leeanne asked.

"I haven't thought about it," I said. "He isn't asking us to pay anything, so why do you already want to think about leaving?"

Leeanne started crying, and even though I was looking out the window at the green hills and the scrub oak and the rows of wire fences that disappeared into nothingness, I knew that she was crying sitting up, crying without wiping at her cheeks, crying openly and without shame so that I would turn around and do something. My shoulders were tired from carrying her weight. I watched buzzards dip in the distance, black birds that carried their wings in sharp Vs.

Leeanne picked up a book from the shelf against the wall and leaned back against the pillows. I stretched out next to her and closed my eyes. She was quiet for a while and I listened to her turn pages, the dry rustle and scrape as they caught on her shirt. I concentrated on the darkness behind my eyelids and tried not to think about things that were familiar to me.

"There's a mark in this book. I can't read it," Leeanne said.

"You can't read the mark or the book?"

"The book, Tyler. I can't read a book that somebody has marked in. It's weird. I don't like using things that aren't mine."

I rolled over onto my side and looked at the open book that Leeanne had balanced on her stomach. In the middle of the page there was a red ink stamp that said EXIT. There were no other marks, just the stamp on the page, and I took the book from Leeanne and flipped through a few pages, and then turned back to the beginning. Inside the front cover there was a name printed in the corner. Deacon. I handed the book back to Leeanne and she looked at it for a second before she dropped it to the floor beside the bed. "It seemed like it was gonna be a good story, too." She let out a long sigh and tapped her fingers against her chest. "I don't know how long I can stand to be this bored," she said. "I can't wait until the baby comes so I can have something to do."

The grange hall was on a narrow strip of blacktop that ran between rows of farmhouses and acreage. The parking lot was half full, and Vivian said that because it was a Friday night, most people would skip the dinner and come after nine for the band. Inside there were tables along one wall, and then a dance floor that led to a small wooden stage at the far end of the building. The tables were covered with checkered cloths and we ordered steaks and beers and Lee-anne asked for a Coke and then Vivian said that Leeanne should live it up and ordered her a Shirley Temple instead.

Chuck wanted to talk cars, but Vivian told him that there couldn't be any shop talk at the table, so he switched to hunting and fishing, which I knew nothing about other than the fact that I had once outfished my father when I was very young, and somewhere there was a picture of me holding up my first—and last—full stringer of trout. They were dull gray in the picture, but I remembered that when I held them up for the camera they had been beautiful with color, like the sheen of oil floating on the top of a mud puddle. Vivian went back to baby questions, and this entertained Leeanne, who had read a book and had never had the opportunity to show just how much she knew.

Chuck excused himself from the table and came back with three glasses of whiskey from a bar that I had not seen. "You don't mind driving, do you?" Chuck said to Leeanne, and he winked at her but I didn't know if the wink was meant to turn his question into a joke or give her thanks in advance. Leeanne was six months away from being legal age for her driver's license, but that was in our other life that we no longer lived.

When the band started playing, we turned our chairs to face the dance floor, and the volume went up suddenly, so that we had to lean in close to each other in order to hear. I held Leeanne's hand, and every so often Chuck would get up from the table and there would be drinks again, and Vivian was always the first to put down an empty glass.

After a while, Chuck took Vivian out on the floor, and they danced to a fast song, and then a slow song, and then half of another fast song before Vivian stopped him and pulled him back in our direction. Her face was pink and there was something about the color high up in her cheeks that made me have to look away from her. Leeanne was smiling, but I could tell that she was using the last of her strength to hold it there.

"You like to dance?" Vivian asked me. She had to lean in close to my ear so that I could hear her, and when she spoke her breath was warm on my skin and she held her mouth close even when I turned toward her and it was as though I could feel her breath in other places on my body so that my hands started sweating and I had to nod instead of answer.

"I'm really glad you two wanted to come out with us," Chuck shouted into my other ear. "I'm really happy."

I smiled and nodded and he gripped my shoulder and pulled me toward him. "I hope you two will stay around awhile. You know? We wouldn't mind that." Tiny drops of spit landed on my cheeks while he talked to me, but I kept my hands in my lap. His teeth were stained from tobacco, but his eyes were shiny and his hand was tight against me. "Maybe we could rebuild that 406 V8," he said.

Vivian grabbed my hands out of my lap and pulled me to my feet. I didn't realize I was drunk until I stood up, and then I had to wait for the floor to settle underneath me before I could walk away from the table. Vivian led me out to dance, and I tried to say no and smile, but she wouldn't let go of my hands, and once we were out on the floor, we were swallowed by the other people dancing around us, and I realized that the only way out was through.

"You know how to two-step?" she asked.

I shook my head. Vivian put her cheek against my shoulder and we shuffled around together. I felt her mouth on my ear. "How old is she?"

I thought I recognized the words to the song. The band was covering something that I'd heard before but I couldn't remember the name. "I know this song," I said.

Vivian pulled her cheek away from my shoulder so that she could look at me, and even though she was smiling, there was something about the set of her jaw that didn't let her lips slide all the way off her teeth.

"How old is she?" she said again.

I looked over Vivian's shoulder toward our table, but the lights were too low and there were too many people between us and them. "She's nineteen," I said. "She'll be twenty in August."

Vivian's mouth was back against my ear. "Bullshit," she said.

I felt something stir in my stomach and I thought it might be the combination of dancing and whiskey and steak and beer, but the buzz in my head went quiet and I kept moving my feet. "Yeah," I said, "she is. People always think she's younger."

"It really isn't any of my business," Vivian said. "I just know what I see, that's all, and I'm not usually wrong." She shifted her weight against me and we turned toward the band. "I just see that you haven't got rings on your fingers and I don't think it'll be too much longer before she busts and you have another mouth to feed. It doesn't seem to me like either of you should be wandering too far from home."

Part of me wanted to give in to her arms, drop my shoulders, and rest my head against her chest so she could hold me until all of the weight lifted and the lies evaporated from my skin like sweat. "I love her," I said.

A steel guitar started up and it was one of those songs that was either fast or slow, depending on the dancer, and Vivian held me in my place and we stayed locked on the floor. She pulled me around in a tight circle and she was strong.

A man in a wide hat danced close to us, and he leaned in and said something to Vivian that looked like "black car," but I couldn't hear and wasn't sure. She laughed and pushed him away.

"He's got a dirty mind," she said to me. Her hands were tight around the tops of my shoulders, and I could smell her against me, her drinks and her perfume. The skin on her neck was white and blank and tight. "I want you to come over to the house and go through Deacon's things. There's a whole lot in there I think you could use—shirts and pants, and a couple coats. Some of that expensive cologne he just had to have," she said. I opened my mouth to refuse her, but she put a finger to my lips. Her hand was dry even though the room was hot as an exhaust pipe and I was sweating through my shirt. "I've been wanting to get rid of it all, but you know how fathers are—they can't give up what belongs to them."

The dancing had become a habit, like Leeanne's hand across her belly, and I wasn't aware that my feet were still moving until I looked down at the floor. "I'm sorry for your loss," I said, but I felt like saying it quiet was the only way to say it, and when I could tell that she hadn't heard me, I didn't feel like saying it again loud.

Her fingers were playing with my hair where it rubbed the collar of my shirt. "You oughta get this cut," Vivian said.

We turned one more rotation and then the lights went up and the drums rolled the music to a stop. The band announced its break and the floor cleared so the crowd could shift to the bar.

"I want you to come down to the house and we'll go through those boxes in the morning," she said. She took my hand in hers so that we could weave through the crowd.

There were more drinks, and more dancing, and at some point I could no longer feel my feet or my face. When Leeanne's good mood finally wore out like a fan belt, I told Vivian that it was getting late, and together we got Chuck to agree that it was time to go.

We were silent in the car, all of us pressed together for warmth until the heater could catch up and take the fog off the windows. I had turned the corner to drunk and was trying to hold myself upright in the backseat next to Leeanne. Once we hit the parking lot, Chuck had decided to drive, and from what I could tell from my one good focused eye, he was doing all right despite the fog and the dark and the turns I could not see coming.

"I hate this stretch of road at this time of night," Vivian said.

"Why do you have to say that? Why even think it?" Chuck rubbed the back of his hand against the bottom of the windshield so that he could clear what the defroster couldn't reach.

"What's wrong with the road?" Leeanne asked.

They were quiet in the front seat, and then Chuck cleared his throat and turned the heater down to cut the roar from the fan. "Go ahead, Viv. You started it," he said.

Vivian turned in her seat so that she could face us. "This is where Deacon died," she said.

"On this road," Chuck said. "In this kind of weather, you know. Rain in the day that goes cold at night so the fog settles in the low spots, but it was nothing new, he'd driven it a million times before."

Vivian turned and looked out her window. "Did we pass it already?"

I watched Chuck squint against the oncoming head-lights, but he didn't look away from the road. "I think it was back there. It was either around that last curve, or the one coming up. I don't remember." His eyes glanced into the rearview mirror and I couldn't tell if he was looking at Leeanne or me.

"That's terrible," Leeanne whispered. She leaned her head against my shoulder.

Vivian turned the heater fan to high again so that the noise filled the car and she had to raise her voice to talk above it. "I guess it isn't true to say he died here—he got farther than this. The police said he had managed to walk a good hundred yards from the car before he finally quit."

There were lights flashing ahead of us and Chuck tapped the brakes so that we slowed and came alongside two cars on the shoulder. There were men standing by the car in front, and even though the hood was wrinkled and the windshield had been busted, and the grill was pushed into the radiator so that all the fluid had poured out onto the road, both of the headlights were still on and shining strong. We could see the deer just beyond the front of the car, its front legs outstretched toward the centerline, the hind end rolled up and twisted at the spine, blood and its insides puddled around it. One of the men waved us on and Chuck swung the car out and crept wide to avoid them.

Leeanne pressed her face into my sleeve and I could feel her breath through my shirt. "I can't look," she said.

"I think it was a deer that got Deacon," Vivian said. She was leaning forward in her seat with her cheek against the window. "I think Deacon swerved to miss a deer and he rolled his car. He was the kind of person who wouldn't want to hurt anything."

The moon came out from behind the clouds and lit the fields and pastures so that the darkness retreated to the hills and I could see fence posts and wire and the white weeds that soaked up the rain. Chuck drove slowly the rest of the way until he made the soft turn and pulled the car near the house. We stood in the driveway and listened to the engine tick and then we moved in different directions. "I will see you in the morning," Vivian whispered into my ear when I hugged her good night, and I wanted to hold on to her, shuffle my feet in that tight clockwise circle, and go back to the dance floor so that I could hear her now that my head was quiet, and I could tell her that I was fine with what I had and what already belonged to me. An owl called out and we were startled and reminded of where we were headed.

"We're opening the shop late tomorrow," Chuck said to me as he walked toward his house. "Maybe we won't even go in at all. I'm gonna sleep like the dead, and it's gonna take a hell of a lot more than the alarm clock to wake me up."

I followed Leeanne up the stairs to the room and then I pulled the covers back on the bed and helped her down, slipped her shoes off for her and tucked her in. "I don't like these people," she whispered. "I want to leave."

The window was still open to air out the paint, but the night was cold and it filled the room with a chill that would probably take a long time to warm. I stood at the window and looked out at the light, the buzzards now gone to roost and replaced by the low shapes of cows on the hillsides. Behind me I could hear Leeanne's breathing turn hollow like a snore, and part of me wanted to press my pillow against her face so that I would not have to hear the sound. Below and beyond us I could see the corner of windows of the main house, the tall shrubs and front door. I could see the mailbox at the end of the driveway, and the road in the distance. I imagined Deacon on that road in this same darkness, and I wondered how close he had really been to making it home.

FIRM AND GOOD

Me and Elbow Ritchie took the corner from Monroe to Jefferson at an easy forty-five and Elbow went deep with his right foot and dropped the Hurst shifter down a gear so the engine turned to a tight whine as the back end slipped out from under us and we fishtailed onto the other side of the street until Elbow led it back to our side with a relaxed left hand and we spit pavement under fifteen-inch radial slicks. Elbow was just showing off and I knew it, but his birthday had been two weeks ago and he had every right to brag, since his father had bought him a '71 Mach 1 and I was driving a Schwinn. He had pulled up to my house the night of his birthday and hit the horn and the gas and I heard nothing but a 351 four barrel blow exhaust at the curb and I knew that fucker had worn his father down to nothing but a wallet who had spilled out the cash it took to put Elbow behind the wheel of too much car and not enough brakes and we had barely been home since. Now we were twenty minutes out of school that didn't end for another sixty-five and Elbow had the short end of some backyard green he had paid thirty bucks an ounce for and I was so high I didn't know if our tires were touching the street as we drove through the neighborhood and took the shortcut to get us home. Elbow had this big-ass smile on his face but everything else about him was sharp concentration and competence, because if there were things about Elbow that I didn't trust, his driving wasn't one of them, and he had a way of cocking his arm out the window, holding a cigarette and the wheel, and cranking up the stereo volume all at one time that looked like some ritualistic form of dance. I almost told him that, had my mouth open and was forming the words over the top of Black Sabbath doing "Fairies Wear Boots," when we hit the cat—nothing more than a black-and-white stone in the street—and I jerked my head out my open window to watch it rebound and spin into the curb and Elbow pulled the cigarette from the corner of his mouth, exhaled, squinted toward me, said something about the paint job, and the Mustang went sixty to zero in a long burn of Goodyear rubber.

It was March and the weather had turned bleak. The sky was milk and there was no warmth in the air even though there had been the threat of sunshine, and we had the windows down mostly because the passenger side didn't roll up all the way and we both got tired of hearing the heavy slapping sound of tire echo if the driver's window wasn't down to match. There were white and weak pink blossoms in the trees, which still seemed as naked as November, and everything was poised on the edge of a spring that just was not coming. The only movement was the sharp wind that bit through our T-shirts, and the trees, and darker clouds that came in from the west and were the color of heavy aluminum and depression, hammered together above us.

Without the ram air hood vibrating across the top of the engine, we were suddenly dumped into more quiet than I had expected and for a minute I wondered if I had seen the cat get hit, or if maybe it was just my imagination and we were still moving forward and blowing back miles.

"We hit that fucking cat," Elbow said, and there were many things I did not trust about Elbow, but what he said around his cigarette was not one of them, and in the empty seconds as side one faded out on the tape deck and there was the quiet pause before side two, I knew that we had killed that thing in the road and I wasn't that high anymore and it would be impossible now to fake it and forget.

"What do we do?" I said. My mouth was as dry as the air that came in through the window, and I could smell burning wood, a distant fire leaking out someone's chimney. For a minute I was reminded of fall and away games when I had played basketball and the team had traveled by bus to a distant town and me and Lonnie Howard would leave the gym when we were supposed to be doing homework while the varsity team played, and we would walk foreign sidewalks of cities we did not live in and there was always a smell that October carried with it—dank and dark and full of smoke and cold and fire and rotten vegetables waiting to be upturned by garden rakes on blustery Saturday afternoons when there was no sun and no heat. But now it was March and Lonnie Howard had transferred schools after freshman year and I was with Elbow Ritchie and I did not play basketball anymore and there was a dead cat behind us and a few months of senior year in front of us and beyond that nothing but the sputter and hiss of dead air like the end of our own tape.

"Well," Elbow said, "we probably have two choices." He shifted his weight in the seat and I could see his right foot rise up from the floor mat and strain toward the gas pedal, and I knew that choice, so I pulled the handle on my door and spilled myself into the street and made choice number two. I heard Elbow make a noise behind me and then I had my legs underneath me and I was headed back along the gutter to the shape and the mess. Elbow gunned the car's engine and I thought maybe he might punch it and run but then the motor cut and there was silence in the street and in thirty feet I was looking down at what we had done. It wasn't as bad as I thought it would be. Other than the unnatural angle of the cat's head and the way that the glassy eyes stared in opposite directions, it looked like it could be picked up and petted. I had seen a squirrel hit by a station wagon one time when I was walking home from school and it had exploded. Crunch and poof. It had looked as if the squirrel had decided to turn itself inside out and go empty in the process.

But the cat was intact. I looked down at it and it looked sideways at me and it said to me five words that I would not forget even after the last of the cheap weed wore off. "It should have been you."

Then a woman in the yard beside the gutter was screaming and Elbow was beside me and the cat continued its accusation and I wanted to reach down and lift it from the thin stream of water it was lying in, but it told me to just step away, leave it alone, let it be. I looked at Elbow to see if he had heard the cat's decision, but Elbow was lighting a cigarette and squaring up against the woman, who was yelling, "Toby, my God you killed Toby," and I shoved my hands deep into my jeans pockets and decided to go as limp as the cat.

She wasn't a tall woman, but she crossed the yard in quick strides, and then the sidewalk, and she was on us before Elbow even had a chance to exhale. Elbow squinted at her and raised both hands in a gesture of accepted defeat. "It was an accident," he said.

"You," she said. "You ran right over him. You didn't even try to stop."

"Ma'am, I didn't even see him. He ran right in front of my car." He hooked his thumb up the street toward the Mustang, which was parked at a decidedly drunken angle in our lane. I could still smell the faint burn of new tire and by now other neighbors had left the warmth of their houses to stand on their porches with their hands on their hips or folded across their chests in a gesture of conviction and I knew that Jefferson Street had found us guilty of the crime and we would never get a jury of our peers.

"I want the names of your parents. Both of you." She said this matter-of-fact, and I realized that she was not hysterical or crying, but her face was flushed and she kept wringing her hands in front of her as if they might escape and do something on their own if she didn't hold them back.

"Everything okay over there, Marianne?" a guy called from two houses down. He was wearing an unbuttoned mechanic's shirt over a white T-shirt and he had a can of beer in his hand.

"These boys ran over my cat."

I heard a woman gasp and suck in her breath and a quiet murmur ran up the street like a wave. We were surrounded on all sides now. There were kids standing on the sidewalk, and crowds forming in driveways. "You want me to deal with them?" beer-can mechanic called. A siren started up in the distance and I wondered if someone had already called the police.

"It's okay, Randy. Everything is under control." She looked at both of us, and Elbow just kept smoking and staring down the street at his car and I kept looking for a place to put my eyes, but in the end they just met hers and I couldn't break away and she wouldn't let me.

Eventually the woman made us write down our names and phone numbers on a piece of binder paper I pulled from my backpack, and then beer-can mechanic came down the sidewalk with a pillowcase and a pair of gloves and everyone watched his performance of pulling the cat from the gutter, dripping water and wrappers, its limbs already stiff, and some of the kids cried and some of the women covered their own eyes from the sight and Elbow grew bored and started taking small steps back toward the car while the cat was bagged and carried away. "Your parents will be hearing from me," Marianne said.

I went home and the evening stretched out in front of me in one long inhale and I choked on my heartbeat every time the telephone rang. The air was cold and my eyes itched from too much weed and the fact that I couldn't seem to close them and rest even though I wanted to.

I had only pushed my dinner around on my plate and when the obligation was over, I went to my room and shut the door and lay on my bed in all of my clothes, right down to shoes and socks, and watched the light leak from my windows and the shadows shift and change on my ceiling. She still hadn't called, and I figured maybe the woman had been all threat and no follow-through—it was an accident. Even Elbow had been saying that the entire way back to my house—"What is the bitch *really* going to do to us? It was an accident. I mean, we weren't driving around trying to kill fucking cats."

When my clock ticked past nine, my eyes finally felt like they could close and I had put it all into justification and perspective and even decided that we hadn't really been that high and it couldn't even be proven that we had actually hit the cat when you got right down to it, and even if she called tomorrow or the next day, there was no way my parents would bust me for being a passenger in a car that had hit a cat—even if we had been cutting school and were stoned and I wasn't supposed to be with Elbow Ritchie in his *too much car for a kid like him* without permission. Those were details—unimportant compared to the fact that it was an accident. Perfectly innocent. Perfectly faultless.

I heard the phone ring the second before it actually did and I heard the television mute in the other room and I kept my eyes shut and pretended that I was blind. I wondered if losing your vision really does increase the strength of your other senses and if my eyes were closed would food taste different or better, could I feel my way from my bedroom to the end of the block, could I hear somebody strike a match in the house next door? With my eyes closed right then on my bed in the darkness of my room I could taste my own fear and smell my own sweat and hear my father's voice on the phone and the sound of my name.

Elbow got his dad to pay her off. He wouldn't tell me how much or how the conversation went, but I figured it was more than a C-note, maybe more than two, and Elbow skated right out of punishment and my parents found another reason to think he was a bad influence on me, and come that Saturday morning I was standing in front of her house, 477 Jefferson, ready to serve three weekends of my time as penance for being high, for cutting school, for being with Elbow, for riding shotgun in a cat-killing machine. Three weekends of work, yard care, house painting, trash hauling, hammering broken stairs, gutter cleaning. Elbow's dad threw her some money and I got to serve the time. "Take this weed with you," Elbow said Friday after school as we headed out to the parking lot and I got relegated to the backseat because guys who didn't have the money to pay to stay out of trouble didn't get to ride shotgun in a cat-killing machine anymore, and now Brock Irwin was in my spot and I was in back like the hired help. Elbow handed me a Ziploc bag with a handful of joints at the bottom, all of them rolled like perfection. "It will make you forget that you're doing a work project." Brock held up his hand and Elbow gave him a hard high five and I rested my head against the back of the seat until the music came tearing out of the speaker behind me and I realized how much I hated that song.

My father woke me up on Saturday morning, five minutes before my alarm was set to go off, and he followed me around while I got ready, monitored my time, supervised my routine, and when he dropped me off in front of her house, he waited at the curb to make sure that I didn't bolt, which is exactly what I wanted to do. She opened the door after the first weak knock and invited me to step past her and into the half-light of her living room. Her house smelled like flowers and cooking and things I could not name but recognized. "You can call me Marianne," she said.

I stood there awkwardly looking down at my old pair of Converse I had worn to work in, and she did not break the silence that followed and relieve me of my shame. I could hear the heavy tick of a large clock coming from a room I could not see, and I wondered if that sound ever got on her nerves, woke her up in the night, made her have to turn the television louder in order to hear her shows. I looked around to see what kind of television she had. I didn't see one at all.

"So?" she said. I shifted my weight and scratched a place on my cheek that did not itch. "You want some coffee?"

I thought about it for a second. The agreement was that I would work for her from eight to five every Saturday and Sunday until the time was served. "It's a good lesson for you, Marty," my dad had said. "And it's a good gesture. She lives by herself. She needs the help."

"I don't know how yard work is going to pay her back for her dead cat," I had said. "I mean, the last time I checked, you can't mow some lawns and bring back grandma if she dies."

"Keep at it, Marty," my father had said. "You want to make it six weeks?"

So the deal was nine hours a day, Saturday and Sunday, all the way into April. It was about serving the time, not the amount of work I got done, and the way I figured it, if she wanted to offer me a cup of coffee, that big loud clock ticking off the minutes was reminding me that for every tick and sip, it was less time I had to haul and scrape and hammer and cut.

"Yeah," I said. "I'd like a cup of coffee. That would be great."

She led me into her kitchen and there was a small table under a window and the room was full of early morning sunshine that was already warm, and I could smell cinnamon and baked sugar, and the table was set with two cups painted with little blue designs, and there was a pot of coffee on a beaded potholder and a white cream pitcher and a cup with sugar and little silver spoons. She pointed me toward a chair and she went to the oven and lowered the door and pulled out a braided loaf of bread, and she set it on the counter while she drizzled icing over the top and then cut it into thick slices, and I could see steam rise out of the bread each time the knife pulled away from it.

"I hope you don't mind raisins," she said.

She took a slice of the bread and lifted it onto a blue painted plate that matched the cups and the saucers, and she drizzled more icing over it and set it in front of me and then took the other empty chair at the table and poured coffee into each cup. When she was finished, she lifted her coffee, sipped at it, added a spoonful of sugar, and then sat back and stared at me. I realized that I had never sat in a stranger's house by myself, never sat and eaten food in front of someone I did not know without the presence of my parents or a friend from school. I had never been alone with a stranger in a stranger's house, and I wasn't sure what to do with my coffee other than to just drink it even though it tasted hot and too bitter, but the thought of adding things to it and having her watch me seemed like too much to go through.

"You don't want cream?" she said.

"It's good," I said. "I'm fine."

"That bread was my mother's recipe," she said. "It was my favorite when I was a girl."

I picked up a small silver fork and held it in my hand, unsure whether I should cut off a piece and take a bite, or drink the coffee, or just pick up the slice of bread and eat it that way. I realized I was sweating and for the first time in my life I couldn't wait to go outside and work.

"Don't be nervous," she said.

I swallowed a too-hot mouthful of coffee and followed it up with another one. "What should I do today?" I asked.

She reached out and before I could pull my hand back or pretend I was cutting into the bread on the plate, her hand was over mine, and it was dry and warm and light. "You haven't even had some food and finished your coffee yet," she said. "Don't be in such a hurry."

In the other room I could hear the clock ticking, tight and hollow and solid, as the sun filled the room. I felt sleepy and wished I was spending this Saturday morning like I had spent the last one—warm in bed, wasting time, surfacing at some point past noon when I got too hungry to sleep. Instead, here I was eating a stranger's cinnamon bread and drinking black coffee and sweating. On the floor in the corner was a small plastic dish of water, and I realized it was a cat's dish, Toby's, and it was still there, still full of water, waiting for the cat that would not come. I wondered if it was the same water that had been in it when he had died, or if she had changed the water since then, refilled it with fresh water out of habit.

"I'm really sorry about Toby," I said. "Really."

"Who?" she said.

In the other room the clock began to chime and it went on for a full ten seconds while it played out the half hour, and I knew that if I had to hear that much noise every thirty minutes I would chop the clock to pieces and burn it up within an hour.

"Your cat," I said. "Toby. I'm sorry."

Marianne poured more coffee into her cup and followed it with cream. "Oh," she said without looking at me. "I know."

I ate quickly and she offered me more but I wanted out of that sunny kitchen, out from under her staring at me. She finally walked me to her backyard and showed me the project for the day. I immediately wished that I had milked more time with a second piece of too-sweet bread and another awkward cup of coffee. Her yard was at least three feet high in overgrowth—grass gone to seed that had withstood the winter and was committed to its takeover; vines crawling over anything that stood still—a birdbath in the corner, decorative rocks, the walls of the house; rosebushes reaching out from the perimeter of the fence; trees, bushes, shrubs. The entire thing looked as if it belonged in a South American movie scene—something from *Romancing the Stone*.

"I guess you can start here," she said. "This will probably take you most of the day."

This will take me most of my life, I thought. "Okay," I said.

She pointed me toward a shed that had yard tools in it, and after wrestling the door from the grips of the grass and vines, I was able to go inside and figure out what to use and where to start. I was hoping she might disappear back into the house and her bread and her smells and her clock, but instead she just made her way to the elevated cement slab attached to her back door, where the grass had to relent its march, pulled a wicker chair forward, and sat down to watch me work.

When I saw the first snake, I was grateful I had started with the lawn mower. The grass was so high that the lawn mower kept getting bogged down and I had to push it forward and backward, forward and backward in a rocking motion until it could chew through the grass and take on the next section. When it nudged the snake free and sent it sidewinding into the deeper grass, I was thankful for the noise of the motor because I was pretty sure I had let out a small scream, and I hoped Marianne hadn't heard. I felt all of the hair on the back of my neck stand up, and a shiver of disgust ran up my arms and slid down my back with the sweat. I hated snakes.

The sun was high in the sky and it felt as if the spring that had been holding its breath had finally exhaled and we were going to take a quick jump over spring and land somewhere in the middle of summer. After two more push-and-pull paths with the lawn mower, an entire tangle of snakes scattered in front of me and the blade caught a small one that hadn't made the quick decision to go forward and right and instead had gone back and left and there was a thick sound from the lawn mower, the churning of the snake, and then it was spit into the grass beside me, the yellow and black stripes now ragged and red. I looked away quickly and pushed the lever down on the handle and the yard went quiet. There was sweat under both of my armpits and I pulled my sweatshirt over my head and walked toward the fence, careful to take only the path that was mowed and not the deeper grass, where the snakes had retreated. I didn't even want my shoes to touch the ground.

I hung my sweatshirt on the fence. "You have snakes back here," I said.

Marianne shielded her eyes from the glare of the sun. "Water snakes, I know. They love that deep grass." She didn't seem the least bit upset by it. Of all days to forget to wear my watch, today was the worst and I had no idea what time it was or how much time was left. I looked up at the angle of the sun and wished I had been a Boy Scout and knew things like how to tell time by the level of the sun or how to rid a lawn of snakes before mowing them down. The one I had hit was sitting on top of the fresh grass.

"I accidentally ran over one," I said.

Marianne stood from her chair and looked down at the grass where I was pointing. She crossed her arms over her chest and shook her head. "The casualties keep adding up," she said.

I lifted the collar of my T-shirt and rubbed the sweat from my face. I could feel pieces of grass sticking to me. Everything smelled green and wet and alive. I was suddenly thirsty but I didn't think it was a good time to ask for anything.

I heard the back door slam and I figured I had finally done enough to piss her off and make her retreat, and in a way I was sorry it had to be over a dead snake, but I wasn't that sorry. I wouldn't be sorry if I ran over all of them,

and if she wasn't sitting back there watching me, maybe I
would. Just rake up all the shredded bodies with the grass
clippings, bag them, and put them at the curb.

I went back to the lawn mower, pushed the lever, and
was just about to pull the cord when the back door opened
and I looked up and Marianne was standing there with
two green bottles in her hand. "You look thirsty," she said.
"Take a break."

I went to the cement slab and she handed me one of the
green bottles. There was no label on it, no identification. It
was just dark green and full and cold. I looked down at it
and tried to guess the contents by the color.

"It's beer," she said. "You like beer, don't you?"

For a second I thought it was a test—something to see
just how far I would go, but she had already sat back down
in her chair and was sipping from her own bottle while staring out across the half-mowed lawn, and not looking at me
at all. I took a small sip. It didn't taste much like beer, at least
not any that I had ever drank, but maybe it was imported.

"My husband brewed it," she said. "What do you think?"

I took another swallow, this one bigger, and it felt good
going down, cold and a little spicy, something like tea. "It
doesn't taste like beer," I said.

"Cardamom," she said.

"What?"

"Cardamom. He liked spices. I'm more like you, though.
I like herbs." She gave me a knowing look. I had one of
Elbow Ritchie's joints of perfection tucked into the front
pocket of my jeans.

"Where is your husband?" I said. "My dad said you lived alone." The beer was going down easily and I was down to half a bottle in another swallow.

"He died," she said. "It's been a while."

I wished there was a label on the bottle and I could pick at it, fixate on it, do something so that I didn't have to look at her and apologize, but I was out of luck and the glass was smooth green, the same color as the lawn, and I watched a trail of ants wander into a crevice in the cement. "I'm sorry," I said. I didn't know what else to say. In the movies they always say, "What happened?" and then there is an awkward and personal moment when maybe too much has been said but there is always some kind of relief in the telling of the story. I didn't ask her that question.

"You want another one?" she asked, gesturing toward my bottle.

I nodded.

We drank the next one in silence, and by then the sweat had dried from my back and the sun had shifted and the wedge of shade that held the cement porch had pulled back and slipped down to the grass. I looked at her from the corners of my eyes, saw the way her hair was so black that it threw off its own glare, and I could remember how in science class we had learned that on the visible color spectrum, darker colors absorb rather than reflect, but her hair was breaking that truth. I could feel my shoulders tightening up and the thought of dragging that mower around the rest of the snake habitat made my arms ache. My Converse were grass stained and my ankles itched.

"Why don't we go inside," she said. "It's actually getting to be hot out here."

"I should finish the yard," I said. The two empty bottles sat beside me on the cement and I could hear other lawn mowers in the neighborhood, the Saturday chorus, and I knew that with the sudden warmth there would be hoses running and cars being washed and phone calls for impromptu barbecues.

"I have been in a battle with Mother Nature for many years, Marty. She always wins."

She stood up and opened the door and waited for me. I picked up my bottles and went in.

The kitchen was warm but not uncomfortable, and at some point she had cleared the table because the coffee cups were gone and I didn't know what to do, so I sat down at the table and folded my hands in front of me. She stepped into the utility room, and I heard a refrigerator door open and then she was back with two more beers. My head felt a little fuzzy from drinking and I figured it was because I wasn't used to working outside. Me and Elbow could put away a twelve-pack together without so much as a stuttered step and I was only on two and already buzzed. I had to remind myself to drink slowly.

"It's the worst kind of sun out there," she said. "It's when the sun is hot but the air is cold that people get sunburned. You don't feel the heat, but it's there—it's just not how it appears and you think if you're not too hot, then you're not getting burned. Then you come in out of the sun and find out you were wrong. You look a little red, Marty."

"This beer tastes different," I said.

"Comfrey," she said. "He was always experimenting."

"It's not bad," I said.

"He died in a car accident," she said. She had taken the other chair at the table and she was watching me drink. "He swerved to avoid something in the road. An animal, a piece of something—no one knows—it was dark and he was on a back road coming home from one of his trips. He liked to disappear sometimes. Drive to nowhere."

The table was made out of grainy wood, natural looking, and I could see small knots in it, trace the raised grain with my finger.

"He left me a lot of money," she said. "I have shoe boxes full of it in my closet."

I looked up at her. She met my eyes and I didn't pull away. I took a long swallow from the bottle.

"I didn't need your friend's money," she said. "When he showed up here with that girl, I had already given him two choices, but I knew which one he would take."

Elbow hadn't told me anything about this. What he'd told me was that Marianne had called his house that night after we hit the cat, and his dad had offered her money, made a deal, and paid her off the next morning. He never said anything about going over there himself, and he sure as shit didn't say anything about bringing a girl. I looked at her like I didn't believe a fucking word she said.

"Oh he came up my driveway in his loud car and that girl was with him and he practically shoved the money in my hands. I'd told him on the phone that he could work one Saturday with you, do those things for me, and that would be enough of a gesture of apology—that's what it's about, isn't it. A gesture. A show of remorse. One day of work and the both of you would be free from obligation." She stood up and opened the back door. The smell of cut lawn was thick and heavy and sweet.

"Or he could pay me one hundred dollars for every weekend he chose not to work and you did the work instead. And he came here, handed me the money. Three one-hundred-dollar bills and that girl holding on to his arm and giving me a look."

"What girl?" I asked.

"The skinny girl. He should let me have her for a month. I could fatten her up."

"Did she have kind of dirty blond hair?" I asked. "Kind of tall, with pretty lips?"

"Exactly," she said. "Kind of tall with pretty lips."

Elbow Ritchie had brought Alyson with him. Alyson had three classes with me—history, English, and biology—and I knew every freckle on her arms and the way she wore her hair depending on the mood she was in and one drunken Friday night right after Elbow got his car I told him that I was going to ask Alyson to prom because the only thing I wanted to remember senior year by was ending it with her.

I felt hot suddenly, cold and hot, and when I reached out to take a drink from my beer, my hand couldn't close around it and I knocked it on its rounded edge, and for one quick second I thought it might regain its balance but it tipped and spun and everything that was left in it spilled out across the table and into my lap. I just sat there and let it, didn't even make the attempt to jump back, move, avoid what was happening.

"I knew that was the choice he would make," Marianne said. "I knew you were different. I could tell that even before he stopped the car that day."

My jeans were soaked in the front and everything smelled like strange flowers and the heavy grass and I realized that all I had eaten was that thick slice of sweet bread and my stomach did a slow turn and I stood up and asked Marianne where the bathroom was and she pointed me down a hallway and I was gone.

I ran cold water into the sink and rinsed off my face and small flecks of grass fell into the water that was pooling around the drain. The cold water made me feel better and I was able to breathe again, and breathing made my stomach drop out of my throat and I knew I was going to be okay. Elbow would explain. It had to be getting late. I could finish up the day here and walk to his house and knock on his door and just say, "Hey, you know what that lady told me?" and I knew he would say, "Man, Marty, not only is she a bitch, but she's a crazy fucking liar, too. Let's egg her house tonight" and everything would be okay.

"Marty, is everything all right in there?" Her voice was close against the door and I tried to picture her on the other side, maybe leaning against it, maybe pressing her ear against the wood to hear if I was sick or crying or still alive.

"I'm fine," I said, and I thought maybe I would have to convince myself of that fact, but I realized that I was. I was just fine.

"I brought you a change of jeans," she said. "You can't go home smelling like beer. I don't think your parents would be too happy about that. Why don't you just open the door a crack and I can hand them in to you."

"I'm fine, really," I said. "I can just rinse them off here in the sink. It's not that much. They will dry out."

"Marty, don't be ridiculous. I can wash your jeans. You can wear a pair of my ex-husband's."

Something in her voice made me realize that she wasn't going to let it go until I at least took them from her, and then I could just tell her that the jeans didn't fit and rinse mine off and go back out to the yard and the sun and finish up this shift so I could go find Elbow and laugh about the bullshit story she had told me. I opened the door a little and she reached around the edge and handed me a pair of faded jeans that were folded so tightly I could see the crease line in the knees. "I'm giving you a T-shirt, too. Just give me all of your clothes. You've been working. If I'm going to wash your jeans, you might as well go home in clean clothes."

"Really, it's fine," I said, but she shoved something else in my hand and then I pushed the door shut and stood in the silence of the bathroom. There was a basket on the back of the toilet with small circle-shaped soaps of different colors, and the towels were deep red, and I could smell lilac or jasmine or one of those scents that you always associate with your grandma or your mom.

I set the jeans down and unfolded a black T-shirt. There was a picture on the front, a beaver with wings, and I tossed it aside. I opened up the jeans and looked in at the waistband. They were 33x31s. I preferred 34s, depending on the cut, but these were damn close, and I thought about folding them back up and setting them on the edge of the bathtub and thanking her anyways, but they were too small, and instead I found myself dropping my own jeans to the floor and kicking off my shoes and sliding out of my pair and into a dead guy's pants. I remembered El- bow's joint in my pocket and fished out the wet and ruined paper that was unraveling and spilling green. I thought about flushing it, but I knew half the time that shit didn't work in movies and I could just imagine it never going down with the water and Marianne back in the hallway, asking if everything was all right through the door.

I pulled off my T-shirt and was surprised to feel how sticky it was and how much it smelled like gas and grass and fumes and sweat. It felt good to get it off my skin and for a minute I stood shirtless in my socks and borrowed jeans and looked at myself in the mirror. I ran more water and splashed it across my chest and scooped it under my arms and leaned forward and let myself drip into the sink, then I took my dirty shirt and rubbed my body off and ran some more water through my hair and when I was done I felt like another person and I pulled on the beaver T-shirt, gathered up my things, and left the room.

Marianne was sitting at the table and there was a full beer in front of my empty chair and the mess had been cleaned and the back door was closed and I could hear the clock ticking in that other room. I found myself wishing that it would go into its overachieving chime to mark a moment of time I could identify, but it did nothing but tick and tock, and I could picture the pendulum swinging. Getting sleepy, very sleepy. I smiled and sat down and Marianne took the wad of clothes out of my arms and went back to the utility room and I heard a washer kick on, the familiar sound of water filling the machine, and I heard dials turning and then she was back and she picked up her beer and looked at me.

"I knew those clothes would fit. I just knew it."

"They're not bad," I said.

"Do you like music, Marty?" she asked. "I have a stereo. We should turn on some music." She clapped her hands together and stood up and left the room. I looked around for a clock, anything to let me know how much time was gone in the day and how much remained. The sun was still bright outside and the shadows did not seem to be lengthening in that way they always do when someone needs to mark the hour.

I heard music, and I could recognize the song, something my parents listened to, something with a lot of guitar, but not the right kind. Acoustic. It wasn't terrible, but it wasn't anything I would ever reach to turn up. "How's this?" she called from the other room.

"I like it," I said. I stood up from my chair and walked around the kitchen. I bent down and looked at the dials on the oven—no clock, just a timer. There wasn't a clock anywhere in the room.

"Do you need something, Marty?" She was standing in the doorway. I could see that she was barefoot and her pants fell over the tops of her feet. Her toenails were painted a bright and glittery purple.

"I was just wondering what time it is," I said. "My dad wants me to call him when I need to be picked up."

She stepped into the room and she smelled different. Sweeter, cleaner. For the first time I noticed that she was wearing hoop earrings, simple and silver, and her hair was tucked behind her ears and I could see her cheekbones and how they held the color up high near her eyes.

"It's one of those days," she said. "One of those days when it feels like it's so much later than it really is. We still have hours. I promise." She sat down and picked up her beer and started drinking again. "You're not anxious to get back out there and work, are you, Marty?"

In all honesty, I wasn't, and part of me was hoping that maybe she would just let me leave early, call it a day; I'd had too much beer, and there were snakes, and maybe it would be best if I came back first thing in the morning, but now I realized I had made the mistake of letting her hold my clothes hostage and I was standing in her kitchen in a dead guy's jeans and winged-beaver T-shirt and I wasn't going anywhere until she gave me back my clothes, returned me to myself, and set me free.

"You remind me so much of Ben," she said.

"Ben?"

"My husband. Who died. Your friend?"

"Elbow," I said.

228 · Jodi Angel

"Elbow—that's such a strange name."

"When he fights he swings with his elbows. Not with his fists. His real name is James."

"Your friend James, he didn't remind me of Ben at all. Too big, too broad. Too much of something in his eyes. But you? It's like I told you. I could tell even before you got out of the car that you were the one."

I couldn't wait to tell Elbow this conversation. And I would tell him about it as soon as I told him about the first one and asked him some questions and got him to tell me just how full of shit Marianne was.

I smiled. "The one?"

She had to be drunk. I was buzzing on those beers and Elbow and I weren't lightweights. I wondered if home brew had more alcohol and I figured it probably did, since there was no government regulation to control what went into the bottle.

"I knew you were someone I could count on, that's all, Marty. I knew that if you were like Ben on the outside, you were probably like him on the inside and I wasn't wrong."

I ran my finger over the pattern in the table. All those lines counting off the stages of development in the tree, tracing the pattern of growth, etching the passing of time. I finished my beer and stood up from the table.

"I really have to see how late it is," I said. I walked past her and toward the room I had not been in before she could stop me. Even over the too-quiet tinny guitar I could hear the clock and I followed the sound.

The room was dark, the curtains pulled, and there was only a thin sheet of light that made the journey past the drapes and it seemed as if it wore itself out in the process and died just beyond the window. The room had the smell of disuse, dust, and forgetting. I could see the red light on the stereo and the light from the dials and I could make out the shapes of furniture, things on shelves. The clock was one of those big upright grandfathers, solid wood and brass and glass, and the ticking was so loud that the window vibrated a little bit every time the pendulum connected with the full extent of its arc—left to right tick, right to left tock. The face of the clock was behind a pane of glass and I could not read it in the faint light so I looked around for a lamp or a switch and found nothing. I walked to the window and pulled back the curtain.

I pulled back the curtains far enough to let in the struggling light and I realized that the room was full of dust, dust settled on everything, everything hidden. I stretched out my left hand so I could keep the curtain pulled with my right, and I wiped my palm across the face of the clock. I couldn't see anything. I rubbed harder at the glass and then I realized there wasn't anything there to see. There were no hands on the clock. No numbers. Just a blank face and the pendulum swinging beneath it marking the passing of absolutely nothing at all. I let the curtain drop and went back through the darkness.

"Marianne, do you have a clock that works?" I said.

Marianne wasn't at the table and the kitchen was empty. I checked the utility room and the only sound was the washer spinning the water from my clothes. "Marianne," I called.

The refrigerator was in the corner across from the dryer, so I pulled the door open and reached in to get a beer. The refrigerator was empty except for rows of green bottles on the top shelf and underneath it stacks of sheets. I took a bright green bottle and bent down to look at the sheets and then I realized that they were not sheets at all and the one on top looked familiar, like a pillowcase, like something I had seen before, and even though I didn't really want to, I lifted back the open end and he was in there, there was no mistaking the black-and-white hair, Toby, only this time he had nothing to say to me like he did the first time we had met, and I remembered that moment, too high and thinking he had given me a message, and now I pulled my hand back as though he had bit me, and then I thought about it and lifted the open ends of the other pillowcases, three of them altogether, black-and-white Toby, a dark silver and gray, a tabby marked just like the one my sister had when we were kids. I returned the bottle to the shelf and quietly shut the door so that it did not even make the comforting noise of a click.

The door to the backyard was not closed all the way and I opened it just enough so that I could look out onto the lawn. Marianne was out there with her back to me, and she was bent over and there was a stick in her hand, a broom handle, the bristles stuck out in a stiff row behind her. She was bent over, poking at something, pushing it around in the mowed and dead drifts of grass I had not gone back to rake, and I realized she was tapping at the snake I had run over, lifting it slightly, rolling it over, letting it fall back to the ground.

There was laughter out on the sidewalk, kids playing, and I remembered that there was a world beyond the yard. I heard the steady clip of a sprinkler and I could smell wet pavement, that unmistakable scent of wet dirt and cement. I had not applied to college, my parents didn't have enough money, and I had none at all, but maybe that would change, and part of me wished that I was going to be someplace else next year and maybe I would be—there was still plenty of time for anything to happen. In the distance I could hear a muscled-up car go by, loud and strong like a 351 Cleveland hitting 5400 rpm and blowing dual exhaust, and somewhere closer, in that same direction, I could hear brakes lock up, the unmistakable squeal of rubber leaving tread across asphalt, and maybe something or someone getting hit.

SNUFF

Halfway through the movie, Lenny Richter leaned into me and whispered *this shit is so fake*, and I wasn't quite ready to agree with him. It was by invitation only, the offer to come and watch, almost a sixty-minute ride out of town at this kid named Billy's house, an hour that had taken more like three to travel, since hitchhiking works better as a solitary sport and I had been tied down with Lenny, who didn't want to go it alone. There was a group gathered in a garage out back of Billy's house, all of us standing around, and Billy had hung a bedsheet up on the wall and propped the projector on a milk crate stacked on a folding chair and we all stood there and watched the film from start to finish, no credits, no title, no names, no sound. When the last jumpy frames of 8mm finally spun through the reels, everybody started talking at once, and one kid said *no fucking way* and I checked my watch and saw that

I was close to curfew and decided to walk back out to the main road and chance getting home on my own. I lasted fifteen minutes walking with my thumb out on the empty asphalt before I bent and broke and went to the pay phone at a two-pump gas station, the only lit building as far as I could see in either direction, and I called home, hoping my dad wouldn't pick up, if anyone did at all. My older sister, Charlotte, answered on the first ring and everything from then on was going to cost me.

Charlotte was seventeen and had been pretty, but not beautiful, but this was the summer she had discovered Fleetwood Mac and something about her had changed. My dad started making rules, more rules than ever before, asking things like "Where have you been?" and everything was a privilege and bedroom doors had to be left open and phone calls were monitored and, as Charlotte liked to say, "privacy was part of the old regime." I did not really know what she meant by that, but I sensed there was a battle brewing, and my dad may have had more power than Charlotte, but Charlotte was smart and quiet as a sniper, and sneaking out had become her specialty.

"Find another ride," she said on the phone. I was leaning forward, trying to cut the wind that had picked up the second I decided to leave Billy's house. It had been Lenny's invitation that I had ridden in on, and I should have figured that the first time Lenny ever found anything good to do, it would be at some place out of town, out the back roads, where the air felt fifteen degrees cooler, and it would finish up hours past the time when there would be any real traffic passing by to get me back, and Lenny would ruin the whole thing halfway through for me anyways by pointing out that everything was probably fake. The other guys had stayed behind at the house, Lenny with them, and talk had been loud, and there had been a lot of clapping and shouts, and by the time I started walking down the driveway, the decision had been made by everyone else to watch the film again.

"I can't get a ride, Charlotte. Please," I said, and I knew that begging wasn't the way to Charlotte's heart and if I stood a chance at getting picked up it was going to come on the back of George Washington, several of him, and probably a Lincoln, too.

"Dad's home," she said. I thought about hanging up then, walking back to Billy's and joining the second viewing, or maybe by then it would be the third and I could just quit trying and get caught up in the mix. "But he's been talking with Johnnie," she said, and I knew she meant "Walker," but she didn't need to say it; it was our code for *drunk.*

I relaxed the phone into my ear and felt its warmth and could see my dad in his armchair, the footrest kicked up, the TV on, the glass empty. The wind took less than a minute to turn from gust to sustained and I felt the edge under it and knew the August night was false and the summer was packing to go. "I'll pay you," I said.

"Stay where you are," she said. "I'm coming."

Billy lived out in what we called "the country," out beyond the city-limit signs, signal lights, stores, and food joints. All we had passed was the one gas station, a skeleton building that offered basic necessities at sky-high prices if what the window signs said was true. According to the cardboard square taped to the door, it kept limited hours, was closed on Sundays, and pumped only one kind of gas. Everything that qualified as civilization was in town, a trip by car, too far to walk from here, and if you didn't have a license you were trapped once you got from one place to the other. I couldn't imagine what Billy might do out here for fun, and then I thought about the film, *nothing but corn syrup and food coloring* Lenny Richter had said, and I felt nervous and pulled as tight as the fence wires that lined the two-lane blacktop and hummed in the wind.

The only other sound was the bugs beating themselves blind against the single overhead fluorescent that lit up the lot. It was a sickly sodium light, too bright and artificial, and the cloud of insects swarming made strange shadows on the cracked cement below. I could smell wet grass, irrigation, farmland, and creosote seeping from the railroad ties that served as the borders between asphalt, fields, and road. In the distance, a dog barked and barked, over and over again, a tired and monotonous sound, and there was no shout to *quiet down*, no hassled owner opening up a door and forcing it to come in, and I wondered what purpose a dog like that served if there was nobody to pay attention. There could have been a thousand things to bark at and nobody to teach it about real threats. In the movie, the girl had dark hair, and she was thin, and she was standing and bent forward onto the bed, and I could see her spine rising up, bony and knobbed, and her skin was pulled tight, her head away from the camera, with just her shoulder blades looking out like hollow eyes. Above me, a bat circled, clumsy and big, and I watched it until its path took it out of the arc of light. I tied my shoelaces, retied them, sat on the curb and chucked rocks, counted moths, listened for a car to come from the distance, and finally it did, the first and only car to come down the road, my parents' Dodge Royal Monaco two-door hardtop that I recognized from the engine whine when my sister drove, the 400 Lean Burn V8 held in full restraint under the hood, and the left hideaway headlight door stuttering like the engine to open up.

Charlotte had the heater on and the music loud and I wondered how she had crept the car out of the driveway, but the very fact that she was there confirmed that she had gotten away with it, and I was happy to slide in and pull the door shut and fold myself toward the warm vents in the dash.

"Thanks," I said.

There were no cars on the road, no headlights in either direction, just house lights, and they were scattered few and far between, set back in the distance, as sparse and dim as city stars absorbed by the night. Charlotte signaled as she left the parking lot, though there wasn't much reason to, and then we were swallowed by the fields on both sides of the road, the staggered fence posts, and even though I had been walking in the dark, I did not realize the immensity of it until it became a throat hold around us and even the broken yellow line was lost beyond the one good headlight.

After the accident, I would wonder if I saw it coming, the shift in shadows, the sudden definition of a shape, a thickening in the air like a premonition, because when something goes terribly wrong there is always a before and always an after, but the moment itself is vague and hard to gather, and time jumps like a skip in a record and so I tried to remember the before, tried to trace what happened during, but in the end, it all came down to after and we were spun hood up into a dry drainage ditch, the broken headlight suddenly finding its too little too late and pointing straight and strong at nothing more than wide open sky, the windshield shattered and fracturing the night into a thousand webbed pieces, and Charlotte bleeding from her nose and me with my mouth open to say something but instead everything just hung quiet and still.

"What did we hit?" Charlotte asked, and she rubbed the back of her hand under her nose and the blood smeared across it, and in the weak light, the blood was more black than red, just like in the movie, and I thought about what Lenny Richter had said, *nothing but corn syrup and food coloring*, and that maybe he could have been wrong.

"We didn't hit anything," I said. "Did we?"

"I saw it," she said. "I just couldn't stop."

The engine was still on, the radio picking up the end of Kiss doing "Christine Sixteen," and I turned around in my seat and looked out the back window at the rise of ditch behind us, tall grass and weeds pressed against the bumper, and I realized that the car was still in drive and Charlotte's foot was on the brake, because the slope of ground was lit bright and red.

"Turn off the car," I said.

It took her a moment to cut the engine and then there was a different quiet with only the headlights telling us nothing except that we were off the road and looking at the stars. I opened my door and I could smell the grass torn up where the back end had swung around when we spun, and there was the sharp burn of fresh rubber on asphalt hanging in the air, but I could not remember Charlotte hitting the brakes at all, and the wind had died down, or we were far enough in the ditch to be out of the gust, and I could hear crickets, a million of them in all directions around us, and the sound of something on the road just over the soft shoulder above where I stood, something ticking out of sync with the noise of the engine cooling, something struggling to get its legs under it, something trying hard to get up and walk.

I heard Charlotte's door open and the angle of the ditch forced her to put her weight into it so she could swing it wide enough to get free, and then she was walking up the short incline toward the road, and I stood there watching her, listening to the crickets, and trying to make sense out of the sound.

"Son of a bitch," she said. And there was a sadness in her voice that made me want to get back into the car and shut my door and slide onto the floor, let Charlotte deal with it and wait it out, because Charlotte was older and had always been the one to take the brunt, but I wouldn't do that this time. I couldn't do that anymore.

My eyes had adjusted to the dark, which had settled and thinned on the road, and even the smallest detail was defined and clear—the broken asphalt where shoulder met road, the yellow centerline, the metal fence posts set back on both sides, leaning and loose with rusted wires marking acres. Behind me, the wide, shallow ditch ran along the roadside, full of nothing more than dense grass gone to seed, trash, and my parents' Dodge Royal Monaco, nose up and cooling quietly with both lights shining into the air. The bugs had already come, gnats and moths in greedy clusters, so that the beams held their movement like dust. The deer was lying in the center of the road, one back leg still kicking out for grip, and Charlotte was standing over it, hands squeezed tightly in front of her, watching the struggle, and from where I stood I saw its head rise up from the pavement, watched the panicked white of its eye roll around and see nothing, and then the deer dropped its head and the back leg tucked in, and all of it went still.

Charlotte crouched down and reached out and touched the deer, and part of me wanted to stop her, tell her not to, yank her back to her feet and down to the car, but I knew that if I had been closer, I would have done the same thing, reached out and touched it, too, and I watched her run her hand over it, ribs to thigh, and I watched the way her hand lifted over the slope of its side, the stomach distended and pulled tightly back from the ribs.

"I can feel it," Charlotte said.

"Feel what?" I asked. Everything around us had gone quiet; even the crickets had slunk back into the thicker grass and the night was still and the air felt warmer than it had before, the breeze now barely strong enough to bend and ripple the fields. I looked at the sky above us and there were a million stars, and all of them seemed as if they were arranged in patterns that I was supposed to understand, but I couldn't recognize anything except that they were brighter and closer than I had ever remembered them to be.

"There's a baby," she said. "I can feel the baby inside." I walked up next to her, careful to keep my footsteps quiet, and then I realized that the deer was maybe dead and there was nothing left to startle. I squatted down next to Charlotte and reached out my hand. I wanted to touch it, let myself feel the hair, stiff and coarse, and I knew I would be surprised by how warm the deer would feel, her skin radiating heat, and I would rest my hand against her rough side and hold it there, waiting for something to happen. But I could not touch the deer. I just stood there with my hand holding air.

"Is she dead?" I asked. I stood up and pushed at the deer with my foot, hooked the toe of my tennis shoe under her ribs and tipped her side up and off the asphalt. Charlotte grabbed my leg and pushed me backward, hard, so that I lost my balance and fell onto the warm road.

"What's wrong with you?" she said.

"I was seeing if she was dead."

"She's dead," Charlotte whispered. From where I sat, I could see around Charlotte to the deer's head resting on the ground, one eye open and fixed and staring up at nothing and her jaw slack, widened just enough that her tongue lolled out and over the darkness of her lips. There was something on the road underneath her, spreading around her shoulders and neck.

"The baby's still alive," Charlotte said, and she started rubbing the deer's side in small, tight circles. "I think we can save it."

The asphalt was comforting and warm, and I was surprised at the way that it held the heat from the day despite the wind and the dark. I could feel small rocks biting into the palms of my hands and I reached forward and rubbed them clean on my jeans and I looked over the deer and down the road, looked in the direction that we had been going before we found ourselves spun into the ditch, and I looked for a pair of lights that would signal the approach of a car, the intervention of someone else to help us pull the Dodge out, move the deer, and get us back on track toward town, someone to interrupt the things that my sister was saying and gently tell her that what she wanted was an impossibility that should not even be thought about, let alone said out loud. But there was nothing around us in any direction, not even the promise of lights, no cars, no more barking dog in the distance, no houses with porches cast in a soft yellow glow, no gravel driveways, no mailboxes marking homes.

"We have to go, Charlotte," I said. "We have to tell Dad."

At the mention of our father, Charlotte stood up and walked back to the edge of the road and down the incline to the driver's side of the car, and I thought for a minute that she might just get in, start it up, and leave me stretched out on the ground, but she pulled the keys from the ignition and kept walking and I could hear them rattling, knocking back and forth on the ring, and then the trunk lid popped up and there was light from the small bulb inside and I could hear her moving things around.

"Dad's tools are in here," she called to me, and I stood up and went down to watch her.

In the light from the trunk I could see the blood drying on Charlotte's face, a cracked thin smear across her upper lip and over one cheek, but there was no fresh blood and she looked all right to me. Our dad was pretty organized and not one to carry anything that he didn't need, but the contents of the trunk had been tossed around and nothing appeared useful and there seemed to be too much and too many of everything, screwdrivers and wrenches, spilled nails, bolts, and washers, drill bits and sockets, some flannel shirts, a water jug, and a half-empty bottle of Jim Beam.

"Perfect," I said, and I pulled the bottle out, unscrewed the lid, and took a long drink and it felt good, and I realized I was thirsty and my mouth was dry and I swallowed all I could before my throat closed up against it.

Charlotte was picking up tools, holding them up for inspection under the trunk-lid light, and setting them back down again. "What about this?" she asked. It was a twelve-inch flat-head screwdriver, and I thought about her bent over the deer, cutting it open with a screwdriver, and how much effort it would take to punch through and saw into the skin, and then I remembered the movie at Billy's, and how they had started with box cutters, the two men who tied the girl to the bed, and how she had been facedown and struggling, but not really, and maybe it wasn't real, or maybe she didn't actually know what was going to happen to her, didn't possibly think it was going to get as bad as it eventually did when they started with the box cutters and they were not kidding around.

"I have a knife, Charlotte," I said. It was a little three-inch Smith & Wesson single combo-edge blade, smooth and serrated, a gift from our dad on my thirteenth birthday, and my mother had been against it, but in the end she had given up and made me promise not to hurt myself or use it on anything that I wasn't supposed to, and mostly since then I had used it to carve my name into picnic tables at the park and once to gut a fish that Lenny Richter and I accidentally caught on an empty gold hook out at his grandpa's pond.

"Give it to me," she said. She reached out her hand and I dug it out and handed it over to her, the black handle scratched and worn down over the past couple of years, and she took the knife and shoved it into the back pocket of her jeans and held her hand out toward me again, waiting, and then I gave her the bottle and she smiled for the first time since she had pulled into the parking lot to pick me up. In the dim light she was pretty, and the shadows made her cheekbones dark and defined, and her lips were full and red, and with her straight blond hair tucked behind her ears, and her face holding colors in a way that I had not seen before, I realized that Charlotte had changed and I knew why our father worried.

"Are you going to help me?" she asked. She took a drink from the bottle and I noticed that its level was dropping fast and I wished there was more.

"This is crazy, Charlotte," I said. "You do know that? You really think you can cut a dead deer open and save its baby?"

Charlotte picked up a flannel shirt from the trunk and used it to wipe her nose off. "I'm going to be in advanced biology next year, Shane," she said. "I've seen movies. I've read books. People do this all the time. Emergency C-sections. It's not that hard."

Above us, on the road, I thought I could hear a car coming in the distance, the drone and shift of an engine rounding a bend. I walked back up to the top of the ditch and looked in both directions, but the road was open and clear and dark for as far as I could see.

"There's no cars out here," Charlotte said. "I learned to drive on this road at night. I was out here for hours and never saw anybody else. It's weird," she said.

"I didn't know Dad took you out here." I tried to think of our dad doing anything after the sun went down, anything that didn't involve the TV and his chair, or the tool bench in the garage, and a drink half full of something named after somebody else.

"I wasn't with Dad," she said.

I walked back toward the deer and looked down at her. From that angle it was harder to see how pregnant she was, if her sides were actually wide enough for her to be carrying something more than herself.

"Come here and help me," Charlotte said, and I went back to the trunk of the car, where she loaded me down with the flannel shirts and a dirty blue tarp and she carried the bottle and a flashlight and we went back to the deer and she lined everything up like a doctor would.

"What are you going to do, Charlotte?"

She spread the tarp out onto the road and tucked it under the side of the deer. I didn't like the sound it made when she moved it on the asphalt, a stiff and artificial scraping noise that made the hair on the back of my neck stand up.

"We're going to deliver the baby," she said. "We have a chance to save it. We killed its mother but maybe we can still give it a chance to live." She took my knife out of her back pocket, opened the blade, held it up toward what little light hung in the air from the headlights that neither of us had thought to turn off, poured some Jim Beam on it, and wiped it clean on one of our dad's flannel shirts.

"I don't think you have to sterilize it," I said.

Charlotte looked up at me. "It's not for the mother," she said. "It's for the baby. Just in case I go too deep."

"Charlotte, what are we going to do with it?" I felt warm inside, maybe a little bit drunk, and the air felt good against my skin and I could hear plants rustling, settling back and forth together in their even rows in the fields, and when the wind died, nothing moved around us, nothing shifted, nothing bent or made noise, and I could feel the stillness like something I could touch.

She laid the knife down near her on the tarp and started ripping the shirts, first one and then another, into long neat strips like rags, and the last one she spread open and wide beside her. The crickets had scattered and were suddenly loud and distant and the only sound that was clear and close was the noise of Charlotte moving around on the tarp.

"Dad can build a pen in the garage," she said. "I can raise it and feed it from a bottle. I can take care of it just like its mother."

A bird suddenly called from somewhere across the road, somewhere deep in a field, and it sounded big and close but I could not see it.

"Nothing works out like that," I said. "You do know that, Charlotte. This isn't Bambi. You can't just cut a baby deer out of its mother and take it home and call it your own." Our dad had never even allowed us to have a dog because he hated pets. He said he hated the noise and the smell and the responsibility to look after something else in the house, and even when we begged and promised that we would do all of the work, he said that it was impossible, that he had been young once, too, and he knew that kids failed, and it would become his dog and he didn't want one.

The headlights behind us had become so much of a presence that I had almost forgotten about them and then the left one sputtered and the hideaway window folded it in with a soft pneumatic sound, a hush like an automatic door closing, and we were cut down to one weak beam staring up at nothing and the darkness filled in. I could hear Charlotte breathing through her nose and the sound was heavy and thick.

She tucked her hair behind her ears, sat back on her heels, and looked up at me standing over her. "You know Dad hates me," she said.

I thought about the way he yelled, the way he put his hand on her arm when she walked in the door sometimes, the way he yanked her around in the kitchen *where have you been?*

"That's just Dad," I said. "You know how he gets. He worries." I felt like our mom, softening my father, making excuses like she always did—*he was just tired, you were just too loud, you have to try harder, you know how much your father works.*

"It's not worry, Shane," she said. "He hates me. He wishes I would just move away and never come back so he could say that he just has a son."

When I saw the girl in the film for the first time, I thought that the men would be younger, that they would be in high school, that for some reason they would be boys, and I hadn't thought about them being anything else, but they had been men our father's age, or maybe even older, and they had tied the girl to the bed and her spine had stood out in a rail of bones and I had seen the shadows of the men first, saw their shapes moving across her white skin like clouds, and she hadn't seemed scared at all, and Lenny Richter had whispered to me *this is gonna be the good part.*

"He loves you," I said. "He's just weird about showing it."

"You know he caught me one time," she said. "He caught me making out in front of the house. It was late and we were parked on the street and I thought everybody was asleep—the house was dark—and I didn't want to come in. You don't understand what I'm talking about, I know, but someday you will, I can't really explain it and it doesn't make any sense, but I just couldn't stop even though I knew I needed to go in. I just didn't."

I tried to imagine who Charlotte had been with and I couldn't. I had never seen her sit with anybody other than girls at school, had never heard her talk to a boy on the phone, had never heard her mention a name, or act strange, or get nervous. I had never known Charlotte to pay attention to anybody except for her best friend, Macy, and with as much time as I knew that they spent together, there didn't seem to be much of a chance for Charlotte to be making out or driving these roads at night with somebody else.

"It wasn't Pete Holbrook, was it?" I asked. He was the only one that I could think of Charlotte liking and that was only based on the fact that I knew that he had liked her the year before, had followed her around at lunch all of the time—I had seen him in the cafeteria, trying to get next to her in line, sit by her and Macy at a table—and I knew he had asked her to a dance once but she had said no.

Charlotte laughed. "Pete? God no," she said. "Not even close." She moved onto her knees and I could hear the tarp shift underneath her and I could hear her take a deep breath and hold it and then exhale. "Hold the flashlight for me, okay?" She clicked it on and handed it up to me and the unexpected heaviness spun the light backward toward me, blinding me for a second.

I pointed the beam down at the side of the deer and I thought I was still seeing spots from the light, but then

I realized they were ticks, standing out like blood-filled moles, and I wanted to look away, but Charlotte was pushing on the deer's stomach with her hand, running her fingertips over the brown skin, pulling the back leg so that she could see the entirety of the white belly underneath. I was shaking badly and I tried to hold the light steady, but it kept jumping around and landing everywhere except where Charlotte was pointing the knife.

"On the count of three?" she asked, and I nodded but said nothing, and she looked up at me, waiting for an answer.

"Okay," I said, and we both took a breath and started counting in unison, "one, two, three," and then Charlotte stuck the knife in, center of the stomach, buried to the handle, and there was blood, a darkening around where the blade went in, and I could hear Charlotte inhale hard through her nose, and she pulled the knife out and there was more blood and it flowed freely, thick and red and staining what had been clean, white, and soft-looking underneath.

I shifted the flashlight and caught the knife in the beam, and the blade was red and there were white and brown hairs stuck to it and I realized that Charlotte's hand was shaking worse than mine and together we couldn't hold anything in focus for more than a second. She wiped the knife clean on a piece of flannel shirt and sat back from the deer, pulled her knees to her chest and hugged her arms around them.

"What time do you think it is?" she asked.

I looked down at my watch and could see the two tiny glowing hands beneath the glass. "It's after two," I said.

"Everybody was asleep when I left," she said. "Mom took her pill at seven. Dad had his drinks." I imagined how it would be when we pulled into the driveway, nobody knowing that Charlotte had left, our parents' windshield smashed, the tires caked with dirt, bumpers full of weeds, and us carrying a newborn deer wrapped in one of Dad's old shirts from the trunk. Part of me hoped that everything would happen like something on TV and our mom would make breakfast even though the sun had not begun to rise and we would be inspected for injury, turned this way and that under the kitchen light, and our dad would take the fawn and come up with a way to feed it, make it a bed in a box, and he would look at the car and shake his head and be happy that both of us were fine, and we would tell the story of how Charlotte had delivered the baby on the road from the deer we had hit and our dad would be so impressed that he would put his arm around her shoulders and say, "That's my girl!" and he would repeat the story to his friends, too proud to keep from telling it over and over again for the rest of the week. But really I knew that it would be nothing like that; it would be something that my mind did not want to imagine, and there were no pictures stored inside my head to give any kind of meaning to how it really would be, and I think that Charlotte knew it, too, but maybe she believed in her own TV version a lot more than I did, or she had more hope, or more need, and maybe those were the things that made her put the knife into the deer again while I stood there, and make another narrow gash next to the first.

"Charlotte, you can't just keep stabbing at it," I said. "You have to keep the knife in and cut."

"I know what I'm doing, Shane."

When the men in the film had the box cutters in their hands, I didn't think that they would really do it, that they would put them against the girl and carve into her back, so that narrow lines of darkness rose to the surface of her skin in shapes almost like words, and Lenny Richter had been standing beside me, and he had put his hand over his mouth, and I thought for a second that he was trying to stop himself from getting sick, and then I realized that he was laughing. He had his hand over his mouth and he was bent forward and he was laughing.

Charlotte had the knife in a tight grip and I could tell that she wanted to drag it sideways, tear through the thin wall of skin that divided the second cut from the first, turn the one-inch slit to two inches, but just when I thought she might do it, go ahead and run the knife the distance of the belly and make a line big enough for her to open the stomach and reach in, find the baby inside, and pull it out onto the tarp, she took her hand off the handle and sat back on her heels, left the knife stuck in the skin. She wiped her hands on the thighs of her jeans and stood up. She turned away from me and started walking back toward the car.

"I need to think for a minute," she said.

I stood there with the flashlight still pointed down at the deer, the beam suddenly steady, the knife just a small interruption in the slight curve of belly that was divided now by a thick line of color. The deer didn't look as swollen as I had thought she was in the dark. She was just a deer, caught in the open between one field and the next, dead on the road. I clicked the switch and cut the light and turned around and followed Charlotte over the embankment.

Charlotte was sitting in the Dodge, drinking, and I wished she had the keys back in the ignition so that we could listen to the radio, but they were still hanging from the lock in the trunk. She passed me the bottle and I noticed that with the door shut the car was too quiet and too still, and I suddenly felt cut off from what I had become adjusted to.

"Would you miss me if I left town?" Charlotte asked me. She pushed the knob on the headlights and the single swath that had cut into the darkness went out and left the gathered bugs to scatter in confusion, and there were only prismed stars above us through the shattered windshield and the slope of the ditch rising around us outside the windows.

"I would miss you," I said. "But I don't think you'd ever do it."

"I might," she said. "I might surprise you." She had a piece of flannel shirt in her hands and she was rubbing at her palm, trying to get it clean.

"Who did Dad catch you making out with in the car, Charlotte?"

I took another small drink and turned my head toward her so that I could see her face. She was staring straight ahead, staring out the broken windshield and into the darkness, and I wondered what she was looking at, since there wasn't anything to see.

"It doesn't matter anymore," she said. "Do you think we can get out of this ditch on our own? I don't want to wait until the sun comes up for someone to drive by."

I looked over my shoulder at the angle of the car in the ditch, the way the back end hadn't slid so far that it was wedged into the slope, and if Charlotte cranked the wheel hard enough and put it in reverse, she could ease us down into the bottom of the gully and we would have a chance at punching our way up and over the incline if she was willing to wind the engine tight and hit the gas hard.

"You could do it," I said.

She took the bottle from me and emptied it in one long swallow. "Help me gather everything, okay?"

We collected the things from around the deer, rolled up the tarp, folded it all together with the torn shirts, put them back in the trunk, and went back to the road. We both stood looking at the deer, and Charlotte crouched down and put her hand on the doe's side and petted her.

"She's cold," Charlotte said.

The air around us was getting thinner and I didn't have to look at my watch to know that somewhere over the horizon line the sun was on its approach and the darkness would begin to soften and give way to light before too long. There were more birds making noise, but they were still too far out to see, and the crickets had almost given up, and I realized that I was tired and ready to be home.

"I'm sorry," Charlotte said. For a second I thought she was talking to me, but then I realized that she had said it to the deer, and her voice was quiet and I knew that she was crying even though I could not see her face. "I tried," she said. She kept running her hand over and over the side of the deer, and then she reached forward and slowly pulled out my knife and she handed it to me, bloody, and thick with matted hair, the handle sticky, the blade too stiff to fold.

I rubbed the knife against the hem of my shirt and was finally able to get it to close, and after I shoved it back into my pocket, Charlotte pointed me toward the front of the deer and she stayed at the back and we each grabbed a pair of legs and pulled and dragged her across the road and over the side and pushed her down toward the bottom of the other drainage ditch, away from the car, so that maybe when she disappeared from sight, she would be out of mind, too. She had settled into the asphalt so that it was hard to free her, and it took us ten minutes to get her across the opposite lane and far enough off the edge to roll. Her legs did not bend and she didn't make it very far down the ditch, but she was out of the way and off the road and nobody else was in danger of hitting her. We both stood on the blacktop shoulder, sweating and breathing heavy, looking at her dark body lying in the grass like nothing more than shadow.

"Why did you give up?" I asked Charlotte. Deep down, I had wanted to believe that maybe we could save the baby, wrap it up, take it home, and make things good like Charlotte said we would, that it was possible, a thin sliver of maybe.

Charlotte bowed her head and said nothing for a second and then she wiped both of her eyes and turned back toward the car. "It wouldn't have lived," she said. "It wouldn't have been natural to force it like that. It wasn't meant to be born yet." Behind her, in the thin light, I could see the narrow stain in the road.

She did just what I told her to do—eased the Dodge into reverse and turned the wheel so that the entire car slipped back into the very bottom of the ditch and we were only at a slight angle with the driver's side high-centered on the incline. I told her to put the car into drive and floor it, get enough forward momentum to push the car up the side and out of the ditch, and to keep a tight grip on the wheel and not let the car slide out from under her in the grass and the dirt, and she did those things, too, and we hit the top of the ditch so hard that we caught air and crossed to the other side of the road and Charlotte had to guide us into our lane without overcorrecting, and she did that, and there was a little bit of fishtailing and the sound of tires breaking loose, and then we were on our side of the road, with one good headlight pointing out the direction.

In the movie the girl had been almost naked, Lenny had said that she would be, but it had taken a while. They had tied her across the bed and she had been shirtless without a bra, her back nothing but blank skin and bone, and she had been wearing panties, white and thin, and when she twisted around on the bed, rolling up off her hips, trying to loosen her hands from where they were knotted above her head, I saw that the panties were the kind like my sister had for a while, the ones my mother used to hang out back on the line to dry, the kind with the days of the week on them, and the girl had been wearing a pair that said *Tuesday*.

I rolled down my window so that the air would keep me awake and I could lean out if I needed to help guide Charlotte down the road. Everything smelled wet and sharp and alive and I was grateful to watch it all fall behind us as we passed, and I knew that we were finally leaving the country, the fields, and the fence lines. Charlotte had her hands gripped tightly around the steering wheel, and she was careful and driving slowly, bent forward in her seat, and I knew that it would take us a long time to get home because it would be hard for her to see.

YOU ONLY GET LETTERS FROM JAIL

The Eberhardts' daughter disappeared the same week they started going to the movies every night to watch the 7:15 showing of *The Exorcist*, and it didn't take long for word to get around that instead of sitting by the phone and waiting for her to call, they were sitting in the dark, watching that possessed girl slam some priests around her room. Suzy Eberhardt disappearing was sort of Page 3 news for everybody—she was the kind of girl who didn't put much stock in curfews and rules, and most of our parents defined "bad crowd" based on who Suzy Eberhardt was with. Everybody knew that she had probably taken off with some guy and would roll home when the money ran out and act like it was no big deal. I hadn't thought much about it until Ricky Riley asked my brother to give him a ride out past the dam, him and this girl I knew from school, and I found myself down a dirt road, drinking warm Lucky Lager on a Saturday.

Ricky Riley had been to Vietnam and was fucked in the head, or at least that's what my brother said, but my brother worked the graveyard janitor shift with him at Mercy and they hung out and were friends. Some people said Ricky hadn't gone to Vietnam, he had just disappeared and run off up north when the draft came around, and some people said he had been drafted but couldn't pass the competency test, and some said his draft number had never come up in the lottery anyways. All I knew was that it was ninety degrees outside and Ricky had on a jungle jacket that had somebody else's name on it, and sometimes he walked with a limp, and he had enough money to buy beer but not fix his van, and he was older than my brother and with a girl I went to school with who told us in the car that she was with Ricky because she didn't have anything better to do.

"Me and Suzy Eberhardt go way back," Ricky said. We had the doors opened on my brother's Duster and he had the hood up so he could show off his 360 and the rebuilt six-pack carb setup to Ricky, who my brother felt should have been sorry for driving a Ford. Debbie from school was sitting in the front seat, playing with the radio, trying to tune in something besides static or country, and I was on my third beer and thinking about wandering down to the lake. I thought maybe I could smell its shoreline like wet thick green, heavy and bug-filled, but guaranteed to be cooler than sitting on the vinyl seats or under the scrub oaks, which were too thin to give more than a weak circle of shade. The trunk was full of gas cans and beer and I was bored and a little drunk and tired of waiting for the sun to set so I could see what Ricky had in mind.

"Do you know where she's at?" my brother asked Ricky. I could tell that he was only half listening because he was focused on the verbal tour of his Plymouth and I had heard his speech enough to know it by heart—he was waiting to get to the good parts: TorqueFlite 727 three-speed reverse valve body automatic, 8¾ posi axles with Mickey Thompsons front and rear.

Ricky took a long swallow from his bottle and ran the back of his hand over his mouth. He had let his dark hair grow long and when he leaned forward, he had a habit of tucking the front behind his ear so that he could see and it had become sort of a rhythmic habit—the farther he leaned, the more he tucked, like a one, two count.

"She's dead in her house," he said.

My brother stepped back from the open hood and I could hear his tennis shoes bend and break the bunchgrass beneath them. Everything around us was a faded yellow, miles of it drifting in soft rises broken only by the occasional grouping of trees, piled rocks, and the purple needlegrass that would give way to sheep sorrel down where the ground got soft by the water. Everything smelled like star thistle and baked red dirt.

"You're full of shit," my brother said.

To the west the yellow hillside fell away in a gentle decline and in the distance we could see the lake, a flat blue expanse with the sunlight rippling and breaking in hard angles off the surface. We were too far away to see if there were people, and on the wrong side of the shoreline to see boats. All of the action was somewhere out of sight. I couldn't remember the last time I had been out to the lake, even though it wasn't more than a forty-five-minute drive from town. There was no reason to go. We didn't have a boat, I didn't know anybody who did, and there were closer places to swim and fish.

"You ever met her parents?" Ricky asked.

My brother had stepped away from the front of the car and was headed to the back, where a case of beer was split open in the shade under the overhang of the trunk. Ricky had pointed the route out, directing my brother through rights and lefts and then finally down a dirt road that thinned out and became nothing more than tire tracks cutting a single-lane path until it emptied out on a crushed circle of grass by rock piles that were growing weeds in the sun. The tire tracks continued in front of the parked car for another twenty feet or so and then disappeared. There were beer bottles and faded cans and wrappers, evidence that we weren't the first ones to hang out there and probably wouldn't be the last, and I wondered if maybe people parked there to fish, but it seemed like an awful long ways to hike down to get to the water.

"I've seen the Eberhardts in town," Kenny said. "I know who they are."

"Total religious freaks," Ricky said. He leaned against the front of the car and started rubbing at his right thigh, the one he favored on the times when it seemed convenient to limp.

"My girlfriend says they're going to the movies every night now, ever since about the time Suzy disappeared. Summer Horror Fest."

"They killed her," Ricky said. "Went crazy with their religion bullshit and took it upon themselves to get the devil out of Suzy."

The radio jumped to life through the four speakers and the sudden noise made me slop beer onto the front of my shorts. Debbie had found some distant rock station to flood the hillsides with, the Eagles doing "Lyin' Eyes," and she swung her legs out of the passenger seat of the car and walked to the back to pull a beer out of the case.

"Do you make this shit up all by yourself, or does somebody help you?" she asked Ricky.

"Why don't you go sit back in the car," Ricky said. "I like you better when you don't talk."

A breeze climbed up over the hillside and pulled itself across our circle and in it I thought I could smell something burning, like smoldering grass or barbecues across the lake, but I knew we were too far away to smell anything but weeds and the faint hope of water.

"Go fuck yourself," Debbie said.

Kenny laughed and Ricky looked up from the open engine compartment and tucked his hair. "Baby, I'm trying to avoid that. That's why I have you."

Debbie shot him the finger and twisted the cap from her beer. She flipped it over and looked at what was underneath. "I hate these puzzles," she said. She threw the cap into the grass and it settled against a Laura Scudder's potato chip bag that was bright yellow and tangled in the weeds.

"It's called a rebus," Ricky said. Everybody looked at him.

"What is called a rebus?" I asked.

"The puzzle. It's got a name. It's like code. We used it in the war, out on field patrols."

Debbie rolled her eyes and bit at the back of her thumb. "Stop with the war bullshit already," she said. "Tell a different story." She shielded her eyes with her hand and looked off to the west. "You want to go swim?" she asked me.

I looked at the lake in the distance and thought I could see a white line moving across it, the wake from a boat cutting across the surface. I imagined how cool the water was, how deep it might be. I was terrible at gauging distance, but the lake didn't look that far away. It was a hard blue stain on the other side of thick trees, high grass, a steep walk down. It could take us ten minutes to get there. It could take us two hours. There would be a lot to step over and through in the process—a lot of things that would like to poke in and scratch.

"Are you sure you want to go?" I asked.

Debbie ran her tongue across her lips. "I'm going," she said. "Right now."

"Don't be gone a long time," Kenny said. "Ricky wants to do this just before sunset."

I looked at the sky and the sun was still far from making the slide toward the horizon line. "We'll be back," I said.

We each grabbed an extra beer and started walking toward the oak trees that marked the slope down to the shoreline. I could hear our shoes trampling the grass and it was dry and brittle and sharp and pieces of it bit into the bare skin on my legs and I had to keep resisting the urge to reach down and scratch. We walked in silence; the only sound was the car radio spilling out the open doors behind us. The music was good and part of me wanted to stay and listen, sitting in the driver's seat with my legs propped up on the open gap between the frame and the door, and just wait for the sun to start setting. I thought that maybe if I stayed by the car, I could keep bugging Kenny enough that he would make Ricky get down to it sooner rather than later and I could find out what he was up to and then we could make the drive back and I could get something to eat, since nobody had thought about the fact that we had all kinds of beer and no food at all.

"You know Ricky is crazy, right?" Debbie said. I had been thinking about a cheeseburger, the kind with shredded lettuce and Thousand Island dressing, and a vanilla milk shake and fries with lots of salt, crispy fries that are too hot to bite into but you do it anyways because you can't wait or hold back.

"What?" I asked.

"He's crazy. He shouldn't even talk about Suzy Eberhardt."

I took a long swallow from my open bottle and slowed down my pace so that I could step over some rocks that were piled in the grass. They had yellow flowers growing through the spaces between them, yellow flowers in the yellow grass, and the rocks themselves were a faded yellow, a flat sea, the yellow of sick skin.

"He seems okay," I said. I couldn't think of anything more to say. When I got right down to it, I really didn't care if he was crazy or if he wasn't—he wasn't my friend, he was my brother's—and maybe he knew something about what happened to Suzy Eberhardt, even though that didn't bother me much either, since she was a girl I had heard of but hadn't known and her disappearing didn't affect me.

The breeze came up again and it was warm and uneven and very slight, but it was enough to dry the sweat. I wished that it would rain, that clouds would just muscle up and unleash, but the sky was as empty, hard blue, and unbroken as the lake in the distance and it was August and rain was nothing more than a dull ache like thoughts of the impending threat of school.

"All that talk about the war? He never went." Debbie finished her beer and tossed the bottle toward a dry skinny pile of broken tree branches. She had been in my English class last year, but she had been gone more than she had been present, and her hair had been different then, darker, and now it was an easy blond and she had let her bangs grow long and straight.

"What about the jacket and the limp and all that stuff? He seems to know what he's talking about," I said.

"He's crazy, not stupid. That's how crazy people are, right? They sound like they're sane but they're really so crazy that when you stop and think about it, nothing that they say really makes any sense."

The ground had begun a gentle descent and I was aware that we were moving downhill and the trees had thickened. I could no longer see the lake and had no idea how much farther it would be until we hit the rock-and-marsh shoreline.

"And the limp, that's a good one. He fell out of a tree. It was the middle of the night and he was across the street from my house, and I saw it happen, I was upstairs in my bedroom, standing at the window . . . Part of it was probably my fault," she said.

"He told my brother that he hurt his leg in the war. A guy in front of him stepped on a booby trap or something and Ricky ended up getting hit."

Debbie laughed and opened the other beer she had brought with her. I was still working on the one I had been drinking in the car and it had gone warm and flat and it was all I could do to keep swallowing it. Even the un-opened one in my hand didn't feel that much cooler and I was sorry that I had carried it.

"He was never in the war. He was in jail."

"Why was he in jail?" I asked.

I could see her smile. "He liked to watch girls." She looked at me from the corner of her eye, but she didn't slow her walking.

"Watch?" Debbie's left arm was close to me and I could feel her skin sharing the same space as mine. I could hear her shoes pushing through the grass and without turning my head I could see each stride, knew the way that her thighs didn't touch at the top of her legs when she moved. She had a habit of tugging on the hem of her shorts after every third or fourth step and she didn't change her pace when she did it, like a small nervous tic that she wasn't even conscious she was making.

"Ricky liked to sneak around our house at night, hide in the bushes. That sort of thing."

Debbie started walking faster and I fell in behind her. We had to turn sideways to walk through the trees and the piles of brush, and the dry branches were naked and sharp and pulled at our clothes. I could see bursts of manzanita, its red branches twisted and topped with thin rigid leaves. I hadn't given much thought to poison oak and I figured I probably should, since this was the perfect kind of place for it, but I wasn't sure if I would recognize it even if I waded through a field. I knew it had something to do with the leaves—leaves of three, let it be—or some rhyme like that, but just about anything can look like it has three leaves and I wasn't sure if it was the absence or the presence of the three that made the difference.

"And they arrested him for that?"

Debbie paused for a second, and I could feel her searching for the next thing to say. "He liked to watch my sister, get her attention, and then—you know. Touch himself."

I tried to picture Ricky Riley outside Debbie's house, ducking down in the bushes in the dark, staring into an open window, watching her sister read or watch TV or eat dinner at the kitchen table, and I tried to imagine what would make him take the next step, what would make him want her that badly.

"He was in love with her," Debbie said. It was as if she had been reading my thoughts and it made me feel weird, as if she had looked inside of me. "That's what he said in all the letters he wrote to her. He wrote to her from jail. According to the police, he was in love with quite a few girls. My sister. Suzy Eberhardt, maybe. I wouldn't doubt it."

I finished a last swallow of flat hot beer and hung my bottle on a dry branch jutting out from a skinny tree. The branch bent but held the weight.

"So your parents called the cops on him?" I said.

"One time we came home and the front door was unlocked even though we never left the house that way, and my sister's dresser drawers were open and some of her clothes were pulled out. Underwear and stuff on the floor. My dad had had enough."

"I'm surprised your dad didn't just shoot him or something." I had seen a lot of movies and I knew how fathers were when it came to their daughters. I had no idea as to how fathers were when it came to their sons. I thought about my own father and how he was always in the garage, working on something—the lawn mower, a carburetor, a set of shelves for the living room—listening to baseball games, drinking beer from the extra refrigerator, never doing much of anything with us except to remind us to mow or take out the garbage or clean up.

"I think my dad thought about it, but what would be the point? My dad thought Ricky would suffer more consequences in jail. Learn his lesson," she said. "I guess he was wrong."

The music had faded behind us and I realized that there were no sounds except for our feet moving through the grass and stepping across the broken branches that had fallen everywhere. The trees formed a thin canopy above us and the sunlight was scattered and the heat had lifted from the air.

"He didn't do much time, and when he got out, he just started coming back around. But he's more careful this time. My parents don't even know yet."

I noticed that my shoelaces were full of foxtails and they were the kind that are hard to remove, the kind that break off and dig in when you pull at them. "I guess I don't get why you're hanging out with Ricky then," I said. We kept walking forward, breaking down the grass.

"God," Debbie said. "Do you smell that?"

I inhaled and it hit me, the unmistakable smell of something rotten and dead. "Probably an animal," I said.

We stopped and looked in opposite directions, inhaling, testing the air. I shielded my eyes to try and see if there was something lying in the grass.

"There are no animals out here," Debbie said. "Haven't you noticed that? I mean, think about it. What have you really seen?"

I thought about it for a second and realized she was right—for some reason I had been convinced that I'd seen rabbits running, squirrels hanging on trunks, birds in the branches. But all of it was things that I expected to see, my imagination filling in the gaps. It was like the first time that I had ever been camping and it had gotten dark and we were sitting by the campfire, Kenny and me, and our parents had gone to bed in their tent and Kenny told me we were in bear country and that bears were drawn to campfires, and I became convinced that I could hear one walking around the campsite, snapping branches, trampling pine needles, and I had felt all the hair on my body stand up, and I had been paralyzed, too afraid to move, and in the middle of the night when I woke up with the strong urge to pee, I was so afraid to leave the tent that I lay in my sleeping bag and pissed myself and in the morning I had to hide my pajamas and Kenny had found out and laughed about it for weeks, called me Piss Boy and made bear sounds every time he passed by my room.

"I guess I haven't seen any animals," I said. "Maybe we have just been making too much noise."

Debbie turned around and we faced each other. "We aren't being *that* loud. There should be *something* out here."

I turned a full circle and looked at everything. The oak trees were a dirty gray with thick, cracked bark and rounded leaves grouped in tight spirals. There were scattered piles of acorns under some of the trees, the nuts themselves split and dry, but apparently untouched by any animal that might wander through. I looked above us and the sky appeared in fragmented shapes between the heavy branches, and there wasn't so much as the dash of a bird to mar the stillness. The breeze came again, slow and insistent, and the leaves around us rustled, moved together in a soft rub. The smell was thick and heavy and I wanted to walk away from it, but Debbie just stood there, staring out over the grass and the trees and the broken branches piled into brush.

"Maybe animals stay away from a place where one is dead," I said.

Debbie took a swallow from her beer and continued walking down the incline. "Maybe it's not an animal," she said. "I want to find it."

"I thought you wanted to go swimming," I said. "C'mon, it's hot."

"I'm not sweating anymore," she said. She finished her beer and tossed the bottle to the ground, where it landed with a soft hollow thump. "Are you?"

I could feel a tightness in my stomach, something more than cheap warm beer, and I thought about how we should have made it to the water by now, that we should be standing on the shoreline, pulling flat rocks out of the wet ground and seeing how far we could make them skip, counting their hops across the surface. I thought that by now I should be shirtless, with lake water around my shoulders as I swam out from the shore to try to see how far I had to go before I could turn around and see Kenny's car on the hillside. I thought that by now I should be swimming with Debbie, seeing how long we could hold our breath, and she would be stripped down to maybe only panties and a bra, maybe, and she would be swimming with me and we would forget about the things that didn't mean anything out here.

"It smells like something big," Debbie said. She had picked up a crooked stick and she was walking with it, poking it into tangles of grass, swinging it against trunks as she passed them so that I could see dust and particles of bark rise up and hang in the sunlight.

"It could be a deer," I said. "Besides, dead animal smells like dead animal. I don't think size matters."

"Really?" Debbie said.

"I'm going back to the car," I said.

I turned around and started walking up the incline, toward where the trees thinned out and went back to grass and rock. I noticed that there were three trails in the grass—mine and Debbie's and one that I hadn't noticed before. It could have been a game trail, my dad had pointed some out that one time that we had been camping and we had gone for a hike, Kenny, me, and our dad, and he had pointed things out to us, things like game trails, but nothing else that was useful. I could hear Debbie behind me, knocking her stick against trees. "I thought we were going swimming," she said.

I looked up at a gap in the overhang of branches and leaves and there was more sky than sun above us. "We don't have enough time," I said. "I guess it was farther than we thought."

I tried to walk slowly in hopes that Debbie would catch up with me, but she just hung back and swung her stick and didn't speak. The sky was changing color and the air had taken on the damp weight of humidity and now there were a few clouds, though they were flat and nonthreatening and far away in the distance. I could hear the music before I could see the car and I tried to hear the sound of voices and I knew that Kenny and Ricky would be drunk since they had had most of the beer for themselves. I had no idea as to how long we had been gone, and there was probably a way to tell time by looking at the shadows, but that was something I had never learned. I felt Debbie's hand on my arm, it was warm and rough and she caught me just above the elbow, on the bare skin below the sleeve.

"Wait," she said.

I stopped and looked at her. I knew that in a few more yards we would leave the stand of trees and be back in the grass that led to the clearing and whatever we had been talking about would be forgotten and I would not think any differently of Ricky despite what I knew.

"He wrote me letters," she said. "That's what you wanted to know, right? Why I'm out here with him?"

She was breathing hard, as if she had had to hurry a little bit to catch up with me. I wondered if she had planned it, waited for me to reach this point on the path before she stopped me, or if it was just an impulse that got to her, and she gave in to the urge to tell.

"He wrote me letters from jail," she said. "I had never gotten a letter from anyone before, you know? And then these letters started showing up—he had some friend of his mail them to me so that my parents wouldn't see the return address—and I know he's crazy, but he can write. There's something about his words. And he said that the truth of it was that he was really in love with me. He just couldn't tell me, except in his letters."

She said all of this in a rush, in a run-on set of sentences that came out like a breath held too long, and even in the weakened light I could see that her face was flushed.

"Now you know," she said.

"You don't love him back, do you?" I asked.

She let go of my arm and I realized that the whole time that she had been speaking, her fingers had been digging in and I could still feel the pressure even as I watched her hand fall away and drop to her side.

"I don't love him," she said. "But if Suzy Eberhardt ran off, I know why she might do it." Debbie shifted her eyes away from mine and she stared off over my shoulder, in the direction of the car that we could hear but not yet see. "It's something to do," she said.

When we got back to the car, Ricky and Kenny were standing by the open trunk, moving things around, pulling out gas cans and setting them on the ground. The sun was low and the sky had gone from blue to violet, with a thin band of green that bled into purple and red as the color leaked toward the foothills. From the car we could see the lake again, untouched and dark now that the sun was setting. I was sorry that we hadn't made it to the shore to swim and I wondered what it would be like beside the lake now, if there would be the sound of frogs calling, the steady low hum of mosquitoes, the splash of fish as they rose from the water to take bugs off the surface.

"If you guys had been in the war, you'd be dead now," Ricky said. "You made a fuck lot of noise as you were walking up here. I could hear you for the past twenty minutes."

Debbie took a beer from the case and opened it, drank half in one swallow, took a breath, and finished the rest of it. She tossed the empty into the weeds. "This isn't the war," she said.

"How do you know we aren't being watched?" Ricky asked.

"Just stop, okay?" Debbie said.

I looked at Kenny to see if he was listening, but he was bent into the trunk, still moving things around even though most of the contents had been pulled out and were scattered around him in the grass.

Ricky grabbed Debbie and put his arms around her and pulled her against him, hard, and buried his head in her neck so that his hair covered his face and I couldn't tell if he kissed her or not. I watched the expression on Debbie's face, but she was as shadowed and blank as the lake in the distance.

He lifted his face from her and tucked his hair back and surveyed the setting sun, the grass around us, the pile of rocks near the car. "It's getting to be time," he said. "We can't wait too much longer."

Ricky pulled a plastic bucket out of the trunk—a white five-gallon one with a twist-off lid and a wire-bail handle. "How do you know I didn't follow you down to the lake? Make sure you two didn't do anything that I wouldn't like," he said.

I thought about the three paths I'd seen, but the third one had been older and fainter than the two that Debbie and I had made. I looked at Kenny again, but he just shrugged and kicked at a faded Schlitz can in the grass.

"You remember that time we stalked those two nurses all night, Kenny?" Ricky said. He had flipped the bucket over and was sitting on it. "Remember how fucking good at it I was? I told you, I was the best guy on patrol—they used to call me Whisper—I could walk across a wide open space without a sound."

Kenny just nodded, but I couldn't tell if it was in agreement or not.

"You remember that one nurse? What was her name? That younger one. Nancy?"

"Diana," Kenny said.

"Yeah, yeah, that's right. Diana. Man, she was a cocktease." Ricky picked up a beer from the ground, twisted the cap, checked the puzzle, and started drinking.

"You scared her half to death," Kenny said. "You broke into her car that time, remember? You were in her backseat when she got off shift." He was smiling and grinding the toe of his tennis shoe into the dirt.

"She liked it, don't you get it? Man, she just thought she was mad. She liked the attention. That's what girls want. A little attention. A little love." He stood up and it took him a second to get his feet under him and I thought he was going to fall, go down on the leg he claimed had been shot up in the war, and I couldn't help but think about what Debbie had told me, how he had hurt his leg falling out of a tree, and how she had said it was partly her fault. Ricky put his arm around my shoulders and pulled himself against me so that we were both unsteady and then I planted my feet and pulled him upright and I could feel his hot breath in my face and smell the beer and hear the words he was saying before they even left his mouth.

"You have to learn how to give a girl the right kind of attention, you get it?" He swayed backward and his left foot swung out and hit the bucket and sent it sideways and rolling across the grass. "You did everything wrong."

I could see spit bubbles foaming in the corner of his mouth and I wanted to look away but I knew that there was no help to make him stop talking. That I just had to wait for him to stop. Kenny was staring down at his toe in the dirt and Debbie had wandered toward the front of the car and was sitting in the passenger seat with her legs out and that was all I could see, her tan legs sticking out from the side of the Plymouth.

"It's time to do this, Kenny," Ricky said. "Turn the headlights on." He loosened his grip on my shoulders and stepped away and he was surprisingly quick and steady and sure on his feet. He grabbed a gas can in one hand and the rim of the bucket in his other and he walked around to the front of the car and set both in the grass, then came back and picked up another gas can and took his beer from the bumper where he had left it.

Kenny reached into the car and there was sudden light and everything that had been dissolving into shadows was pulled back into place. The sun was still visible on the horizon, a thin white band between the hillsides and the violet dark above, and the few scattered clouds that I had seen before had thickened and become heavy as a wedge on the far side of the lake.

Ricky pulled Debbie from the car and she stood up and he shuffled her against him in an awkward hug and I watched to see if her muscles would tense and pull him close in return, if her hands would move, slide the distance of his back, if she would bury her head in his chest and hold on to him, but it was all over before I had enough time to read the signs.

"Okay, the only way this is gonna work is if everybody clears their heads and gets rid of fear. You can't be afraid. No matter what. No screaming and no fear. Got it?" Ricky asked.

He put his index finger under Debbie's chin and lifted her face up so her eyes could meet his. "Got it?"

She nodded and then he let go of her and she sat back down in the seat and I watched a red line form under the frayed edges of her cutoffs where her shorts cut into her thighs.

"So what's the plan?" my brother called over to Ricky.

"Just follow my lead. No screaming and no fear. Keep the bucket close, okay? All I need are three. That's what the Holy Roller told me. He'd give me a hundred bucks for three."

"What is he talking about?" I whispered to Kenny. Ricky was climbing up the rock pile with a gasoline can in his hand.

"Holy Roller homecoming tomorrow out near the Four-square church and some guy offered Ricky good money to get him the snakes. He's giving me twenty bucks for the ride."

"Snakes?" I said.

In the distance the sky lit up, a sudden flash that turned the clouds the color of ripe plums and reflected the hill-sides on the lake. "Jesus," I said.

"Heat lightning," Kenny said. "Listen."

I wanted to know how many times Ricky had been out here before—he knew the way without hesitation—I wanted to know if he had ever brought a girl with him. I thought about Suzy Eberhardt and whether or not she knew the way out to the emptiness of this dead yellow grass, too, if she had ever taken off for the lake, and if Ricky was with her, if he stayed two steps behind her and kept falling back until his footsteps didn't make sound and he watched her walk while she tugged at the hem of her shorts and crushed a path for him to follow.

I strained my ears but all I could hear was the radio turned down to a mumble, and the sound of Ricky climbing up the side of the boulder pile, shoes scraping rock, and the occasional metallic ping of the gas can banging into jutting edges. "I don't hear anything," I said.

"Exactly," he said. "No thunder. That storm is miles away."

"Man there's a lot of flowers up here," Ricky said. "It's strange how something like these would try so hard to stay alive when it seems impossible for them to live."

When Ricky reached the top of the boulder pile he unscrewed the lid on the gas can, tipped it upside down, and started pouring. "Let's hope it only takes one can," he said. "Fucking government and their gas prices." Even from the distance I could smell the gas, sweet, wet, and heavy. I could see the yellow rocks darken as he pointed the nozzle in the gaps between the boulders and tipped the can over and over again.

"What's he doing?" I asked Kenny.

"Forcing the snakes out. They've been holed up in there all day, soaking up the heat from the sun. So Ricky is dumping some gas into their nests. The gas will piss them off and out they'll crawl."

"Is he going to light it on fire?" I asked.

"No need to—check it out."

"Here they come," Ricky shouted, and then he remembered his own rule about no screaming and let go of a whisper that was little more than a hoarse yell. "Get the bucket ready."

"Go sit in the car," my brother said. He shoved me toward the driver's side and I stumbled that direction, and then I heard Debbie screaming and I saw her scrambling to pull the door shut and there were snakes on the ground, quite a few of them, sidewinding across the dead grass in shocked knots of twos and threes, their yellow-and-green-patterned bodies tangled and taut.

Ricky had jumped from the rock pile and he was on the ground now, running in circles, and there were shouts, and I watched him bend over and pull his hand back and I could see snakes grouped tight in the wide spread of the headlights, confused and ready to strike, their tails thin brown points rising up from the coils. The sky lit up again, a double shotgun blast of light, bang and then bang, but soundless in the distance, and I wondered how many miles away it was, the storm that we could not hear.

I felt Debbie's hand on my arm and the radio was still tuned to the out-of-town rock station, and I could hear the music but not the words, and Debbie's hand was cool and her grip was tight in that familiar way that I remembered from before. Through the windshield we watched Ricky and Kenny run around the snakes, turn in circles, and run back again. Kenny's job seemed to be to hold the bucket and he was swinging it in such a way that had there been anything inside it would have been spun out and tossed a distance, but as it was the bucket was empty and Kenny was staying close to the front of the car, where maybe he could jump on the hood if he needed to get out of the way.

It was Ricky I was most fascinated with. He moved almost gracefully, and there was a fixed expression on his face, something beyond concentration, and his eyes were dark and everything about him was poised to strike with just as much potential threat as the snakes. He was using one hand to distract them, get their attention, misdirect, and the other hand would come in at a quick angle, almost from behind, and reach for the neck. I watched him miss over and over again, but he never lost his position or the look of focus on his face. Then I saw something behind him, just to the edge of where the headlights reached, and I realized that the Laura Scudder's bag had been kicked from the grass and what had been underneath it was now tossed into the light—a thin brown sandal with a heavy sole, lying on its side, caught in the grip of weeds.

It was over in a matter of minutes, the rock pile emptied of snakes, all but three of them scattered to the darkness and the thick dead grass beyond our lights. The slow unlucky ones were in the bucket, twisting over and over on themselves, tails buzzing, striking blindly at the plastic. Kenny spun the lid on them and all we could hear was the sound of their heads beating against the sides.

"I got bit," Ricky said. He held up his hand and turned the back of his wrist toward us and I could see that it was red and already puffed up and there was a thin smear of blood running down his arm and dripping into the dirt.

"Shit," my brother said, and he took Ricky's arm and held it in front of the headlights so he could get a better look at the damage.

We got out of the car and Debbie helped me kick the beer bottles out of the way and we put the gas cans back, and even though I was afraid to touch the bucket, I made myself pick it up and put it in the trunk because Debbie was watching me. We helped Ricky get into the backseat of the car, and then I went around and got in the front passenger seat, and Kenny handed Ricky a beer and said something about making a tourniquet, but Ricky just shook his head and took a drink. "I gave in to fear," he said. "The Holy Roller told me that I wouldn't get bit if I kept fear out of my heart and believed in Jesus, and I guess I didn't. And he said that if I didn't, then that was Jesus's way, too."

Debbie was in the backseat with Ricky and I could hear her shifting around, feel her knees press into the back of my seat, and part of me wondered if it was deliberate or not, if she was sending me a message through code.

"This would be a good time to call in a chopper, take my ass out of this war," Ricky said.

"There is no war," Debbie said. "You weren't ever there." I could hear her voice take on an edge and I was waiting for Kenny to start the car so we could chew up back road to cut the distance between here and home.

"Don't talk like that," Ricky said. "You don't know anything," he said. "You know less than nothing." And then he made a sound that I had never heard before, something high-pitched and like an animal in pain, and I jerked around in my seat and saw that Debbie had her hand around his wrist and I could see that her nails were biting into Ricky's swollen skin.

"Be honest about one thing," she said. "Just be honest for once. Admit that you don't know anything about Suzy Eberhardt."

There were tears running down Ricky's face, I could see their shine in our little bit of light, and he raised his left hand and I thought for a second that he might hit her, just pull back and knock her off his arm, but instead he tucked his hair behind his ear and wiped the back of his good wrist against his face.

"Scooter Tabor was in front of me," Ricky whispered. "We were in double canopy and he took a step and I was thinking about smoking, and wishing I had a cigarette stuffed into my hat, and there was a sound and all the air got sucked up and then I was flying, lifted right up off the ground, and Scooter Tabor got blown up and I took the scatter in my leg." He wiped his eyes again and then Debbie let go of his hand and he put it against his chest and cradled it and began a slow rocking motion, back and forth, in his seat.

"Forget it," she said.

Kenny flipped the key forward in the ignition and at first there was the tired sound of the starter turning and waiting for the engine to catch and then the sound faded out to a click, and the headlights dimmed and then died. "Fuck," Kenny said.

In the darkness I could hear things but they all seemed to be coming from inside the car. When we had gone camping, there had been crickets, thousands of them all around us, their noise a constant wall of sound, but out here there wasn't anything, no crickets, no bugs, no frogs.

Kenny turned the key again and this time the starter didn't even try. There was just a sputter of dry clicks, and then one click, and then nothing at all.

"What's going on, man?" Ricky asked.

"Fucking battery, I guess," Kenny said. "We shouldn't have had the radio on all day. The doors open. The dome light was on. Shit, I don't know. How long did we run the headlights?"

Nobody said anything, but I thought that I could hear Ricky crying, or not really crying, but breathing heavy and making a low noise in the back of his throat. The heat lightning went off again, lighting up the lake so that it looked as flat and reflective as smoked glass. I looked out toward the front of the car and tried to see the potato chip bag, the marker for the brown sandal I had seen in the weeds, but there wasn't enough light from the sky to see much of anything except for the vague sense of shapes. The windows were down and the breeze from the afternoon was back, the residual of down-canyon winds, and I thought that I could smell wet ground and rain, but I knew that we were still weeks and miles away from storms.

Debbie shifted behind me, but this time I could not feel the pressure of her knees into the back of my seat and I wondered if that was part of the code, too. Kenny turned the key again and there was nothing. "Let's just keep everything off," he said. "The battery will charge itself and then we can get the car started and get the fuck out of here." Kenny looked over his shoulder toward Ricky. "Hold your hand above your heart. It'll slow the shit down." In the fall my brother would move away to college, and he wanted to be an architect and build things and when my father had asked him why didn't he want to be a doctor, he had all of that experience in the hospital, my brother just said that his job was to push a mop through things that spilled out of bodies, and he couldn't imagine spending the rest of his life in that smell.

Out beyond the hood of the car, near where the stand of scrub oaks began, I thought I could see a shape move past, a shift in the shadows, maybe a deer, but I knew that my mind liked to play these tricks on me and it was probably just my imagination. Kenny said we would sit there and let the battery charge itself, it would just take a little while, and even though I knew that wasn't true, it sounded good to me.

ACKNOWLEDGEMENTS

This collection would not be possible without the help of many people who have contributed to the construction of these stories in many ways. I would like to thank Corinne Litchfield, Kevin McKenna, and Deborah Meltvedt for inspiration; Jan Haag and Shelby Angel for reading and cheerleading; Kate Asche for opportunities; Dylan and Molly Gyurke for laughter; Jan and Scott Winnett, Jim Baker, and Suzanne Barnett for family; Melinda and David Ruger for much support; Pam for getting me started many years ago; all the people at Tin House Books for their hard work to make this book beautiful; Nanci McCloskey for tireless effort; Rob Spillman and Danielle Svetcov for taking chances and believing in my writing; and especially to Meg Storey, who found the best in every page of these stories, and then made them better.

PHOTO: © KEVIN F. MCKENNA

JODI ANGEL's first collection of short stories, *The History of Vegas*, was published in 2005 and was named a San Francisco Chronicle Best Book of 2005 as well as an LA Times Book Review Discovery. Her work has appeared in *Tin House*, *Zoetrope: All-Story*, *One Story*, the *Sycamore Review*, and *Esquire/Byliner*, among other publications and anthologies. Her stories have received several Pushcart Prize nominations and "A Good Deuce" received a special mention in *The Best American Short Stories 2012*. She grew up in a small town in Northern California—in a family of girls.